"Devin, I need to—" Spark fell silent when he felt her arm moving around his arousal. She moved her arm so slowly and with enough pressure that he could have sworn it was done intentionally.

"You need to what?" Devin kept her head down to hide the smile that slid onto her face.

Spark leaned his head to the side, trying to comprehend exactly what was going on. If what he thought was happening was happening, she he let it continue? *Hell, yeah,* he reprimanded himself before any gentlemanly thoughts could come forth. "Um, I think I need to move away from you for a minute."

Devin sat up and looked him in the eyes. "You don't want me lying on you?" she teased. "I was resting comfortably."

"Yeah, that's the problem. I wasn't comfortable at all."

"What's wrong? Maybe I can fix it."

Spark smiled. She was good, really good. "You think so, huh?"

"I know so."

WAITING IN THE SHADOWS

MICHELE SUDLER

Genesis Press, Inc.

INDIGO LOVE STORIES

An imprint of Genesis Press, Inc.
Publishing Company

Genesis Press, Inc.
P.O. Box 101
Columbus, MS 39703

ISBN: 13 DIGIT : 978-1-58571-364-6
ISBN: 10 DIGIT : 1-58571-364-3
Manufactured in the United States of America

First Edition

Visit us at www.genesis-press.com
or call at 1-888-Indigo-1-4-0

DEDICATION

This book is dedicated to
My Aunt
Brenda Louise Henry of
Smyrna, Delaware

ACKNOWLEDGMENTS

To my children, whose unconditional love keeps me strong on those days I want to just give up.

To my friends and family, for your words of encouragement and constant support. I love you all.

To Sidney Rickman, thank you for all your hard work.

To the Genesis Press family and anyone who has ever read any of my books. Thank you.

And to anyone I might have missed, I'm thinking of you.

CHAPTER 1

Devin ran through the hospital's emergency room entrance at top speed with her brother Charles right on her heels. He was the first person she'd thought to phone once she received the call from a nurse at the hospital stating that her husband had been taken to the emergency room and that she should come down right away.

In her hysteria, she hadn't thought of calling her brother Troy, who was a surgeon at the hospital. She just knew that she had to get someone to watch her girls after school and get to the hospital as quickly as possible.

Troy was waiting for her when she walked through the hospital doors. He was the rock of the family's eight children, especially the five younger than himself, always trying to take their pain away and carry the burden himself.

When she saw him, Devin rushed straight into his arms. "Troy, what happened? Where is Chris?" she asked, panic coloring her voice.

Troy glanced at Charles. "Let's go over here into this room," he said, ushering them into a private area.

"No, I want to see Chris," Devin said. "Is he okay?"

"Devin, have a seat." Troy practically forced her into the empty chair. He wished that he didn't have to be the one to tell his baby sister the bad news. "Devin, listen to me," he began, looking into her frightened eyes.

Devin sensed the truth, but she was fighting the reality of it. The tears rolled down her face faster as she looked at her brother for answers.

She was breaking Troy's heart, but he had to tell her. He sat close to her, briefly glancing at Charles, who stood in the far corner helplessly. "Devin, baby, he didn't make it. He died on the operating table."

Devin stood straight up. Hearing the worst hurt far more than thinking it. Devin's heart seemed to stop beating; her lungs burned, and she started to slide to the floor.

"Devin," Troy said, catching her in his arms and easing her down. "Devin, you all right? Charles, go get the nurse." Troy began to check his sister's vitals. "Devin, can you hear me?"

"Yes, Troy, I hear you," she replied calmly, too calmly.

"Devin, let's get off the floor. Let's get you in a chair. Do you have a headache?"

"No," she replied.

"Let me look at your eyes."

"No. I said I was fine." Her voice was filled with determination. With Troy's help, she got off the floor and into a chair. "I want to see my husband now, please."

"Okay. Um, let me see if they are ready for you. Charles," he said, motioning to the seat next to her. "I'll be right back."

Charles sat next to his sister and put his arm around her. "Baby girl, everything is going to be all right."

"How can you say that, Charles? My whole world has fallen apart. Don't tell me that everything is going to be all right."

"You know that you have the whole family behind you, and you have two beautiful daughters. You can not let this destroy you." He brushed the tears from her cheek.

"But it already has, and I can't pretend that it hasn't." She looked at the door to the room, expecting Troy to walk back in, but saw a stranger standing at the door instead.

The stranger walked in. "Excuse me, miss. I'm Detective Daniel Cummings. I hate to bother you at a time like this, but I have to ask you a few questions. Is that okay with you?"

Charles stood to oppose the intrusion, but Devin stilled him with her hand. "I guess. I'm waiting for them to allow me to see my husband, so—"

"I understand. I just have a few questions. Um, do you know who might have wanted to harm your husband?"

"Harm my husband? No, of course not. Why?"

"Has he recently argued with anyone or had any kind of confrontations that you know of?"

"No, what?" She glanced at Charles. "Why are you asking me questions like this?"

"Um," he said, glancing at Charles, "maybe it would be better if you came down to the station in the next day or two and had a talk with us."

Devin realized that she didn't know how Chris had died. She hadn't thought to ask. All she knew was that her husband was dead. "How about if you tell me what's going on right now. Did someone hurt my husband? Was Chris murdered?"

The officer suddenly looked uncomfortable. "Haven't the doctors talked to you, Mrs. Aldridge?"

"All I know is that my husband is dead. Detective Cummings, please tell me what happened."

The officer sat down opposite them. He had assumed that the doctor had already explained everything to her. "Mrs. Aldridge, your husband was found shot in the parking lot of the Oak Park Industrial Park by a co-worker, a Mrs. Shannon Ross."

"Chris is a manager at the Technical Card Processing center. I don't understand. No one would want to hurt Chris. Everybody loved him. He didn't have any enemies."

"Okay, ma'am. I'm not going to trouble you any further. Here's my card. If you think of anything over the next couple of days, please give me a call. And please accept my condolences." He looked at Charles. "Can I speak to you for a moment?"

"Sure," Charles said, following him out of the room.

"Sir, are you related to Mrs. Aldridge? Will you be watching over her?"

"I'm her brother. Our family will take care of her."

"And the doctor?"

"He's one of our older brothers."

"I didn't want to tell Mrs. Aldridge, but I'm sure your brother knows. Mr. Aldridge was killed execution style. Whoever killed him knew exactly what they were doing, and they obviously were watching him because they knew where he would be and got him while he was alone. I'm telling you this, Mr.—"

"Avery."

"I'm telling you, Mr. Avery, because I would like you to be forewarned of possible danger to your sister. I'm giving you my card as well." He handed Charles his business card. "Please don't hesitate to call me if necessary."

"Thank you, I will." Charles put the card in his pocket and watched the detective walk over to someone he guessed was his partner.

"Charles?" Troy said, walking up to him. "What's going on?"

"I was just speaking with the detective. He told me what happened to Chris. Are you going to tell Devin?"

"I don't want to. I know she needs to know, but I don't think she's ready to hear it."

"Are you ready to take her to him?" Charles asked.

"Yeah," Troy replied. "You ready?"

"Yeah," Charles answered. There was no question that they were going to do this together. Devin was going to need all the support she could get. Unfortunately, out of their eight siblings, only the two of them were there. When they got her back to their parents' house, there would be a crowd of people smothering her with love and support.

"We need to call the house, too," Troy said. "I promised Mom."

Charles stood near the door to the room, watching as Troy slowly walked their sister to her husband's body. He hated to hear any of his sisters cry, any woman for that matter. Devin's grief was almost more than he could bear, but he knew he had to be there for her. Troy had always been the strongest of the three brothers, Charles was the most sensitive and easily angered, and John the oldest fell somewhere in the middle.

The closer she got to Chris's body, the louder wept. Then she simply collapsed on her husband's body. Troy stood over her, rubbing her back, trying to comfort her.

"Um, we're going to let you have some privacy, Devin," he said after a few moments.

She didn't answer.

"We'll be right outside, baby," he finished, turning toward Charles.

In the hallway, the brothers stood across from the door to the room, but could still hear her sobs.

"Damn," Charles breathed out heavily. He ran his hands over his face. "I don't see how you can do this for a living. Deal with death everyday."

"Well," Troy said, "I don't deal with death everyday. I mean, granted sometimes there is nothing that you can do, but I think that I'm fighting death everyday. It gets hard sometimes, but if I didn't do what I do, death would win a whole lot more. Unfortunately, there was nothing we could do for Chris. He was dead on arrival. Chris's was murdered. Devin is going to have to talk to the police once she gets past this."

"If she gets past this," Charles corrected.

"I think she'll be okay. Devin is strong, and she has the girls to take care of. She won't let this keep her down for long."

"I love your optimism. I guess that's why you're the doctor, and I just sing songs."

"Well, you bring people together with your music, and I try to keep them together with my hands."

"You think she's okay?" Charles looked at the door.

"No, but I think she'll be okay," Troy replied.

For the umpteenth time, Devin wiped her face with the wad of tissue in her hand. This was unbelievable. How could this be happening? Just last night, they had been in each other's arms, making love and talking about their plans for the future. Just last night, over dinner, they had been looking on the internet for the perfect house to move into with their twin daughters. He had been joking about getting a house with enough rooms, just in case they decided to have more kids in the future. They'd planned, laughed, kissed, and loved, all just last night.

And now, this. He looked so peaceful, sleeping. What was she going to do? How could she tell their daughters? The girls were only five. Would they understand what had happened? How could she expect them to when she didn't understand herself?

Devin wiped her eyes again. She lifted her husband's hand and held it to her cheek. "Oh Chris, why did it have to be you? What am I going to do without you?" Devin closed her eyes and prayed for strength.

They had met seven years earlier when she was in college. When she took him home to meet her family, they'd welcomed him immediately. Even her father, who usually gave the gentlemen callers a hard time, had liked Chris from the start. Chris was new to the area, but he was very knowledgeable, and he showed her how to enjoy life. Neither of them had much money when they met, but Chris worked long hours first at the nursing home, then the processing center. His hard work was the reason he was able to buy her the pricey engagement ring and wedding band. He'd said that she deserved the best because she was the best woman to ever come into his life.

Tears continued to fall as she mourned the years that they would never have together. Devin didn't know what to do next. She supposed she would have to call his family, but she didn't know too much about them. He'd only spoken about a brother named Al, whom she'd never met.

Chris had always told her that he and his parents were not close. As close-knit as Devin's family was, she couldn't comprehend the concept of not being close with one's family. The couple of times she broached the idea of bringing his parents out for a visit or to meet their grandchildren, he simply said no and moved away from the conversation. Then one day he came home and told her that his father had died. He displayed little emotion. He said that his brother had handled everything and never brought the subject up again.

Devin didn't know Al's number. Maybe it was in Chris's papers somewhere. She would look through his desk.

Devin kissed her husband on the cheek.

"Good-bye, love," she whispered, kissing him again and then walking out of the room.

"You okay, baby girl," Troy asked, extending his arm for her to move into.

"As well as I can be. Thanks for letting me see him."

"You going to the house?" Charles asked.

"Yeah. Um, I need to figure out the funeral arrangements and stuff. I need a minute to think."

"Well, good luck getting that at Mom and Dad's house. It will be packed by the time you get there," Troy said.

"I know, but that's what I need. It will help me being around family."

"Okay. I'm going to stay here for a bit longer. I'll see ya later." Troy hugged and kissed his sister.

"Troy, what will happen to him now?"

Troy looked at his sister. He didn't want to tell her the truth, although he figured that she had an idea. "Well, the nursing staff will take care of him and they will take him downstairs until the funeral home comes to pick up his body." That was the easiest answer for both of them. There was no need for her to know that the medical examiner would be handling the body first to remove the bullets and such. "Don't worry, he will be fine."

"Come on, Devin, let's get you to the house."

Charles led her out of the hospital. Devin didn't notice that the detective who had questioned her earlier was still there and talking to two men in black suits. However, Charles did notice. He also noticed that they seemed to have more authority than the detective. The detective pointed towards them as they walked by.

CHAPTER 2

Two days later, Devin's head was pounding and her eyes were swollen beyond repair, but here she was on her way to the funeral home to make arrangements for her husband. She sat in the back seat of her oldest sister's Mercedes, looking out the window, thinking about the past and contemplating the future. And no matter how hard she tried, she couldn't stop crying.

If her mother patted her hand one more time, she was going to scream. Devin knew her mother had good intentions, but she really just wanted to be left alone.

When they got to the funeral home, Devin felt lightheaded. She took a few deep breaths to calm her nerves before getting out.

"Good afternoon, ladies. My name is Mrs. Crawford," the lady at the door said, extending her hand to Devin's mother.

"Hello, I'm Brenda Avery, and I am here with my daughter, Devin. We spoke over the phone."

"Oh, yes, please come in. So young. Please accept my condolences. Come, sit." Mrs. Crawford led them into the office and pulled out a folder. "I have already sent my coworkers to the hospital. Would you like anything to drink?"

Devin didn't like the feel of the funeral home. It was an ordinary building with offices on either side of a long hallway. The doors read like storefronts: Flowers, Programs, Music, Chapel. She supposed it was a business just like every other place, but on television, the funeral homes always looked like giant houses. There was always mournful elevator music playing overhead, and the lights were usually dimmed.

"Um, no, thank you," Devin said, sitting back in the chair. "Um, can you just explain the, um, process to me?"

"Sure, dear. The first thing is to decide the type of memorial service you would like for your loved one. Did he leave any instructions?"

"Um, no, this was kind of sudden," her mother stated.

"I want something simple, nothing out of the ordinary. Chris was a simple man."

"Okay, I have a sample of a basic service. Do you have a burial plot?"

Devin was stumped. She hadn't thought about that.

"Is there a burial ground that your family uses?"

Mrs. Avery spoke up again, "We have family plots at Jacobs that we can use." She pulled paperwork out of her purse.

Devin and her sister Tia, who had insisted on coming along, looked at her mother. They'd had no idea that the plots were there.

"Their father and I bought plots for the kids and their spouses once they were married."

"You never told us that," Devin said, wiping at her eyes again.

"Well, it's not the sort of thing you tell your children on their wedding day. Roberta and John, Jr. were the only ones that we told. They know where all of our paperwork is. At any rate, here is the information for the plot."

"Perfect," Mrs. Crawford replied. "Now, Devin, is there a church where you would like the services performed? We also have a chapel here that can be used if you wish."

"Um, I'd like to use the chapel. I don't believe there will be that many people, just my family and friends. My husband wasn't close to his family," she answered sadly.

"Okay, dear. That's no problem. We can pick a date that is available and suitable for you for the services. Now, did you bring your insurance information?"

"Yes." Devin handed her the paperwork.

"Good." Mrs. Crawford looked through the papers. "It looks like a substantial amount. I just have to contact the insurance agency to confirm the validity. Did you have a chance to prepare an obituary for the newspaper and the memorial program?"

"No, not yet."

"No problem. But if you could work on it, we'll have it put in the paper. There usually isn't a fee to have it run once, two days before the service. And they will run it again the day before for a small fee. Now, I would ask that you bring his clothes to us at least two days before the service. In fact, just bring them along with the obituary. Bring in a full set of clothes, including underclothing and any jewelry. We like to offer the family a private viewing the night before the services."

Devin listened intermittently to the woman. Her mind was running all over the place. She couldn't seem to keep it focused on any one particular thing.

"Devin, would you like to look at the coffins now? I understand if you would rather wait, but I find that it's best not to put things off."

"I can do it. I have to." Her mother patted her hand again. Devin shut her eyes, silently accepting the gesture.

It wasn't until after they got into the room that Devin realized it had been a very bad idea to try to be so brave. As soon as she saw the large room showcasing the latest models in coffins and their accessories, her vision blurred and her steps grew unsteady. Her mother was right beside her offering support. Tia, unfortunately, needed help, too. She was crying just as hard as Devin. Roberta had to help her out of the room.

"Baby, we don't have to do this. We can pick something out of the home's catalog. I think this is a little too much for you."

"No, I'm okay. Mom, I'm okay. Please, let me do this." She walked through the line of coffins, looking at each slowly. Her mother walked behind her.

A phone rang, causing Devin and her mother to jump. "I'm sorry," Mrs. Crawford said. "I'll take it in the hallway. Excuse me."

"Mom," Devin said, "I know you're trying to help me, and I appreciate it. I appreciate what everyone is trying to do for me, but it's just too much hovering. I know I have to go through this, and I will. I'm going to come through it okay in the end."

"I'm sorry. It's just the mother in me. I hate to see you going through this. I wish I could take all the pain away, but I know that I can't. Just know that I'm here for you. We all are."

"I know. Thank you, Mom." She hugged her mother. "Thank you."

"Excuse me, Mrs. Albridge," Mrs. Crawford said, coming back into the room. "Um, excuse me," she repeated timidly, uncomfortable intruding on such a private moment.

"Yes?" Devin answered, focusing her attention on Mrs. Crawford.

"Did you happen to call another funeral home before calling here?"

"No," she replied, a chill moving up her spine. *That was an odd question.*

"Well," Mrs. Crawford continued, visibly unnerved, "it appears that when my co-workers went to the hospital to retrieve your husband's body, someone had already taken him." She moved forward quickly as Devin swayed at the news. "Mrs. Albridge?"

"Devin. Devin," her mother said, supporting her daughter to the best of her ability.

"Move her over here. To the sofa."

Mrs. Crawford began fanning Devin frantically as Tia and Roberta rushed back into the room.

"How could this have happened?" Mrs. Avery asked. "What is going on?"

"I don't know. I was just as surprised as you are."

"What happened, Mom?" Robert asked.

"I don't know, but I think we are going to need April. We need to get Devin back to the house and figure all of this out." Their sister April was an attorney with a lot of connections. Hopefully, she could get to the bottom of this mess faster than anyone.

The whole family was gathered at the house, trying to figure out why Chris's body had not been at the hospital morgue. They were waiting for Troy, who had volunteered to go to the morgue to get answers since he was already at the hospital.

When he finally showed, the deafening noise level inside the house ceased instantly and they heard the playing children, who had been ushered to the backyard. He came in and kissed his mother and sister, who were sitting next to each other on the sofa in the large family room.

"Well?" Devin said, wiping the tears that formed at the corner of her eye. Her tears, she noticed, had switched from those of grief to anger. "Who took him? Who took my husband?"

"Devin, have you taken any of the pills I gave you?" Troy was worried; he could see the signs of an approaching nervous breakdown. Devin hadn't slept, had been forced to eat the little she ate, and was constantly in tears.

"No. Troy," she said, turning her sorrowful eyes on him, "tell me."

Troy let out a defeated breath. "They said that a man who said he was Chris's brother came in early yesterday morning and claimed the body. Said he was taking Chris home to be buried with his parents. They said the man stated that was Chris's wishes."

"And they just gave him the body, without any identification? They just give bodies to anyone?"

"Apparently, he came with morticians who did have identification. They signed for Chris's body. I called the morticians from the hospital, and they said that a Mr. Bowen flew the body to Delaware for burial."

"Delaware?"

"That's where Chris's parents are buried."

"Chris told me he was from Ohio. Why would he lie about that?" Devin's confusion grew the more she tried to figure out what exactly was going on.

"Maybe his parents moved to Delaware, and he just didn't tell you. You said that he wasn't close to his family," Tia suggested.

"But his brother should have talked to me about this. How do you just take someone's husband?"

Her mother put her arm around Devin's shoulder. "Dear, don't worry. I'm sure that April's police friends will get to the bottom of everything. We'll figure this all out. Everything will be okay."

"No, Mom, it won't." Feeling like she needed to get away, break free of the suffocation she was feeling, Devin jumped up from the sofa, almost hysterical. "My husband is dead, and I don't even have his body. I can't mourn him; I can't bury him; and I have no idea what the hell is going on."

"It's not going to do you any good to lose control," her mother calmly replied.

Tears fell uncontrollably from her eyes as Devin stood in the middle of the room, the focus of her siblings, cousins, and family friends. Devin knew that she had already lost control. She was in the middle of a nightmare that seemed to get worse and worse by the moment.

Just when she didn't think she could take anymore, April walked in with a look of disappointment on her face. She threw her briefcase in a corner, and then turned to the room. "They wouldn't tell me anything. I don't know what's going on. I couldn't get any information on Chris, his murder, or this brother of his. My contact did tell me, however, that this was now a federal investigation." She looked at her sister. "I'm sorry, Devin. I don't know what Chris was into, but whatever it was, the federal government has their hands all over it. There's nothing more I can find out."

April hugged her sister tightly as Devin cried out more of her frustrations.

"What else can I do?" Devin asked.

"I don't know."

"Devin, dear," her mother injected, "we should still have a memorial for Chris. I think that would be a good idea. We have a lot of family and friends here. And you and the girls need closure. They need to understand what has happened to their father."

"How can I explain it to them when I don't understand what's happened myself?"

"I think you know all that you need to know for now. You know that the man you love has died. He was your husband, your soul mate, and the father of your children. Baby, you have to be strong for your daughters. I know it's hard right now, and we don't understand everything that is going on, but Chris was a good man and a member of this family. We are not going to let his life, our memories of him, not be honored."

Mrs. Avery guided her daughter back to the sofa. Someone had to take charge here, and it was obviously not going to be Devin, nor should it be with everything that was going on. "Tia, get the notepad. We have work to do. Roberta, call one of your caterer friends. Charles, musicians. John Jr., we need a hall. April, call Mrs. Crawford and tell her that we need to put the obituary in the paper and we will need programs. Devin, you are not going to crumble on me, on your daughters. You are a strong woman with a whole family willing to support you."

Devin was awakened from her drug-induced sleep by the shrill ring of her cell phone. She scrambled to answer it before anyone else in the house was awakened. Devin had slept in the family room of her mother's house, while her daughters slept in one of the four back bedrooms with most of the other grandkids, who often spent nights at the house.

"Hello?" she answered groggily. It was 1:30 a.m.

At first, there was no answer, and then she heard what sounded like someone sniffling on the other end of the line.

"Hello?" she said again.

"Hello, Devin," the man answered. It was almost a whisper. "Please forgive me. I shouldn't be calling you, but I know you're confused, and you deserve better than this."

Devin sat up on the sofa immediately. "Who is this?"

"I had to take him back to Delaware. He made me promise, and he wanted to keep you and the girls safe if anything should ever happen to him."

"Are you Chris's brother?"

"Chris? Um, yes. I guess I am the closest thing to a brother that he ever had. I just wanted you to know that he is fine and that he loved you and the girls very much. I'm sorry that I can't tell you more than that, but you made, um, Chris very happy."

"Why did you take my husband?"

"Devin, please don't ask me more right now. After everything blows over, I will contact you again, and hopefully, I'll be able to explain everything to you. Right now, I have to go. Please, continue to be strong. Take care."

"But wait—"

CHAPTER 3

Two years later . . .

A gentle breeze brushed through her hair and held her troubling thoughts at bay as Devin watched her innocent twin daughters ride the merry-go-round at the crowded Six Flags Great Adventure theme park located only an hour from her home. In a rushed panic of indecisiveness and fear, she had bundled them up early that morning and whisked them as far away from the house as she could. Though she had no evidence of it, she'd felt instinctively that someone was watching her home.

Her first instinct had been to run to her parents' home, but it was only ten minutes away. Anyone who knew her would know that her parents' home would be her first choice for refuge. Although she kept the worry from her face for her daughters' sake, smiling a little brighter every time the circular ride swirled them in her direction, deep inside, her heart pounded, and her head ached as she continued to turn scenario after scenario over in her head.

Was she going to return to her home? And if so, would she, should she, take the girls with her? Should she just take them to her parents until she figured out the mess that was somehow related to her deceased husband? She unconsciously fingered the teardrop-diamond necklace she'd received as a second anniversary gift. It was time for her to decide what her next move was going to be. The sun was starting to drop behind the horizon.

Devin ran her hand through her black shoulder-length locks in despair. She'd thought that after getting through the past two years things were finally starting to get better. And now, this. Seemed as if Chris's past was determined to keep interfering with her future. Devin had thought that if she stayed strong and moved on with her life, everything would eventually fall into place.

She'd never looked for the answers that she needed for closure to Chris's murder. That night, after the phone call, she'd been concerned about the girls' safety. Devin had gone along with her mother's suggestion and held the memorial for family and friends, and then worked hard to focus on her girls and her future.

Since Chris's murder, she had managed to build herself up, overcome her insecurities, and maintain a stable life for herself and her girls. She had forced herself to remain strong and focused. With the help of Chris's life insurance money, she'd been able to pay off their home, purchase a new car, and provide adequately for her family.

Now six, her twins, Tionne and Dionne, were the most important people in her world, and it was her duty as their mother to protect them from the lies that were apparently Chris's legacy to them. Pulling out her cellular phone, she dialed her parents' house while waving mechanically at the girls on their fifth trip around on the ride.

"Hello, Mom," Devin said into the phone cheerfully, trying to disguise her anguish.

"Devin, baby, hold on. I got Tia on the other line. Hold on just one second."

Devin could almost hear her mother's smile. Waiting patiently, she knew that it would take more than a second for her mother and older sister to say their goodbyes. She continued smiling at her girls as the ride went on.

"Devin?"

"Yeah, Mom, I'm here. How's everything going with Tia?"

"Great. She and Jeff and the kids are leaving tomorrow for their vacation to Disney World. They're all so excited. I told her that she would probably have a hard time getting the kids to sleep tonight, especially Kevin. I can't believe he's eight years old. Seems like just yesterday she was giving birth to him. They've all grown up so fast."

Her nephew, his father's image, was a little helper, constantly taking care of his younger siblings, three-year-old Kayla and seven-month-old Derrick. She was happy that Tia had been able to finally find happiness with Jeff Daniels, her high-school sweetheart, even after he found out that she had kept Kevin a secret for the first four years of the boy's life. Devin had thought that she herself had also found that happiness, but the reality had been horrifyingly the opposite.

"Mom, I wanted to ask you if the girls could stay with you for a week or two."

"Week or two? Um, sure, baby, sure," her mother said, concern filling her voice. "Is everything okay, Devin?"

"Yes, I just need to get some things straight, Mom. That's all."

"Okay, dear." Brenda Avery didn't pry. She wanted to desperately, but putting a tight rein on her lips, she decided to simply give her daughter what she needed: time. In her opinion, Devin had never truly dealt with her husband's death. "Whatever you need, dear."

"Thanks, Mom. I just need to get some things straight." She exhaled loudly, letting some of the negative energy escape her weary body. "I'll bring them over later."

"Okay. Your father and I would love to have them. Don't worry about a thing. It will all work itself out."

"Thanks, Mom. I really appreciate this." Sometimes, whether you believed it was going to get better or not, just hearing your mother's reassurance made it seem possible.

"You know your father and I are here for you." Brenda was convinced that if Devin was asking for this favor from them, she truly needed it. "We'll see you when you get here, baby."

"Thanks, Mom." Devin slid the phone into her hip pocket, grazing the folded white envelope there. That envelope and the letter inside it had frightened her more than she had ever been in her life. She remembered opening it one night the previous week after bringing it into the house, along with the rest of her mail. She had been curious about the fancy writing on the front of the envelope and even more curious about the return address.

From the graceful handwriting on the front of the envelope, Devin assumed it was from a woman, a woman named C. Harrison, and it was addressed to Devin. She didn't know a C. Harrison, especially one who apparently lived in Delaware. The return address was a post office box in Wilmington, Delaware. Simply stated, the letter said that C. Harrison had been trying to reach Devin since Chris's death. According to the letter, that was when C. Harrison found out that her husband Richard had used the alias Chris Albridge and married Devin. C. Harrison went on to say that she was Richard's legal wife, had been married to him for thirteen years. She also stated they had daughters, identical thirteen-year-old twins named Christina and Christal.

Out of all the things Devin had found out about Chris since his death, this was the hardest pill to swallow. The fact that their marriage was not legal and that he hadn't loved her at all tore through her heart like a cannon ball.

Devin forced a smile as her daughters happily bounced toward her, oblivious to the turmoil their father had inflicted on their lives. Since their father's death, they had been dealing with missing him as best as little girls could. Thankfully, the crying and yelling stages were past. Devin continued to keep memories of him alive for their sake, even when what she really wanted to do since getting the letter was curse the day he came into her life. It was important to her that they never know the ugly facts about their father.

"Mommy, Mommy, you should have rode with us. It was fun," Tionne shouted as they reached her, both girls throwing their hands high.

"I'm glad you enjoyed it," she replied, hoping that her cheerful façade held. "Are you guys ready to grab something to eat?"

"I want to get on another ride," Dionne said, "the rollercoaster."

"Are you sure, Dionne? You were afraid of it earlier."

"I'm ready now, Mommy. TiTi said she was going to hold my hand." The pleading in her voice made Devin smile at her wide-eyed innocence. Dionne wasn't going to let them leave until she had finally gotten up the nerve to climb the high steps and ride the twisting, curling track. Both girls had been tall enough for the ride when they walked to the height scale earlier, but Devin had kept her fingers crossed, hoping for a change of mind. Motherhood made her fear what her daughters didn't.

"After this, I'm taking you to Grandmom and Grandy's house. They want you to stay a week or so with them. Isn't that great?"

"I guess," Tionne said.

"That'll be fun, Mommy," Dionne, the youngest by four minutes, commented. "Grandy spoils us."

"Good, now let's get to the big rollercoaster before it gets too dark. This is the last ride, ladies. Then we really have to go." The *big* rollercoaster was actually the log flume ride. Dionne had watched the other riders scream as they took the final plunge and the huge splash that followed and had hesitated earlier when it was their turn.

"Okay, Mommy," they said in unison, rushing ahead of her toward the ride.

She watched them, amazed at how the years had gotten away from her, how grown they seem to have gotten almost overnight. Her babies weren't babies anymore, but she still had to protect them from the cruelty of the world for as long as she could.

Their dark mocha skin and thick, naturally straight jet black hair revealed their father's half-Hispanic heritage. The two girls were blessed with thin limbs and long torsos, unlike their five-foot, six-inch mother, and glowing facial skin. Devin dreaded them coming into dating age. Surely she was going to have to hire bodyguards for her daughters. They were so lovely. Luckily, they'd received their brains from her side of the family. Their father surely hadn't been thinking when he got himself into the mess that took his life.

"Hello . . . Mom, Dad," Devin yelled as she opened the heavy wooden door to her parents' large, ranch-style home. By the number of cars in the driveway and parked in front of the house, she could tell that the house was in its usual full-to-capacity state.

"We're back here, dear, in the kitchen," her father yelled. The laughter coming down the hallway belonged to her eldest brother John Jr., the dentist.

Being the youngest of eight children had its advantages and disadvantages. She had been spoiled by all of her siblings, but in most ways she felt that she had never truly lived up to their success. Even after finally receiving her teaching degree and getting a job at the local elementary school, she still felt that she didn't live up to any of their successes.

In the family circle of success were three brothers, John, the dentist; Troy, the doctor; Charles, the multimillionaire recording artist who'd married a doctor; and four sisters. Roberta had married a publication tycoon; April was a lawyer who'd married a lawyer; Kristal was a toy store chain owner and entrepreneur; and Tia was a child psychologist. Basically, she was the sibling without letters before or after her name. That fact, along with her girls, kept her in school fighting to get the doctorate she so desperately craved.

"Hello, everybody, we're here," she said, making sure to smile as she walked into the crowded room to find four of her siblings sitting around the large kitchen. Immediately, relief filled her, and the pressures of the day seemed to lift off her shoulders, not high, just enough to ease her a little. There was nothing like home.

"Hey, baby girl," her father yelled from across the room. He was a five-foot, eight-inch, thickly built dark-skinned man with a small potbelly from a little too much beer. He was handsomely groomed with wavy hair that he loved to joke could make you seasick.

"Hello, Daddy," she replied as the girls pushed past her to run to their grandfather and bestow hugs and kisses on him. "Mom, thanks for doing this. The girls couldn't wait to get here."

"Of course not. They love the way their grandfather spoils them," Brenda Avery replied, watching her husband take the cookie jar down from its shelf. "Come with me, dear. I have something to talk to you about."

Obediently, Devin followed her mother toward one of four bedrooms, moving away in the nick of time from the punch her brother Troy threw at her leg.

"Punk," she mouthed, rushing past him. They had been trading punches for the last fifteen years. Fortunately, at the age of thirteen, she became smart enough to try to get out of the way rather than go toe to toe with him.

"Devin," her mother was saying when she walked into the room, "your father and I want you to know that we are here for you. The whole family is here for you."

"I know," she answered, reaching for her mother's hand. The last thing she wanted or needed was for her mother to get emotional on her. "Mom, I know that you're worried about me. But I'm fine. I'm fine with everything that came out about him after he passed, and even with the stuff coming out now, two years later. I am fine."

"But he was still your husband, the father of your children, Devin. You loved that man. No matter how much you might be hurting right now, you have to mourn your loss so that you can move on."

"I have mourned him, Mom. In my own way I have, but I've got two little girls that I have to be strong for. If I fall apart, then who will they have?"

"Baby—"

"Mom, I don't want to talk about this anymore. I have to get to the bottom of all of Chris's lies. That's the only way I'll truly be able to put him to rest and move on with my life."

"I believe that he did love you, Devin. Anyone who saw you together could see it."

"Yeah, well, there is a lot that you don't know, Mom, and there is a lot that I still need to find out." Devin let a small laugh escape in order to cover the pain resting very closely to her heart.

"You just be careful, baby. Are you sure you don't want us to do anything to help you? I'm sure your brothers would help you out."

"No, this is something I have to do on my own. That's why I need the girls to be with you. Once and for all, I need to get to the bottom of this."

"What are you going to do?"

"I don't know yet, but I don't need you to be worried about me."

"Baby, I'm your mother. What would I do if not worry? You know, all of the secrets and stories that swirled around after Chris's death makes all of this seem so dangerous. What if someone doesn't want you snooping around?"

"I have to get to the bottom of it all. I'm only interested in his personal life, not anything else. Maybe I could at least find this 'brother' of his. Either way, I know that this is something that I have to do."

"Are you sure?"

"I'm sure. I just want to get down to the truth about his personal life. I've got to talk to the woman who wrote that letter."

"I understand, Devin. Just know that we're all here for you. If you get into any trouble, you call us. You hear me?"

"I will. April told me the same thing when I talked to her earlier." April had offered the help of one of the investigators she employed.

"Okay. I guess I can't stop you or change your mind, huh?" Brenda held her daughter's hands tightly between her own, wishing she could do much more.

"Mom, I have to do this."

"Okay." Pulling her close, Brenda held on to her youngest child for a moment while sending up a silent prayer for her safety. She realized that Devin was going to have to find her own way out of her dilemma. No matter how much she wanted to help her, the only one who could solve this problem was Devin. "You take this." Brenda pulled out a roll of money from her bra and placed it in Devin's hand.

"Mom, I don't need—"

"Take it," her mother repeated, kissing her on the cheek before releasing her.

Holding hands, they walked back into the kitchen where John Sr. was waiting with his arms full of his granddaughters. "Is everything all right, dear?" he asked his wife as she walked past him.

"Yes," Brenda replied. "Everything's just fine."

"So, Devin," Troy, the overprotective brother, began. "What's going on?"

She nodded her head toward the living room, beckoning him to follow her. "Look, I got some investigating to do into Chris's past."

"Devin—"

"Don't—" She threw her hands up in frustration, putting a stop to his forthcoming words. "Don't say it. I've got enough to deal with."

"Well, what are you going to do?" He lowered his voice significantly, trying to express urgency in his tone. Troy was worried for his sister, not for her physical safety, but for her mental safety. "Have you thought this out—any of it?"

"No, of course not. Hell, no. But for my daughters' sakes, I have to find a way to come to terms with what is happening in my life, and the only way to do that is to get to the bottom of everything dealing with Chris. It's been two years since his death, and I don't know any more about my husband than I did the day he died."

"Well, we all thought that moving on would be the best idea for the kids. Maybe we shouldn't have forced you to let it go."

"No, it's not your fault," Devin protested. "You're my family, and you only wanted what was good for me. At the time, it did seem like the best thing to do."

"So where do we go from here?" Troy asked. She definitely wasn't going to do this on her own. "I'll take some time off from the hospital and help you."

"Troy, no offense, but you're a doctor."

"Hey, I've got connections. Besides, you're a teacher. That doesn't exactly make you Nancy Drew."

"Well, this is my life and my business. I don't want anybody else involved."

"So, what are you going to do, go see whoever wrote you the letter? You don't even know that she was really his wife. This could be a trap."

"I'm going to get the answers that I need, and if it leads to her then so be it. She didn't give me too much information in her letter. She didn't seem to know too much about him herself. She said they married shortly after high school."

"How do you know that she's even telling the truth? Maybe she's setting you up or trying to find out information about Chris, too. Devin, I really don't think you need to be doing this all by yourself. Maybe we should call the police and show them the letter."

"No, no police." Devin sat down on the sofa, putting her hands to her face in deep thought. "They didn't help before; I doubt very seriously if that has changed. One thing's for sure. There is only one way to find out if she's telling the truth, and that is to go to her."

"But who even told her he was dead?"

"His brother, I guess. I can't give you an honest answer because I don't know any of these people. I'm going to assume that the brother would have known his first wife, if he had one. For all I know, he took Chris's body to her."

"Now you're just throwing out a bunch of theories. That's not going to get you anywhere. Have you heard from him since he called you that night?"

"No."

"Not even to see how the girls are doing?"

"Nope. And I don't wish to hear from him. He's not Chris's real brother. I know that from the shock in his voice when I asked him. And he doesn't need to be calling to ask about my girls."

"And he never once mentioned that Chris was married?"

"Not to me. But I could tell from the whispered words that he was trying not to stay on the phone long."

"I just don't understand, sis." Troy rested a hand on her knee. "How could this man have been married to you for seven years and her for what . . . thirteen, fourteen without once getting things mixed-up, or letting guilt about the whole situation choke the hell out of him? I just don't buy it."

"It just goes to show you that you've got to be careful who you marry, don't you?"

"Devin, I'm sorry. I didn't mean—"

"I know you didn't. It's all right." She patted his hand to reassure him. "Look, I gotta get out of here. I've got a lot to do before morning."

"I can help you," Troy said in a final attempt to accompany her.

"I'll be all right, Troy. I'm a big girl now. Don't worry about me."

"That's easier said than done." He stood, pulling her into his arms. "Just be careful, and if you need anything, call me. Me, John-John, Charles, call one of us, okay?"

"I will," Devin replied, hugging him tightly. "I will."

CHAPTER 4

In the darkness, a cigarette glowed brightly in the parked 2008 Malibu as the man inhaled. Uncertainty about whether he should be there in the first place, staking out this woman as a favor to his sister, was beginning to drive him crazy. He was only on day two, and already it was getting the best of him. Minute by minute, disgust for his assignment filled him. His stomach ached from clenching and unclenching.

Reaching into the glove compartment for a stick of gum, he accidentally knocked over the can of Pepsi that sat on the armrest. It spilled onto the other half of the Italian sub he planned to eat.

"Damn it," Spark hissed as he rushed to clean the mess before it made a permanent stain on the cloth interior of the rental car. *Why the hell am I putting myself through this?* If he weren't still in debt to his sister for twenty thousand dollars, he wouldn't have to be sneaking after this woman, spying on her and her kids. Twin kids. That Richard, he sure did know how to pick 'em. At any rate, after this they would be even, and Carlissa could stop holding the fact that he owed her money over his head.

At thirty-seven, he was finally starting to get his life together. He'd stopped gambling and had managed to obtain a good job at the local oil refinery. But as soon as he didn't need her to bail him out of jam after jam, his sister had begun to throw the countless times she had been there for him in his face.

In all honesty, he did owe her. If she hadn't coughed up the money that he owed for gambling debts to the Atlantic City loan shark, he'd probably be dead right now. Instead he'd only received a bruised face and broken arm. That life was behind him now, and it hadn't taken any programs to get him out of it. All it had taken was a .45-caliber handgun pointed at his temple on the balcony of the penthouse suite at the Bogotá Hotel. That had sobered his ass up real fast.

Since that fateful night, when he'd called his sister at 3:45 a.m. asking for her help, he had stayed far away from Atlantic City. Gambling was so far out of his system that he didn't even like to go to Christiana Hospital, which was located across the street from the Delaware Racing Park and Casino. He began to panic every time he got too close to the place. And he was glad for it. Those little attacks helped to remind him how far he had come. Four years clean. No, it wasn't drugs or alcohol, but it was an addiction just the same.

Suddenly alert, Spark jumped as he saw the headlights of her 2008 Nissan Altima flick on. *How did she get in the car without me seeing her?* He had told his sister that she was crazy for even thinking he could do this job. But she'd insisted because he had seven days off, and he was free.

Quickly, he started his car without turning on his lights. He allowed her to pull off and then followed her down the street. After she made her first turn, he brought his lights fully on. When he turned the same corner, however, he no longer saw her car on the road. The street was completely empty. Glancing at his watch, he assumed she was headed back to her house. He would just go there. *Now, which way was her house? Right or left? Damn.* Pulling the car over at the nearest corner, he pulled the map out from under his hip, spread it and tried to find his location.

Devin rifled through the desk drawer for all the papers she thought she would need on her trip to Delaware to track down the woman who had written the letter. Only the light from the desk lamp glowed in the dark room.

She dug deeper into the drawer until she found their marriage certificate. For a few minutes, she sat down in the leather chair, allowing her feelings to engulf her. Although she willed herself not to completely break down, Devin couldn't stop the convoy of tears that coursed down her cheek as she thought of the years that had been wasted loving a man who couldn't have possibly loved her.

In the darkness, a car's headlights flashed past her window. She nervously went to the window and looked through a blind slit. She recognized the car as Dana Jones's new car.

The teenager had worked for two years after school, saving every penny she could get her hands on in order to pay cash for a new car on graduation day. The neighborhood had been so proud of her dedication that they'd pulled together, held bake sales, yard sales, and even sold dinners in order to present her with a $1,500 check toward her college expenses.

Dana's headlights did provide her a glimpse of a silver car parked under a streetlight one house down from her ranch-style home. In the car, she briefly saw the outline of a man. From the bright red dot she saw after Dana passed, she figured he was smoking a cigarette.

Who the hell is that? Devin thought as panic raced through her. *Was it somebody watching her?* If so, she had made the right decision in sending the girls away. Without thinking, she grabbed the rest of the papers in the drawer. She would have to go through them after she got wherever she was going. Right now, she had to get out of the house.

The thought that someone was watching her, that it hadn't been her imagination, pissed her off. What did she have that they wanted? The answer had to lie in either the papers that she hastily stuffed into her shoulder bag or Delaware.

For the past two years, no one had contacted her about Chris. She hadn't learned anything about his past. All she knew was that her husband went to work at a car processing center and came home every night. They had a good marriage and loved each other very much. So why had he been murdered so brutally? And why hadn't the police been able to tell her more?

When Chris died, the man who went to the morgue and claimed his body had called her and said that she shouldn't worry. He'd even told her that he would be in contact. That had never happened. So, if she wanted to learn about Chris's past, it would be up to her.

After putting out his second cigarette, Spark became bored with waiting in the darkness. Staring at a dark house wasn't his idea of fun. She was in there. He knew because the chrome rims on the Nissan Altima parked on the street marked it as hers. Auto detailing had been one of his many temporary gigs.

Getting out of the rental, he decided to take a closer look and jumped when he let the car door slam shut. The loud noise reverberated down the street.

"Damn," he whispered as he gritted his teeth and pounded his fist against his thigh. He looked up and down the street before dodging behind a tree when he realized he was standing in the middle of the road.

Even if he did know what to look for, he didn't know how to start. *This is crazy.* He didn't know anything about spying on people. Spark moved closer to the dark house. He edged up the side, careful to stay as far in the dark shadows as possible. He didn't trip over the bikes that were lying in the middle of the front yard, but he did fall into the bushes at the side of the house when his foot got tangled in the hose. Trying not to make any more noise, he hoisted himself up on his hands and knees and was about to stand when he heard a car door shut. Seconds later, he heard an engine start.

"Oh, hell," he said, racing back to the street. He made it just in time to see the taillights of the car turn the corner.

"Oh, hell," he said again, loudly, running to his car. He quickly jumped in and started the car, then made a U-turn in the middle of the street. If he lost her this time, there was no way he would be able to find her again. God only knew where she was headed. *Why hadn't he parked the car heading in the same direction as she had parked hers?*

Spark had no qualms about running a few stop signs or breaking the speed limit. He did everything he could to catch up with the red taillights he saw in the distance. He couldn't lose her.

"Damn, damn," he repeatedly exclaimed. The urgency of the situation mounted in the pit of his stomach, and he slammed his fist over and over on his right leg. Releasing a long sigh, he relaxed when he realized that she was heading onto Highway 64 West. That would give him a chance to catch up to her.

Boldly, he moved over into the left lane to pass a car and a truck. Picking up speed, he was preparing to pass another car when he saw that she had turned on her right blinker. She was moving into the turn lane, making a right onto Highway 171 North.

"Jesus," he exclaimed, slamming his foot onto the brake pedal. Unconscious of the fact that he'd almost caused an accident by his actions, Spark maneuvered behind the car he was about to pass. He missed seeing the fingers being thrown at him by his fellow drivers. His only focus was her Nissan Altima.

Devin patiently stood in line. Three people were in front of her and four others to her rear. She swayed back and forth, shifting the weight of her well-formed body from her left to her right foot. She blew out a long breath as her patience waned. The people in front of her at the Southwest Airlines ticket counter seemed to be taking forever.

She'd thought that nowadays most people purchased their flight tickets either online or at a travel agency. Her situation was different. It was an emergency. As she looked behind her again, she saw a woman in a navy business suit step into the line. She shook her head. Surely not all of these people were trying to purchase last-minute emergency flights. But even as her patience began to wear thin, her determination grew stronger.

The man behind her bumped her none too gently. Caught off guard, Devin tensed. She wondered if she should be taking her situation more seriously. As she turned to face the man who'd bumped her, she caught the faint but familiar scent of Ishi Miaki cologne for men. For a moment, the scent reminded her of a trip that she and Chris had taken to St. Louis just to get away for the weekend. He had worn that cologne. She shook the memory off. That was another time.

"Excuse me, miss," the stranger behind her apologized. "I didn't mean to bump into you like that."

His voice wasn't deep, but it vibrated through her. Devin looked at the man. They stood toe to toe, eye to eye, exactly the same height, which wasn't tall for a woman and even shorter for a man.

"It's no problem," she replied, more concerned for him than herself. He seemed more uncomfortable with the incident than she was. She smiled when she saw another airline attendant walking in their direction. Hopefully, he could help the line move a little faster.

Spark was embarrassed. So engrossed in trying to take a peek at the slip of paper in her hand, he had tripped over a crack in the floor tile, which had caused him to accidentally push her forward. But he could tell by the look on her face that he hadn't been caught spying. He'd thought the paper in her hand would give him some idea of where she was headed. It hadn't. It appeared to be an envelope, but he hadn't seen the address.

Having accepted his apology, Devin turned around to resume her mission. She was going to get to the bottom of her deceased husband's deceit once and for all. And her first step was to get to Wilmington, Delaware, and have a talk with the writer of the letter that she was holding.

Finally, she thought, moving forward to take her turn at the counter. Glancing behind her, Devin noticed that the short, dark stranger turned his head away. Had he been watching her?

"Hello, ma'am," the man behind the counter started. "How may I help you?"

"I would like to purchase a ticket to—" The loud crash from behind her made her jump. Turning around, she watched with wide eyes as the short, dark man pushed himself off the floor, then bent down to pick up one of the metal poles that was used to hold the rope that formed a pathway for the line. He must have knocked it over when he fell. With her hand to her heart, she said, "You scared me to death." A brief moment of sympathy for him flashed through her as she turned back to face the airline representative. "Um, a ticket to Wilmington, Delaware, please."

"Round trip?"

"Um, no. Make it one way. I don't know when I'll be returning," she answered.

"I'm very sorry," Spark said, moving closer and hearing her destination. *Delaware.* "For scaring you," he continued innocently after she turned towards him.

"You will have to fly into Philadelphia International, ma'am," the counter attendant stated.

"Is that close?"

"That's the closest airport that this airline flies into. I don't know how close it is to Wilmington," he replied.

"But how—" Devin started, suddenly realizing that she hadn't taken the time to map out her trip or even think about the money she would need. She didn't know anything about Wilmington, Delaware. Once she got to Philadelphia she would be walking around with blinders on. Unconsciously, she clung to her purse as she thanked God for the extra money her mother had slipped her. This was a journey that she had to take, regardless of the outcome or the expense. She could always call home for more money if she needed it. "Okay, that will be fine," she said to the attendant. "Do you know where I can purchase a map?"

"Maybe at one of the shops on the next level," he answered, pulling her tickets from the printer and placing them neatly into a courtesy envelope.

Back in his spot in line, Spark waited to be called. He was filled with relief, ecstatic that his trip would soon be ending. He had done his job. It had taken only two days. Now he could get his irritating sister off his back. But soon the excitement subsided and his stomach began to tighten. *Why was she going to Delaware? Who was she looking for? What did she expect to find there?* He began to speculate as he watched her walk away from the counter, realizing that he was a long way from being finished with her.

Devin was disappointed to find that she would have a three-hour wait before her flight was scheduled to depart. Moving cautiously through the terminal, she examined the people around her. A father was struggling with luggage as he hurried his weary children through the crowded airport. A young couple stood snuggled closely together as they rode to the top of the large escalator. A man standing to the side, out of the way of passers-by, caught her attention. Their eyes connected through the crowd. She thought of the man sitting in the car in front of her house. If someone were watching her, surely he had followed her to the airport.

"Damn," she mouthed through clenched lips as she refocused on her reaching her departure terminal and quickened her pace. Once at the correct terminal, she looked over the rows of partially filled seats and found a spot close to the corner. With her back to the wall, Devin was satisfied with her selection. It gave her a full view of the sitting area and anyone approaching the area.

She sat tense and focused, watching every move from others for almost an hour before beginning to think that maybe she was taking the situation a little too seriously. No one had approached her; no one had even given her a second glance. The man she had noticed standing in the terminal had already passed by her and into the next terminal with a mildly attractive woman on his arm. Maybe she was overreacting just a little bit.

Letting out a sigh, she reached over to pick up her purse, which was in the seat next to her. As she did, a shadow fell over her. Instantly, she straightened in surprise, then relaxed when she saw that it was the same man who had been standing in line behind her.

"I'm sorry. I didn't mean to frighten you," he commented, his apology authentic.

"It's okay," she smiled, relaxing a little as his voice caressed her. He was an attractive man, with visibly muscular arms and a strong build. He obviously worked out often. The scent of his cologne was now mixed with the distinct smell of cigarettes. Tobacco odor had always been a turn-off to her, but his brown eyes with their honest shyness held her attention.

"I just wanted to apologize for earlier."

"Do you do that a lot?" she asked.

"What?"

"Apologize."

"Well, um," he started, a small smile curving his lips. "Yes," he confessed.

"I thought so. I've only seen you twice, and I've gotten three apologies." The more they talked, the more handsome he seemed to become.

"Can I buy you a drink or something to make up for earlier? I've upset you twice already today, and we don't even know each other." Spark's smile widened and showed dazzling white, perfectly even teeth as he tried to hide the fact that he was uncomfortable approaching a stranger, trying to trick her into thinking this was a fluke meeting. He wasn't used to acting, nor did he do it well. If she had been a chick at the bar, he could have handled himself a lot better.

Devin, the notes from his sister's private investigator had said, was a pretty woman of average height. But he hadn't expected beautiful. No, she wasn't all flashy and high maintenance like his sister's friends, who were constantly slipping him hints of seduction. Although her hair was thick and long, she had it drawn back in a simple ponytail. She wore no makeup, no fake nails. And she was wearing a gray T-shirt and blue jeans. All she had beside her was her purse and a carry-on bag. Devin seemed comfortable in her skin. He liked that.

Upon closer examination, Devin noticed that his teeth were a little too perfect, but that was none of her business. Although she had two hours to spare, she didn't want to bother with the man.

"No thank you. I'm fine. And you don't owe me a thing."

"Oh, but I do. I've bumped into you. I almost scared you to death. The least I can do is buy you a glass of lemonade."

Devin was about to hesitate again when he continued. "I'm not going to take no for an answer."

She had two hours to spare. Why not spend the time with a nice looking man and possibly make a new friend? She nodded her head and accepted his offer for drinks.

"So, you from here?" he asked, pulling out a chair for her. Best to start the questioning out simple and see where it went from there.

"Yes, all my life," she replied.

"My name is Darnel Miles." He extended his hand. "I know it seems like we've already been introduced since I've talked to you three or four times now."

"Hi, Darnel. I'm Devin Albridge. I mean Avery. Devin Avery," she corrected. Noticing Darnel's left eyebrow raise in question, she said, "Don't ask. It's a long story."

"Hey, none of my business," he replied, holding up his hand in mock surrender. The information he had from his sister said that she had taken her maiden name back. He wondered why. Maybe she'd found out that Albridge wasn't Richard's real name. But Richard had always been a stand-up kind of guy in his book. He was sure that Richard would have eventually explained everything to her. "What would you like to drink?"

"I'm so tense," she openly confessed, then hesitated. She didn't know this man enough to be letting him in on her business. Still, she felt comfortable around him. "I'm sorry." Devin let her eyes fall to the table.

"Hah," he laughed, trying to ease her discomfort. "Now look who's apologizing."

"I know." She laughed. "This is a nice table," she said, running her forefinger across the slate and granite tabletop.

"Yeah, it's a cute little bistro-like setting they got working here." He looked around at the five circular tables placed strategically around a tall counter. Next to the serving counter was a large cooler filled with juices and soft drinks. There was a refrigerated counter with cold cuts, salads, and cut-up fruit. It was quaint and cozy, decorated with fake trees and flowers.

Devin took advantage of his distraction to study him. She was surprised at how clear his complexion was. The full beard he sported was neatly shaven and trimmed to perfection, which only added to his overall attractiveness. Before he caught her, she turned her head and tried to act as if she were looking at the crowd of people entering.

"Darnel, it seems to be getting crowded in here," she said, bringing his eyes to hers.

"Yeah, it is. And please, call me Spark. Do you need to go?" he asked, already knowing the truth and hoping she didn't feel his nervousness.

"Hah, I wish," she answered unsuspectingly before glancing at her watch. "Actually, I still have a two-hour wait. Spark? That's a strange nickname."

"Just one of those childhood things that sticks with you. Two hours, you said? My flight leaves in two hours, too. That's great. We can keep each other company." He paused uncomfortably. "That's if it's all right with you."

"Uh, sure. I don't see why not." She could do with some company. Sitting in the airport alone wasn't exactly a thrill. And what harm could it do? They were surrounded by hundreds of people. Evidently he was close to his departure terminal, or he had time to get to it. "What terminal do you leave from?"

"This one," he said simply, waiting for her response.

"This one?" she questioned.

"Yeah, I'm catching the nine-thirty flight to Philadelphia," he answered. "What do you want to drink?" he asked, realizing that he had never gotten up from the table.

"Um, I'll just have a water," she answered, forcing down her craving for a Pepsi. Not a Diet Pepsi, but the classic, original Pepsi.

Spark made sure not to ask her where she was going. He didn't want her to think that he was that curious. That was why he rushed to get her a drink. But when he returned, he could tell by her expression that she was full of questions. His nervousness mounted. What would he say to her?

Fortunately, his clumsiness came to the rescue. The leg of a wrought-iron chair from a nearby table wrapped around his foot, causing him to stumble and spill his fountain lemonade on the floor.

Devin was stuck between laughter and pity. *The poor man.* How in the world had he made it this far in life? But at the same time, he wore a comfortable smile of embarrassment. The smile seemed to be as familiar to him as his hand or his foot. Obviously, it had become an integral part of his life, and so had his awkwardness.

Spark was the first to let loose a small laugh, but Devin quickly joined in. As he moved out of the way so that the counter girl could clean up the mess, he offered an apology.

"I didn't think I would be apologizing again so soon."

"It's okay. I didn't think I'd be accepting another one so soon." Devin continued laughing, but tried to get herself under control.

"I'm afraid that I'm equilibrium-challenged."

That set off another round of hysterics in both of them.

"Is that what it is?" Devin said when she got her breath. "I thought you were just clumsy."

Sitting back down across from her, Spark was suddenly struck a little harder by her beauty. It was the first time he had seen her truly smile in the few days he had been spying on her. Damn. He had almost forgotten that she wasn't just someone he had happened to meet at an airport terminal. She was his job, his detail, and his suspect. Call it what you wanted, he wasn't supposed to start liking her. But it was already too late. He did like her—more than he liked his sister.

CHAPTER 5

Because the nine-thirty flight to Philadelphia International Airport wasn't full, the stewardess informed the thirty-five passengers that they could sit wherever they chose. Devin felt a little relief when Spark suggested that they sit together. She was very uncomfortable on planes. Even though she was unsure of what she was doing, Devin felt that Spark's company would ease her tension. They seemed to talk comfortably to each other. Besides, he was pleasant on the eyes.

Once the plane was in the air, Devin's apprehension grew. Was she making the right decision by going to a strange place on a whim? How was she going to accomplish her goal when she didn't know the first thing to do after she got off the plane? Devin fell silent, lost in her thoughts, and missed the beginning of Spark's question.

". . . when you get there?"

"I'm sorry. What did you say?" she asked, blinking her eyes to focus on him.

Spark looked at her strangely. "I asked who you're visiting when you get to Philly. Family?"

"No," she answered quietly, her uncertainty clearly present in her voice. Her purpose for being on the airplane was private. Looking at him, she could see he was curious, but she had only met this man a few hours ago.

Once she landed, she would just take her time at the airport until she figured out what her next move would be.

The small map she'd purchased at the airport in Chicago didn't give much detail about the area she would be visiting. She still wasn't sure exactly how far she would be from her destination once she got to the Philadelphia airport. She was certain that she would have to buy another map or ask for more specific directions.

"You don't sound as if you want to talk about it," he stated, backing off to convince her that he could be trusted. In the big picture he was a liar and a manipulator, but he wanted her trust. And he knew that it was asking too much—was—ridiculous really—but still, he wanted it.

Spark found his guilt clogging his throat. He wished that he could let her know who he was, but she would hate him. And he liked her too much to take the risk. Instead, he would try to help her in any way possible to get where she was going. He couldn't let her wander around aimlessly in the airport.

"It's not that," she said. Letting out a deep breath, she tried to decide what she could afford to tell him and what she should keep to herself. "I'm not going to Philadelphia," she confessed. "Once I land, I have to find a way to Delaware."

Spark tried to look at her with as much shock and amazement on his face as he could muster. "Really? I'm going to Delaware. What part are you going to?"

"Wilmington, I guess."

"You guess?"

"I'm going to Wilmington."

"Well, I go through Wilmington on my way home. I live in Bear." He kept his comments short and to the point. It was best to let her talk if she wanted to. "Maybe I know your friends."

"No, actually, I don't know anyone there. But I have to find a way to get there."

"Well, you can ride with me. My car is at the airport. Long-term parking. I'll give you a ride to wherever you're going."

"Ha," she laughed. "I don't know where I'm going."

Spark just looked at her.

"I'm sort of on a mission," she finally stated.

"Mission?" he repeated.

"Yeah. I'm looking for somebody, but I don't want to talk about it."

"Okay."

"But could I ask a favor?"

"Sure, what is it?" Spark figured that helping Devin would only help his cause. He needed to find out what she was up to even though he truly liked her. She was beautiful, seemed intelligent, and held his interest with her conversation. She didn't berate him for his clumsiness as so many of his former lady friends had. He felt comfortable around her.

"Could you help me find a hotel room once I get to Wilmington?"

"Sure," he readily answered. He was going to have to keep an eye on her. He was pretty sure that the only connection she had to Delaware was his sister. Spark imagined that Devin was going to Delaware to look for her.

He wondered if he should call his sister when he landed. He hadn't told her that he was coming back so soon or that Devin was the reason. He supposed that he should tell her, but he really wanted to just back out of the whole situation and let his crazy-ass sister handle facing Devin.

At the same time, he wished he could turn back the hands of time and stand up to his sister. He wished he had told her no—told her he wasn't going to do her dirty work. Spark hadn't wanted to go to Chicago in the first place, and now that he'd met Devin, he really wished he hadn't.

The pilot was announcing that the plane was making its descent when Spark gently nudged Devin awake. He smiled as he watched her hand automatically go to her mouth to wipe away any drool. She did it almost as if she thought she was still at home, until . . .

"Agh . . . ," Devin yelled, grabbing blindly for him as the plane began to drop in altitude. "What's wrong? What's happening?"

"Devin, calm down," Spark quickly replied, trying to hide the humor that filled him. "It's just that the plane's about to land."

"Land? We're there already?"

"Yeah. After you nodded off, I just let you sleep. It seemed better for you." The plane dropped again. She grabbed his hand.

"You should have let me stay asleep."

"Then you would have woken up in a complete panic when the plane landed. No, this is better. No heart attacks."

"Thanks, since you put it like that," she replied, gripping his hand tightly.

"It will be okay," Spark said, squeezing her hand in return and finding that he enjoyed the touch, palm to palm, skin to skin. He was content to sit silently next to her and hold her hand for the remainder of the flight.

"It wasn't that funny," she said, following him off the airport parking lot bus, struggling with her carry-on bag, suitcase, and purse.

"Yes, it was," he answered, stopping to take her suitcase from her. "And why doesn't this suitcase have wheels? When did you buy it, 1970?"

"It's my parents' suitcase, thank you very much. And don't change the subject. Where is your car parked anyway?" She glanced briefly in the direction he pointed. There were cars everywhere. "Where?"

"It's the black Camry," he replied, shifting the suitcase to his other arm.

"Like I can see that."

"Well, you asked. We're almost there." He started laughing again. "I just can't get over the look on your face when the plane landed."

"Let it go. That was an hour ago."

"But it's still funny." Five minutes later, he said through laughter, "Here we are."

Devin moved past him to stand by the trunk of the car. She didn't say a word to him, hadn't spoken in five minutes. Just listened to the stuttering snorts that filled his laughs. She watched him place her suitcase in the car's trunk. She didn't care that she was standing in the middle of a humongous and nearly deserted parking lot with a strange man whom she had met only a few hours earlier and was dependent on for a ride and a brief tour of a strange place. She didn't care. He wasn't going to keep making her the butt of his joke. Damn it, she'd said it wasn't that funny, and it wasn't.

Spark didn't pay any attention to her. He just kept on snickering as he unlocked the car door, but his amusement was short lived when he slipped as he got into the car.

Surprised to see him drop out of sight, Devin rushed around to the side of the car to find Spark lying on his back with one leg in the car, the other under the door. "Oh," she exclaimed. "Are you okay?"

"Um . . . yeah," Spark replied, embarrassed but accepting her proffered hand. "Ow, ow, ow. Easy," he stated, sitting up.

"Are you sure that you're okay?" she asked again as he got to his feet. She smiled broadly once she realized he was all right.

"Don't do it . . ." Spark pointed a finger at her as he got into the car.

Try as she might, Devin couldn't hide the big smile when she walked back to the passenger side of the car. "Unlock the door," she shouted.

He didn't do anything.

"Unlock the door, please," she replied patiently.

"I thought you were laughing at me," Spark confided as she slid into the passenger seat. His insecurities were expressed on his face as he stared straight ahead.

She could see his face more clearly as they neared the lights at the pay booth. It shocked her that he was so sensitive, but then she remembered his clumsiness earlier in the Chicago airport. Devin wondered if he had a problem that she should know about. After all, she was in the car with a virtual stranger in a strange city, in the middle of the night.

"Why would I laugh at you?" she asked, turning her face stone serious. "Unlike some people I know, I don't think it's funny when someone might have hurt themselves."

"Okay, point taken. I apologize for earlier," he said, glancing at her briefly. "Look, it's about a thirty-minute ride to Wilmington. You can either go back to sleep or I could tell you a little about the place."

"I'm going to lie back, close my eyes, and listen to you talk about Wilmington. I like your voice." Devin adjusted her seat a little, crossed her arms, and shut her eyes.

"You like my voice? Don't you want to see some of the place? At least you could look at the Wilmington skyline as we ride into it."

"I'm all right. I'll hear about it later. Just let me know when we get to the hotel."

"Okay."

Fifty minutes later, Devin was awakened gently by a tugging on her arm.

"Devin, wake up. Devin?"

"Hmmm," she replied. "I was listening," she lied.

"No, you weren't," he laughed.

The car was stopped in front of a sign that read Doubletree Inn. Stretching, she started to get out of the car but he stopped her.

"I already went inside. They're booked up."

"All booked up? Well, we'll just try someplace else." She glanced down at her watch. "I'm sorry to have you out so late."

"It's no problem, but I'm going to tell you this. The local university is having graduation tomorrow. Ten chances to one, we won't be able to find a room for the next few days." Quietly, he waited for her response.

Devin was silent. She didn't know what to say or do. She'd assumed that it would be easy to come to Delaware and just as easy to get a hotel room. Completely at a loss, she hunched her shoulders in defeat. What could she do but ask him for a ride back to the airport and wait for the next flight home?

"Look, it's one in the morning. Why don't you just stay at my house tonight?" Spark suggested, sure that she wouldn't agree and unsure of why he'd offered in the first place. He should be trying to get her out of Delaware as soon as possible, suggest that she take the next plane back. But he didn't want her to leave. He liked her more and more.

"Are you sure?" Devin asked, like she had other options. She knew she didn't. "I mean, I don't want to be an inconvenience. Will your wife mind?" Okay, it was corny and obvious, but she asked anyway.

"I don't have a wife, so no one will mind, and yeah, I'm sure. It's too late for us to ride around looking for the last hotel room in town. I don't live far from here." He started up the car and headed toward the traffic light.

This time Devin didn't fall asleep, she couldn't. Her mind began to race, and her heart beat erratically. What was she doing? Everything her mother had ever warned her against. She was going home with a strange man in a strange town. She wondered why she wasn't the least bit nervous about her circumstances. In a way, she felt a relief at having to go home with him. If she had been able to get a hotel room, she might not have ever seen him again. He didn't owe it to her to help her while she was there. Maybe now she could ask him for a little assistance or at least a push in the right direction. He was from the area.

"Here we are," Spark said, pulling her out of her daze as he turned the car off the highway into a huge apartment complex. Driving toward the back, he parked in front of a building with what appeared to be six townhouses.

Devin waited for him to get out of the car first, watched him retrieve their luggage from the trunk, and then followed him to the last door on the right. "These are nice," she stated, looking around and stepping into the apartment. From the outside it looked like a two-story home, but now that she was inside, she could tell that instead of six townhouses there was really a row of twelve apartments, stacked by twos.

His apartment was spacious. They walked down a hallway. Spark opened a large closet and threw his carry-on bag inside of it. He kept Devin's in his hand. Devin followed him into the living room, which was tastefully decorated with black leather furniture, end tables, and lamps. A huge black and glass entertainment center occupied one wall. It was filled with a stereo, DVD player, 32-inch flat screen TV, a Playstation set, and tons of games and DVDs. The artificial plants that took up the corner spaces were beautiful and large.

She looked around the room and decided that it suited him. It was neat, clean, and organized. He must have cleaned the place before he left. "A confirmed bachelor pad," she commented as she walked toward the kitchen.

"What?" he questioned as he continued toward his bedroom. He opened his door and saw that the bed was made; a sigh of apprehension escaped his mouth. When he left, he'd purposely left his bed unmade. Damn it, Vivian still had a key. He'd known she wouldn't be able to come into the house and not fix the bed, especially after he had taken such care to clean everything else in the house. When he had broken things off with her and asked for his key back, he'd suspected she had made copies. This was proof of it.

"I said your place looks just like I would imagine a bachelor pad to look," Devin yelled from the other room.

"Well, I am a bachelor," he admitted. "Make yourself at home. There should be something to drink in the fridge. I'll be out in a moment." Suddenly remembering, Spark walked into the living room.

From the top of the entertainment center, he picked up the few pictures he kept out, one of his twin nieces and another of him and his sister before he began to resent her. Just as fast he walked back to the bedroom.

Devin didn't see what he had in his hand as she turned back from the refrigerator. It looked like pictures, but she wasn't sure. Whatever they were, he didn't want her to see them. She hunched her shoulders. They were probably pictures of some girl. She twisted the top to a Snapple Green Tea bottle. As good as he looked, it would be stupid of her to think there wasn't someone in his life, regardless of what he said.

"Okay, I'll take the sofa," Spark was saying when he walked back into the living room. He was carrying two sheets, a blanket, and a pillow.

At first, she didn't say anything. Her eyes were glued on him. Spark was a sight for sore eyes in his wife-beater and pajama pants. The arm and chest muscles hidden earlier by his T-shirt were now on full display. No, he wasn't cut like a bodybuilder, but you could tell that he wasn't a small man. The wifebeater looked damn good on him.

"Uh, you sure? I can sleep on the couch," she argued.

"No, I wouldn't think of it. The bed's all yours," he smiled at her, "unless you want to share."

"Ha, ha." The thought had crossed her mind about four times, and each time, she'd reined it back in. "No, thank you. Where's the bathroom?"

"Through there and to the left," he answered, spreading the blanket out over the sheets.

"Spark, I really appreciate this," Devin said.

"It's no problem. What kind of man would I be if I left you out there on the rough streets of Delaware to fend for yourself? Tomorrow I'll help you find whatever you're looking for, and you'll be straight."

"It's not really whatever so much as whoever," she confided, leaning against the doorframe, watching him watch her.

Spark had figured as much, but decided not to push it. He wanted to make sure that she trusted him enough to let him in on her secret. "Well, whoever, then. We'll find them tomorrow. I put a washcloth and towel in there already."

"Thanks again." Devin unpacked her nightclothes and went to the bathroom. She was exhausted, but instead of taking the time for a leisurely bath she opted to shower and dive into bed. It was late, and she wanted an early start.

Spark sat on the edge of the sofa wondering how he was going to work through this mess. He knew that he was dead wrong for helping her. He should have never even approached her at the airport. It would have been better if she didn't know who he was. The only reason she could be in Delaware was to look up his sister and the girls.

God, he had forgotten all about the pictures. If she had seen them, she would have known. His nieces looked exactly like their father, just as her girls did. She wouldn't have missed the strong resemblance. His nieces were just a few years older than her daughters. Tomorrow, she would ask him to take her somewhere. He didn't know for sure if it would be to his sister's house, but all roads had to be leading to her.

As he listened to the shower run, Spark imagined being the beads of water dripping down her wet skin and navigated a path that he would take. The path started from her shoulders, ran through the valley between her ample breasts, over the little pudge of her stomach, and down through the little black forest between her legs.

Rocking forward to stand, he walked around the living room trying to relax his arousal. He blew out a long breath just as he heard the door to the bathroom open.

Spark dived onto the sofa and quickly covered himself to hide his erection. He was lying sideways, looking at the floor, when she stepped into the room wearing a robe that came to her knees. He could see that her legs were still a little damp and wondered if she wore anything under the robe. She was so close all he had to do was reach out, look up, and he would know.

"Good night, Spark," Devin said.

"Good night, Devin," he replied, watching her retreat. In a huff, he fell on his back and tried to put the image of her lying in his bed, between his sheets, out of his mind.

CHAPTER 6

Sun splashed into Devin's face and awakened her. She wasn't sure what time it was, but it felt too early to be getting up. She was still exhausted. Devin quickly said her morning prayer, a practice that she had started as a child, along with the rest of her siblings, at her parents' insistence. 'Before you move, before you think or act, you thank the Lord for waking you this morning.' The instruction was still as clear as the first day she heard it.

And she was thankful because today was the day that she was going to get to the truth about her deceased husband. Somehow, she was going to get the strength to find out who belonged to the post office box on the envelope and find out exactly what was what.

With her determination renewed and thoughts of her deceased husband's deceit put aside, Devin got out of bed and opened the door with only thoughts of C. Harrison on her mind. She looked around the apartment only to find that she was alone.

"Spark," she called, walking from the living room to the kitchen. He was nowhere to be found. Looking out the window, she saw that his car was gone, and wondered when he'd left.

Back in the living room, saw a piece of paper on the living room table. It was a note to her. *Had an appoint-*

ment, will be back as soon as possible. Food in frig. Make yourself at home. Devin decided to follow his directions.

She showered and dressed, then made herself a quick breakfast of scrapple, eggs, and toast. After eating, she called her mother to let her know that she was fine. She knew that her mother would worry herself sick if she didn't hear from her on regular intervals.

"Do you need anything?"

"No, Mom. I'm fine. Hopefully, I'll be on my way back home in a couple of days. This shouldn't take me long. How are the girls?"

They talked for a few more minutes before Devin ended the call. Bored, she turned on the television and surfed the channels until she found something of interest.

"So, when did you get back in town? I thought you would be gone for the week."

"Late last night," Spark answered. He was standing outside of St. Mark's United Methodist Church where he had been attending Gambler's Anonymous meetings for the past four years. Spark didn't believe that he needed the meetings for gambling anymore as much as he did for his decision-making. In these meetings, he was able to sort out his confusion and slow down his thought processes, or even bounce his ideas off others, if necessary. The meetings were his safe haven whenever he was unsure about the things happening in his life.

Now was one of those moments. He knew that he should not have gotten involved in his sister's craziness. And now, he didn't know what to do about the lady staying out his house. Should he help her, or should he just help her find a hotel and then leave her to her own devices? He lit the cigarette that he'd been holding between his lips.

"Are you okay, man?"

"I'm as good as I can be, right now. Man, you stay safe," he said, shaking the man's hand and walking toward his car. The cigarette seemed to give him more comfort than the meeting had. After an hour, he still hadn't come up with any idea of how to fix his problem.

He headed home.

Devin was sitting at the sofa, watching *The View* when he walked in. She jumped up as he approached.

"Everything okay?" she asked, noticing the tightness of his brows. "You look like there's a problem."

"No problem. I just had to get to that meeting. Is everything okay with you?"

"I'm fine. I was just watching television until you got back. Listen, I really don't mean to put you out here. I don't know why I thought coming here and doing what I needed to do would be so easy."

"Oh, you can't find who you're looking for?" he asked curiously.

"More like, I don't even know where to begin to look. I think I'm going to have to contact my sister. She's a lawyer. I should have never come here in the first place. I don't know the first thing about finding people." Devin sat back down on the sofa.

"Wait, wait. Don't go beating yourself up." Spark removed the cell phone at his said, tossing it onto an end table, and sat beside her.

"No. I shouldn't have come. I acted like the spoiled brat I've always been. Just dropped off my kids, picked up a suitcase, and traveled all the way here like the answers to all my questions were going to fall at my feet. Oh, God. I left my kids with my parents, as if they don't have enough to deal with. And I know better than that. That's not the kind of person I am."

"I'm sure that if your parents couldn't handle it, they would have told you so."

"No, they wouldn't have. They would have just done it because I asked them to. My parents don't ask too many questions when it comes to their grandchildren."

"Okay, listen. I'm off work for a couple of days. I'll help you look for whoever you need to find, and we'll get you back to your children as soon as possible." Spark couldn't believe he had just said that. Apparently, he had unconsciously made up his mind already.

But now that it was said, how was he going to do it? He looked at his watch. 11:30 a.m. "So, who are you looking for? Somebody you used to date? A family member?"

"No, nothing like that, I'm afraid. Someone wrote me a letter, and I need to locate them to talk some things through." She wasn't going to tell him too much. Although it would have been easy to unburden herself,

Devin had to remember that she had only known this man one day.

"Well, I'm not sure if it's a good idea to just roll up to a stranger's house and start asking a bunch of questions. Would you classify this person as a friend, or will they have a fit when you knock on their door?"

"Probably the latter. I can't imagine that we will have a civil conversation once we finally meet."

"Why did they write you if they didn't want to meet? That doesn't make much sense to me."

"I don't know. There's just a lot to it, and I don't feel right bringing you into my problems. If you don't mind, all I need is for you to help me find the person, and I'll take it from there."

"Okay, no problem."

"I really do appreciate your help."

Spark nodded his head. He was busy trying to figure out if it was possible to help Devin without getting his sister involved. Maybe he could just run her around for a few days and then concede defeat. Devin could go home, believing that they'd tried their best. At any rate, it was better having her close so that he could keep an eye on her.

"What's the address you're looking for?" Carlissa had not told him that she had written Devin. The least he could do was make sure that she wasn't stupid enough to write her own address.

"I don't have an address. I have a post office box number."

"A P.O. box? That could take forever to find. Do you realize how many post offices are around here? No, of course you don't. Well, there are a lot. Okay, let's think. How can we narrow down the search for a post office box?"

Devin thought for a second, and then snapped her fingers as the simple solution presented itself. "Why don't we just call one of the post offices in the area and see if they will tell us where the box might be located?"

"It's worth a shot. I'll get the phone book." While Spark walked to the kitchen, Devin walked to the bedroom to retrieve the letter.

After getting the post office number, Devin made the call. "Hello," Devin said after the post office worker answered, "I am trying to locate the owner of a post office box that might be in your location."

"I'm sorry, but we don't give that information out."

"Of course, I apologize. Can you tell me if you have this box number?"

"Um, I'm sure that you could just walk in and look at the numbers on the boxes, ma'am."

"Well, the problem is that I'm from out of town, and I'm not very familiar with Delaware at all. I just received a letter from a long-lost friend with P.O. Box 527, Wilmington, Delaware, as the return address."

"I can tell you right from the door that number is not here. This post office is located in Bear. You would have to call one of the Wilmington offices, and I doubt very seriously if they will give you any information over the phone either. Your best bet would be to go inside and look at the numbers, like I said."

"Okay, thank you for your time," Devin said, hanging up the phone. "We called a post office that's not in Wilmington."

"Right. I'm sorry. I figured that the post office here would be able to help us. So, what do we need to do, call a Wilmington office?"

"Basically, she said that they won't help me over the phone either way. I need to go inside and either look at the boxes myself or beg for assistance. I got the impression that the post office isn't going to be too helpful."

"Well, it is a federal office. I'm sure they're not able to just give you someone's information because you ask for it."

"I'm hungry. You hungry?" Devin asked, wanting to suggest that they go out and pick up something to eat. Maybe even stop by the post office. Wilmington couldn't be that far away. But she didn't want to seem as if she was taking advantage of him. He was already being kind enough to let her stay there for free.

"Okay, well, we can get something to eat and ride to Wilmington to check out a post office if you wish."

"Are you sure that's okay? It's not far out of the way, is it?"

"No, but we need to hurry. We don't want the post office to close before we get there." He glanced at his watch. "We should have plenty of time to pick up some seafood and then go to the post office down the street. Do you like seafood?"

"Of course. But it's my treat. The least I can do is feed you since I'm staying for free."

"Hey, I won't argue with that logic. Let me run to the bathroom, then I gotta stop and get gas real quick."

Devin went into the bedroom while he was in the bathroom to grab her purse.

Ring, ring . . . ring, ring.

"Spark, love?"

Instantly, Devin froze at the sound of the female voice vibrating from his answering machine. She strained to listen.

Spark flashed by as he ran out of the bathroom to get the phone. Whoever she was, she must be important. *Damn,* Devin fussed on the inside, *right when she was about to start getting some answers.*

Spark couldn't get to the phone fast enough. Turning off the answering machine, he hurried to speak before she said anything else.

"Hey," he said, his heaving breathing filling the line.

"Damn, what you doing?"

"Nothing."

"Stop lying. Are you screwing?"

"No," he replied. His sister's language was harsh and vulgar, but only when she talked to him. To anyone else, she was the perfect picture of the delicate lady, the perfect mother. See, he thought, thirty seconds, that's all it took for him to remember how much he disliked her.

"Yes, you are. You nasty bastard. You're supposed to be keeping an eye on Ms. Devin Avery."

Harrison, he said in his head, before remembering that Richard hadn't been able to give Devin his real name. "What do you want?" he asked. Irritation filled his voice.

"I want to know that you're doing your damn job."

"Goodbye." Spark hung up the phone. He looked at it with a grimace as if it was his sister that he was frowning at. Even if he couldn't do it to her face, he could do it behind her back.

A movement in the hallway caught his eye. It was Devin walking to the bathroom. *Dammit.*

Spark followed her, but the door was shut when he got to it. "Devin."

No reply.

"Devin."

No reply.

"Hey, you ready?" he asked, nonchalantly. "That was my damn sister. We need to hurry if we're going to make the post office."

"Okay," she said, emerging from the room. Unfortunately, Devin had never been one to keep her mouth shut when it was necessary. She knew that what Spark did was none of her business. And she didn't know why she was upset that the woman had called him. He was doing her a favor, and she needed to just accept his help and move on. "I thought you said that you didn't have a woman."

"I don't," he said, sensing the conversation was going to get worse before it got better. "I said that was my sister."

"Oh, and you hurry to answer your sister like that," Devin continued once they were seated in the car.

"You don't know my sister, Devin."

"No, I don't, but I do know my sisters, and I don't hurry to answer them like that. I'm sorry." She put her hands up in surrender. "I apologize. It just caught me off guard."

"Are you sure that's all it is?"

"Yeah, I'm very sure."

"Oh, I thought for a moment that you were sitting over there sulking because you were a bit jealous."

"Jealous? You have to be kidding. I don't know you enough to be jealous of you being with anyone else. No, hon, I'm not jealous."

"Okay. Dang, you sure do know how to kick a man when he's down."

She crossed her arms. "I just wanted to make sure that you know where I'm coming from." Devin glanced in his direction, making sure that he believed her.

He didn't. But that was okay. She had no intentions of going there with Spark. As attractive as he was or she might have been to him, Devin knew that she couldn't let that deter her from her goal.

The flavorful buttery garlic sauce that smothered her shrimp and vegetables did little to subdue the disappointment of not making it to the post office on time. Devin sat in the booth quietly and watched Spark devour his corn on the cob. She was excited on their way into the city until the traffic jam delayed them.

"Come on, Devin, cheer up. We'll come back here first thing in the morning and find out everything. You won't have to be here much longer. That is why you're upset isn't it?"

"Yeah, but you're right. Tomorrow is a new day, and you're sure we can start first thing?"

"No problem." Spark smiled when she began to pay attention to the steamed broccoli on her plate. "I was hoping that you were still jealous from this morning."

Devin looked at the handsome man across from her. "I told you this morning that I was not jealous. If I wasn't jealous then, why would you think I was jealous now?"

"Because I didn't believe you this morning. I know you thought my sister was some other woman."

Now Devin smiled. "You're delusional. Maybe I shouldn't be staying at your house. You might be dangerous and crazy."

"Come on, now. You're still sitting over there jealous as hell. As soon as my sister called, your whole mood was ruined."

"Like I said, crazy. And I still don't think that was your sister."

"It was my sister. You really don't believe me?"

Devin picked up a newspaper that she pretended to read. "It doesn't really matter who was on the phone. That's none of my business. You're not my man."

"You know what, Devin Albridge-Avery or Avery-Albridge, or whatever your name is, you're a trip. I think that you are jealous, and you should be willing to make me something to you. I don't see a ring on your finger, unless you have a man back in Chicago. And I doubt that because he wouldn't have let you come all the way to Delaware by yourself."

"What I have in Chicago is none of your business."

"All I'm saying is don't sit there and act like you haven't thought about it." He stood over her. She had a nerve. He was being a complete gentleman to her, and he was truly a nice guy.

"I haven't, and if I have, it's because I wasn't thinking clearly. But now that I am, I just want to find who I'm looking for and get the hell out of here. Like you said, whatever my name is, right? Why are we even having this conversation seeing as how we don't even know each other?"

He knew she was lying to both of them. It might have been only a day, but she was feeling him. But she would keep it to herself. And he would do the same, only for a different reason.

They didn't talk to each other on the way back to the apartment. Spark pointed out different landmarks, and Devin would occasionally look in the direction he was referring to, but it seemed as if he was talking at her, not to her.

CHAPTER 7

Once they returned to the apartment, they went their separate ways. They only spoke when necessary for the rest of the evening. Spark excused himself when he almost bumped into her. Devin asked if she could get a bottle of water.

She called her mother and her brother Troy before going to bed, needing them to cheer her up a little.

"You ready to come back home?" Troy asked, hearing what he assumed was defeat in her voice.

"No. I haven't found the woman yet. I've only been here a day, Troy."

"Well, by the sound of your voice, I figured that you hadn't found what you were looking for and were coming back."

"No. I'm just tired. It was a long, wasted day. Hopefully, tomorrow will be a better day."

"So, you're going to stay?"

"Yes, Troy. I have to do this. Why can't you understand?"

"It doesn't really matter if I understand or not, baby girl. If you believe that you have to do this, than I'm behind you. I guess I'm just as worried about you as everyone else. Just call me every night, so I'll know that you are okay. And come home as soon as you can."

"I promise I will, Troy. Tell everyone that I asked about them."

Devin stayed in the bedroom for most of the evening, only venturing out to the bathroom around eleven. She didn't look in Spark's direction, but she knew that he was still awake. She had heard him turn off the television around ten-thirty. He wasn't asleep yet.

When Devin came out of the bathroom, she ignored him. Devin understood that her anger might have been mistaken for jealousy. And maybe she had felt a twinge of jealousy when she heard the other woman's voice, but now was not the time for any of that. She really shouldn't be mad with him at all, but she had to take her anger out on someone, and he was there.

For an instant, Devin felt that she should apologize, but quickly decided against it when she saw his head raise off the couch pillow.

"So where to?" Spark asked. Anger was prevalent in his voice, but try as he might Spark couldn't get the picture of her lying beneath him out of his head. He had dreamed about her all night. And even though she sat in the passenger seat all smug and confident as if she had lived in Delaware all her life and knew where she was, he could see her jaw shaking. Her uncertainty was undeniable, and he wished he could comfort her in some way.

"To the post office, I guess, " she replied. She was disappointed and a little heartbroken. In her arrogance,

Devin had actually thought she was going to come to Delaware, find C. Harrison, give her a piece of her mind, and be on her way with her pride and dignity still intact. Sadly, it wasn't turning out that way.

She pulled the envelope out of her pocket. Then they got stuck in traffic again. It was hot, and even with the windows rolled down, no air was circulating through the car. But even then, she didn't talk to him to pass the time away. Instead, she turned the radio up when he made an attempt at conversation.

Devin looked straight ahead, stubborn as the spoiled baby girl that she was. When she got a chance, she glanced over at him. And through the anger, she felt a strange sensation bubbling in the pit of her stomach. He was so handsome, almost too handsome, but she was still mad at him. If she were to be honest with herself, Devin would have admitted that she was jealous, but then, she would have to also admit to the feelings swirling inside her. She'd only known the man two days, for goodness sake.

All the way to the post office, she wondered how different yesterday would have been if that woman hadn't called his phone. Surely, the possibility of a much closer relationship with him was there. How good of a lover would he be? How good could he have made her feel? And who the hell was that woman anyway? He'd said his sister, but was she really?

At the post office, Devin was disappointed. When she finally had her turn at the counter of the small, snug room that served as the service area, she was informed that they were at the incorrect post office. Apparently, the city of Wilmington had five post offices. She was crushed when the postal employee told her.

Fortunately, they were able to narrow the search down to two offices by pinpointing the zip codes. She left the building with Spark right on her heels. She still wasn't speaking to him, but she was thankful for his help. She just couldn't tell him. As if reading her mind, he simply hopped in the car and pulled off. Before she knew it, they were at another post office.

She didn't make a move to get out of the car. Devin wanted to say something to him, but she didn't know how to go about apologizing. Spark hadn't been anything but generous to her, offering her shelter, food, and transportation.

"Um, Spark—" She wanted, needed, to say something to him.

"Go on inside, and see what you can find out," Spark said, cutting her speech short. Once she got out of the car, Spark pulled out a cigarette and lit it. His mood was darkening. What had he done that was so wrong? He shouldn't even be helping her. Common sense told him that she was looking for his sister even though she hadn't told him. Why was he the one driving her around on her wild goose chase? If Carlissa found out about this, she would never let him live it down.

He felt the connection that he and Devin had made. He could feel the intense heat that simmered between them, and he knew she had to feel it, too. She had to. If he could hold her in his arms for just a while, it would make dealing with Carlissa worth it.

Damn. He banged his hand against the steering wheel of his car. He didn't like the way he felt about Devin. He didn't like it at all. But when she came out of the door with the disappointed look in her eyes and the small pout on her face, his groin tightened. He wanted to put his arms around her and fight away all her troubles. But he couldn't.

Devin got in the car and slammed the car door shut.

"I'm sorry," she said, apologizing as she sat back deeply into the seat. "For everything." That was her way of getting it all out.

"What did they say?" It was obviously not good.

"They said that the box is here, but they weren't at liberty to give me any information on the renter."

"Okay, so let's get a bite to eat and go back to the house to think about the next step."

"I really want to thank you for all your help. I mean, you didn't have to do any of this for me, a total stranger. I really appreciate it."

Spark didn't say anything. He wanted her to eat crow for a few minutes longer. He was enjoying it.

She stopped and looked at him. "You can stop me at any time, you know."

"I was rather enjoying myself. It's not often a man has a woman so apologetic. There was no way I was going to stop you."

"Anyway, this little bit of running around has me tired. It's almost noon, and I'm still where I was when I left Chicago."

"It's only been a few hours, Devin. Sometimes these things take time. Just be patient. You'll find her." He had slipped, and as soon as the words fell from his lips, he knew she had heard it.

"Her? How do you know I'm looking for a woman?"

"I'm assuming it's a woman." Spark glanced at her quickly as he maneuvered through the city and back toward his house. "I hope you're not staying with me while you're looking for a man."

Devin smiled at him. "It is a woman. I need to find her and get some answers about—"

"Devin, if you're not comfortable talking to me about it, I'll understand." He was just happy that she believed his little white lie. "I'll still help you any way that I can."

"I just didn't think it would be this hard." She sat back in the car, frustrated and disappointed at the outcome of her day. In her head, she realized that she would have to enlist the help of her sister after all in order to get to the bottom of things. April was the only one she could think of who could help her get the information she needed. The post office was not going to give her access to the box renter's information, which by law and by right they shouldn't. But a private investigator could dig up information like that easily. Between one of her investigators and her contacts at the police department, April should have no problem at all. And she had already offered the help.

"Um, this is the best curried chicken I've ever had," Devin said, raising the fork to her mouth to take in one of her last bites. She shut her eyes to savor the taste of the spicy mixture of seasonings.

"You sound like you're really enjoying it." Spark sat across from her at the dining room table. He had stopped eating himself in order to watch her take a bite and slowly chew. With her eyes closed, her moist lips working in unison to finish the bite, Devin looked as if she were in utopia. Every few chews, he was treated to the sight of her tongue sliding through her mouth to pick up a stray morsel. Shaking his head, he brought his mind out of the gutter.

"This is so good. I'm serious. When I leave, we're going to have to keep in contact so you can send me this on a regular basis."

"On a regular basis? You're crazy," he laughed. "And you would eat it?"

"All you have to do is freeze it and send it overnight." She was very serious. "Why are you looking at me like that?"

Spark didn't answer. Instead, he got up from the table to clean his plate and put it in the sink. He needed to get his mind off of the swell of her breasts, the curve of her hips, and the scent of her body. Her fragrance surrounded him.

The loud clank of the plate hitting the floor made him jump, but luckily, he came out of his daze in time to catch himself from hitting the floor hard. His wrist hurt, but his face was safe.

"Oh, Spark, are you okay?" Devin jumped up from the table when she saw him falling. *What was wrong with him?* She raced around the table and knelt beside him. "Are you okay?" she asked again, concern filling her voice.

"I'm fine." Spark turned around and held his wrist. "Damn, this hurts."

Immediately, she went to the bathroom, stopping at the hallway closet to grab a washcloth, which she soaked in cold water at the kitchen sink. *How in the hell has he survived this long?* She looked over at him and a smile formed on her lips.

He was so handsome, so considerate and helpful, and so damn clumsy.

"Here, Spark, let me help you." Lifting his arm, she let him put his weight on her as he stood up from the floor. "Just sit on the sofa. I'll get some ice for your wrist."

"I think I might have broken it, again," Spark commented.

"Again?" Devin lifted his wrist and slowly moved it from side to side. Spark winced, but he wasn't in excruciating pain. "I don't think so. You probably just sprained it."

He rested back against the sofa cushions and closed his eyes. There was no embarrassment, no excuses. He had given up the silly reactions to his equilibrium disorder years ago. Now, it was just how it was. He was clumsy. His day was a success if he got through the day without harming himself. Obviously, today wasn't one of those days. Luckily, he hadn't had any incidents at work, at least not yet.

Spark worked at an oil refinery. Although his job wasn't stressful or strenuous, there was some high risk involved. He had to take several safety classes a year and continuously train to operate upgraded equipment. At work, he stayed on constant guard against himself, always moving slower than usual, and always conscious of his surroundings.

"Does it still hurt a lot?" Devin sat next to him and placed a Ziploc bag of ice on his wrist.

"Thanks, Devin. I'm okay."

"Well, I can't be letting the only person I know in Delaware kill himself."

He laughed easily with her.

"Want to watch some television? We don't have anything else to do." She stayed next to him, trying to change the atmosphere in the room. It was only 2 p.m., and they had done all the running around they could. Devin had left a message on April's office phone and was waiting for a return call.

"Yeah, let's watch something. I don't know what's on during the daytime, but if you can't find anything just put in a movie."

Two hours later, the credits for *Madea Goes to Jail* were rolling over the screen. Spark was leaning on the side of the sofa with Devin lying across his chest in a peaceful sleep. When she first lay against him, Spark stayed tense for fifteen minutes. The feel of her next to him and the scent of her body floating through his nostrils had him immediately on edge. His body was still hard—his whole body.

As the credits continued to roll, he pondered moving her to stop the DVD, but he was enjoying her closeness too much. Spark stayed in his spot and didn't move anything—except the hand that moved slowly up and down her arm. He didn't understand what was making him have these feelings for her. At first, he'd thought it was purely sexual attraction. They had known each other for only two days. That was not time enough to develop anything but lust. Nevertheless, what he felt for her was more than that. He was beginning to care for her.

Spark didn't want her to be hurt by his sister's actions. Carlissa's perception of her life was very different from the reality of her situation. For some reason, she believed that her husband had wronged her when he went through with the divorce that she had often threatened him with. Richard had refused to keep their mock marriage intact. Spark knew for a fact that they had only married because she was pregnant with the girls. Richard had never loved her, and he'd never pretended otherwise.

Carlissa was a manipulator. She had wanted Richard and had done what she needed to do to get him. And now she was manipulating Spark in the same way. Any other sister would have settled the debt and insisted that her brother get help. Of course, he would have had to listen to her complaints and threats of abandonment if he continued on the same road. Carlissa hadn't complained or threatened him. She hadn't tried to intervene in his best interest. All she'd said was that he owed her big time. She had definitely collected.

He looked down at Devin sleeping peacefully against his chest. His hand moved from her arm to lightly stroke her hair. Guiltily, he closed his eyes. *What was he going to do?* He didn't want to deceive Devin, but no matter how he felt about his sister, he didn't want to betray their bond—as weak as it was.

At the feel of his hand on her hair, Devin snuggled closer to him. Bringing her arm up, she wrapped it around his midsection and held on as if he were a pillow.

Spark inhaled a small breath as he felt himself growing harder. He was uncomfortable as hell, but he wasn't about to move her away. He tried to change his position slightly so that his boxers wouldn't be so bunched up around his scrotum.

Devin awoke slowly at his movement. Against her arm, she could feel his hardness. She wondered how long he had been in that state and if she had been responsible for it. Inside, she smiled to herself.

"Um, Devin," Spark began. He couldn't take it any longer. He needed to adjust himself. "Could you excuse me for a moment?"

"Hmm," she moaned, wrapping her arms around him tighter. As she squeezed, she nuzzled her breast deeper into his crotch.

"Devin, I need to—" Spark fell silent when he felt her arm moving over his arousal. She moved her arm so slowly and with enough pressure that he could have sworn it was done intentionally.

"You need to what?" Devin kept her head down to hide the smile that slid onto her face.

Spark leaned his head to the side, trying to comprehend exactly what was going on. If what he thought was happening was happening, should he let it continue? *Hell, yeah,* he reprimanded himself before any gentlemanly thoughts could come forth. "Um, I think I need to move away from you for a minute."

Devin sat up and looked him in the eyes. "You don't want me lying on you?" She teased. "I was resting comfortably."

"Yeah, that's the problem. I wasn't comfortable at all."

"What's wrong? Maybe I can fix it."

Spark smiled. She was good, really good. "You think so, huh?"

"I know so."

"Devin, I don't think we're talking about the same thing so I'm going—" Spark froze when her hand reached for the waistband of his jeans. "Okay, maybe we are talking about the same thing. But maybe—" He stopped his own damn self this time. He looked at her.

Okay, maybe she was going about this the wrong way, Devin thought to herself, but right now, she needed him this way. At least, she needed to release some of the frustration she'd been harboring since receiving the letter. Spark was exactly what she wanted and needed. Even though she'd fought hard against the feelings she thought might be growing between them, she felt he was her friend. She didn't want to admit the feelings were more than friendship because it didn't make sense to her that true feelings could develop so fast for another person. Love at first sight just wasn't in her realm of reality. Quickly, before she changed her mind, she made a bold decision.

Pushing her nerves aside, she stood up and extended her hand towards him. Would he take it? Devin looked him right in the eye to let him know how serious she was. Her mind was made up, and her desire was high.

It didn't take Spark as long to make up his mind. As soon as she offered her hand, he accepted it. He stood beside her.

"Are you sure?" He had to ask. If she were going to have any kind of regrets later, he'd rather wait until she was sure she was making the right decision. *Lord, I can't believe I'm thinking this way.* Why was he second-guessing himself? Any other time, he would have jumped, or rather, dived into her without a second thought.

"Come with me and find out," she replied with a smile and pulled him toward the bedroom.

"Okay." He followed easily, stopping inches behind her when she reached the bed.

Devin turned around to him. The look on his face made her smile. She saw hesitation in his eyes. She realized that she needed to erase any doubts that he might be having. Devin didn't want his insecurities to prevent him from enjoying their time together.

"Come here, " she said, extending her arms wide for him to move in close to her. Lifting her head, she waited for him to kiss her.

He obliged her. Surrounding her plump lips with his own, he slowly suckled her bottom lip before releasing her. Spark kissed her again, deeper this time. He wrapped his arms tightly around her midsection as he felt a connection with her begin to form.

Devin returned his kisses with a strong passion of her own. She was at first surprised by the energy she felt flowing between them after the first kiss. It was different from anything she had experienced before, different and overwhelmingly pleasant. Her arms went around his shoulders, and she found herself filling with the strong emotions his kisses provoked.

"Devin, this is nice," he said between kisses. *Funny how his wrist wasn't hurting any more.*

Together they sat on the bed. Then he leaned her back. Slowly, Spark's hands moved under her shirt until both breasts were filling them. He deepened the kiss.

Devin moaned. Her excitement rose, and she felt the jittering in her stomach begin. Her hands moved to the bottom of his shirt. Devin began pulling at it to get it off him.

Suddenly, they both froze as the tune of "We Are Family" by Sister Sledge echoed through the room. Devin knew instantly that it was one of her family members calling to check on her. She began to move.

"No. No. Don't go," he whispered.

"It might be important. It might be my kids." Regretfully, she got up from the bed.

Spark's head fell heavily onto the mattress. *Damn it.* Jumping off the bed in frustration, he wondered if he should just go jump into a cold shower and go to sleep. He wanted Devin so bad. He liked her so much. This wasn't anything like his past relationships. This felt different, like it could really lead to something.

CHAPTER 8

Instead of the bathroom, Spark walked into the living room where Devin was taking her phone call. He sat at one end of the dining room table and listened to the conversation. He could tell that she was talking to the sister that she had called earlier; April, he thought Devin had said her name was.

"That was fast. I didn't expect to hear back from you so soon," Devin said.

"Well, all you needed were addresses. Mind you, I'm not guaranteeing that any of these are who you're looking for. I got the names and addresses of three women living in or near the Wilmington, Delaware, area who may have used that post office to rent a box. There were no other viable choices as the addresses were too far away. It wouldn't make sense for them to rent from that location."

"Okay, just give me what you have." Devin pulled a pen and notebook out of the little carrying case that still held all of Chris's important papers. Over the last few weeks, she had used the notebook often to scribble down thoughts about her dilemma.

"The first name is Crystal Harrison of 1272 Newman Street, Claymont, Delaware. The second is Chelesa Harrison of 417 Lobdell Street, Wilmington, Delaware. And lastly, Carlissa Harrison of 1120 Christiana Road,

New Castle, Delaware. Devin, I really wish you would let my guys handle this for you. You didn't have to go all the way to Delaware to solve this problem. I could have sent someone over there for you."

"April, I appreciate your offer, but this is something I have to do. Don't you understand? That's why I wouldn't let Troy, John, or Charles come with me. I need to see this woman, talk to her myself, and ask the questions that I have for her."

"Well, are you all right? Do you have enough money? You find a nice hotel?"

"I'm fine. Don't worry about me. Have you seen the kids? Are they having a good time? I'm going to call them later."

"I was over at the house yesterday. You know Dad went out and bought another pool. Troy and Charles were putting it up. The girls told Dad that they needed a bigger pool since they are older now. So, he moved the smaller pool to the side for Tia's kids, since they're the only little ones left for now."

"It's a good thing that there are more teenage grand-kids than youngins." Devin spent the next couple of minutes talking about family matters, and then let her sister off the phone. She watched Spark walk back and forth from the bedroom as if he were trying to check up on her, but not listen directly to the conversation. "Okay, April. I'll call you later and let you know what I find out. Thanks again."

As soon as she hung up the phone, Spark walked, or tripped, back into the room. Devin shook her head back and forth, trying to stifle the laugh that rose in her throat. How one man could be so good-looking and so clumsy at the same time was beyond her. Either God had played a cruel joke on him, or the devil was having one hell of a laugh.

"Well, I got three names and addresses," she said to cover the laugh as she moved over on the sofa to give him room.

"That's good. So what's the plan?" He didn't want to seem too anxious to find out if his sister's name was on the list. Instead of trying to take a peek at it, he figured that he would just ease her into a light conversation.

"I guess the best thing to do is to just stop by each address and ask if any of them was married to a Richard. Hopefully, when we pull up, we'll see twin girls playing in the front yard, and the problem will be solved." She pushed the paper towards him.

"Sounds good," he replied, glancing down at the writing. Sure enough, Carlissa's name was the last one on the list. *Damn, you could find just about anything you wanted to on a person nowadays if you knew where to go.* And April obviously did. "I just hope no one gets upset that we're knocking on the front door and asking crazy questions."

"They're just going to have to be upset. That's the only way we're going to get our answers."

"You mean your answers. I still don't know exactly what's going on." He thought that would prompt her to go into further details; it didn't. She stayed quiet. "I heard you mention on the phone that you have a lot of nieces and nephews. Why don't you tell me about your family?" He settled next to her on the sofa, and waited for her to start. Spark figured that this was one way to get to know her a little better. He found himself not wanting to think about the fact that tomorrow she could find the answers to her questions and be leaving him for good.

"Um, let's see. I'm the youngest of eight kids."

"Eight?"

"Yeah, so I was pretty spoiled growing up. Um, let's see. Roberta is the oldest. She never worked a day in her life. She's a socialite, if you will. Her husband Carlton owns a big publishing house. She chairs a lot of committees. You know the type."

"No, actually I don't. But I get the picture."

"They have two kids. Pamela, we call her Peaches, is 23, and Carlton IV is 21. They're both in college. Then there's John Jr. He's a dentist by profession, but a chef by choice. He can whip up any meal you ask for. He and Anna have four kids. The oldest, John III, is starting his first year of college this year."

She looked at him briefly before going on. He was looking right back at her. Could he really be this interested in what she had to say? In her family? In getting to know her better? Soon she would be gone. Was it really necessary for them to get to know each other better?

"Please, continue," Spark said softly.

"Okay. April, she's next. I was just talking to her."

"The lawyer."

"The lawyer. She's married to Thomas, also a lawyer. Started their own firm. They have two teenage daughters.

Brilliant kids who will probably end up lawyers, too. After April is Troy, the doctor. He's the rock of the family, always trying to put the weight of our problems on his own shoulders. He and his wife, Stephanie, have four kids."

"Sounds like you got a lot of professionals in your family. That's good. A lot of kids, but a lot of good role models, too."

"Yeah, great role models. Kristal's next. She's a businesswoman, owes a toy store that specializes in ethnic items. She has two stores in the state and is thinking about buying more. Her husband helps her run the businesses. He used to be in advertising, so you know he knows how to promote business. They have two younger kids."

Devin hesitated. It was always hard for people who didn't know the family to believe that Charles was her brother, so she had stopped telling people a long time ago.

"Charles is next. He's married to Shelia, who is a doctor. Charles is a recording artist."

"Really? Anybody I know? I mean, is he famous? Does he have an album?"

"Charles Avery."

"Charles Avery? No way. That's your brother?"

"Yeah. We keep it kinda quiet, so please . . ."

"Hey, don't worry about that. My lips are sealed. I just never met anyone related to someone famous before."

"He and Shelia have two kids, too. They've been in love forever. My sister Tia is the child psychologist. She's married to Jeff, who is a co-owner and operator of three nightclubs in Chicago, along with my cousin Chauncey. They're vacationing right now in Disney with their three kids. And then, there are my two girls, Tionne and Dionne. You already know my story."

"Actually, I don't, but I figure that you'll tell me when you're ready."

Devin looked at him. She wasn't ready. "You know, I just don't put my business out to complete strangers like that."

"Complete strangers?" Surprisingly, that hit him in the heart.

She could tell that what she had said hurt his feelings a little. Maybe she hadn't phrased it right.

"That's what I am, a complete stranger?" Spark wasn't sure why he was suddenly so upset, but he was. He felt as if she had just stabbed him in the heart, slapped him in the face. This made him even madder, at himself. She was right. They had only met two days before, and technically they were complete strangers. But didn't she feel the connection that was between them? "We've almost had sex, and now I'm a complete stranger."

"Spark—"

"Forget it, Devin," he said, getting up and walking toward his bedroom. He slammed the door shut.

Devin sat back on the sofa, flabbergasted. She couldn't believe that he had acted the way he did. Hell, they were complete strangers. She crossed her arms in front of her. *Who the hell did he think he was? So what if she was about to have sex with him. She was a grown woman. She could have sex with whomever, whenever she wanted. Without explanation.* It hurt the way he'd said it. As if she was easy or something. And if she was easy, so the hell was he.

She punched at the sofa pillow. By tomorrow night, she planned to be the hell out of Delaware. First thing in the morning, she would find this C. Harrison person, give her a piece of her mind, and then be on the next plane moving.

Devin stood up and walked to the sliding glass doors that led to his balcony. She leaned her head against the pane and wondered what she was going to do to pass the rest of the day away. Looking at her watch, she saw that it was only six o'clock in the evening. The sun was still high.

She'd thought she would spend the rest of the day lying in Spark's arms, but it appeared that she was in for a lonely night, and on the sofa at that. Going to the linen closet, she pulled out the sheets and blanket that he had used the night before and made her bed. She would shower and make use of the vast DVD collection that filled one side of his entertainment center.

In the bedroom, Spark walked over to the door as soon as he heard her turn off the shower. He listened to the bathroom door open and waited for her to knock on the bedroom door for her suitcase. Her clothes were sitting on the chair in the far corner of the room. He expected her to come knocking any second, unless she was going to sleep in the nude. Quickly, he pushed that thought out of his head. *She wouldn't . . . yes, she would.*

After waiting ten minutes, then hearing the television come to life, he realized that his second thought had been right. It was only seven o'clock. How was he going to get through the whole night without thinking about her spread out all over his sofa? And he was hungry. He didn't want to face her after reacting so childishly to her statement. Childish or not, it was honest. He cared for this girl, even if he didn't think he wanted to.

Standing in the middle of the room, Spark happened to get a glance of himself in the mirror. He moved closer to his image. *Man, don't do it. Stop yourself from falling for this girl. Just stop it.* But talking to his reflection didn't work. Spark realized that it was already too late, and now he was in the middle of something that was going to backfire on him big time.

His sister had him by the balls, for lack of better words. And when Devin found out that the woman she was looking for was his sister, she wouldn't want anything to do with him. If she ever found out that Spark had been in Chicago for the purpose of spying on her, she would hate him.

Spark's mind began to work overtime. He didn't know what to do, which way to turn. On the one hand, he wanted to just go to Devin and tell her everything, at least everything that he knew about Richard. He wanted to help Devin find out the truth so that she could finally let go of the past, and then maybe, just maybe, they could have something together if she forgave him. But he wasn't willing to take the chance that she would be able to forgive. She would still probably hate him.

But Carlissa, as much as he couldn't stand her, was his sister. And even though she was twisted and evil, she was his sister. He couldn't let anything happen to her for his nieces' sake. They had already lost their father.

Spark fell across the bed in defeat. No matter which way he turned, he was damned. And either way, he would lose someone.

Two hours later, still frustrated by his circumstances, Spark went into the bathroom hoping that a shower would help him.

As soon as she heard the water come on, Devin went to the bedroom to rummage through her suitcase for something to put on. If he hadn't decided to shower, she had been prepared to sleep in the nude. There was no way she was going to knock on the bedroom door after the way he had acted. It was completely uncalled for, and she believed that Spark needed to apologize to her this time.

Devin walked out of the bedroom just in time to see Spark walking out of the bathroom wrapped only in a towel, a small towel that didn't quite close all the way around him. Part of his right thigh was visible.

"Excuse me," he said, planning to walk past her in the narrow hallway. He tried to ignore the fitted tee that failed to hide her protruding nipples and the thin night pants showing off the curve of her hips. "Did I wake you?"

"No," she said in a whisper, still trying to get over his masculinity. "I, um, I wasn't asleep. Needed to change into my nightclothes."

"Devin?" Spark said, cautiously. "It's pretty silly for us to be in here like this not talking to each other. We're acting like a married couple."

"Really? You think so? I hadn't noticed that we weren't speaking. I was under the assumption that you weren't speaking to me."

"Are you hungry? I can throw something on the stove. See, this is what you call making nice." He reached in the hallway closet and pulled out a new stick of deodorant. Spark was about to put some on when he realized that he couldn't hold onto the towel while doing it. Trying to remain cool, he put the deodorant back on the shelf, firmly wrapped the towel around him, grabbed the deodorant with one hand and raised the opposite arm. It was no big deal. They were both adults. The more comfortable he seemed with her being there, the more comfortable she would be.

"Making nice?" Try as she might, Devin's eyes just wouldn't stray from the towel. She watched him work the deodorant under one hairy arm. "I thought it was more like trying to apologize without the apology." She watched the edge of the towel begin to loosen. "But since I am hungry, I will make nice, too." She watched him switch the deodorant and lift the other arm.

"Good," he said.

"Oh . . ." She watched the towel shift right and fall to the floor.

Spark's composure left him as he struggled to pick up the towel with the hand that was holding the deodorant. His other arm was still high in the air. He couldn't grab the towel. Common sense didn't tell him to drop the damn deodorant until after the whole incident was over.

Devin tried to hold in her laughter as she picked up the towel and held it around his nakedness. The deodorant was still in his hand.

"Now, this is funny," she admitted. "And ironic."

"Ironic?" Spark had to laugh at it himself.

"Yeah, never in my life did I expect to be trying to cover up a man," she explained. On their own accord, her eyes glanced down again, hoping to see the excellent piece of God's creation they had just witnessed.

"I'm sorry, Devin. I didn't mean to embarrass you," he replied, finally putting the deodorant back in the closet and leaning against her to do so.

"Don't worry about it, Spark. It's not your fault that your coordination is challenged." She laughed again. At least his accidental exposure had released some of the tension between the two. "Hope you're not embarrassed."

"Who me? Not likely," he contended. "I just didn't want to offend your sensibilities. Well, um, I'm going to get dressed," he said, hesitating in his movement when he looked into her eyes. For a split instant, he thought he might have seen something more than interest there. *No, this isn't a good idea.*

"Okay," Devin said, realizing that she was the one still holding the towel. "Here, you're going to need this." She put the ends of the towel in his hand and moved away, cautious not to touch him.

Spark still didn't move. He let the towel fall from around him.

She made the swallow as inconspicuous as she possible could. Devin knew that she was playing with fire, and she was about to get burned. Maybe she needed to. It had been a long time since someone had set off a spark like this in her.

When she looked back at his face, she could see the desire and lust he was feeling. Devin didn't move when he stepped closer to her. She admitted to herself that she wanted his attention.

She was beautiful, he thought, feeling himself grow even harder. Damn, he wanted her so bad. Blindingly bad, he thought, grasping her outstretched hand, the look on her face telling him that she wanted him just as bad.

Spark wrapped his arms around her tightly as he pulled her into the circle of his arms. Excitement rushed through him as he felt her thigh against his, her breast against his hairy chest and his penis pushing through the tiny passage between her legs.

An unsteady breath passed from Devin's lips as she stood in his arms letting each second of pleasure build on top of the last. It had been so long since a man held her close, since she felt the lips of a man on her cheek, her neck. Oh, God, he already had her insides melting with the work his hands were performing on her body.

With one breast weighing heavily in his hand, Spark suddenly stopped. Against his wishes, the gentleman in him came to the forefront. With all his soul he wanted to bend down and plop her dark nipple between his teeth, but he didn't. Instead he glanced up at her, looked in her eyes, and even though he saw the passion flicker there, he had to make sure.

"Devin," he started on a heavy breath. His passion was barely restrained. "Are you sure?"

She didn't open her eyes, just let out another long breath, nodding her head erratically up and down. "Yes . . . yes." The electrical charge she was receiving from his hands was more than she could bear. "Yes," she repeated when she didn't feel him responding to her plea. With her eyes still closed, Devin guided her mouth to his. She started walking backward into the bedroom.

Spark tried to follow her, but he was so engrossed in the kiss that he accidentally stepped on her foot and almost tripped.

"Ow," she laughed, lightly hopping on her foot.

"Um, sorry," he replied, letting go of the softness of her lips. In frustration, he swooped her up into his arms. He'd be damned if he'd embarrass himself any more right when she was about to give him what he had been craving all night. He didn't trip, fumble or fall at any time during the straight line to the bed.

When he laid her down and fell on top of her, he wasn't clumsy; he was gentle. Reaching for the same breast he'd held in his hand earlier, Spark quickly slid the hard stubby nipple between his lips. He heard her gasp and lavished the nub more. His right hand worked its way down her side until he had a tight grasp on her hip. Then he shifted and used his knee to spread her legs apart.

Devin held her eyes tightly shut, basking in the feel of his obviously experienced hands. Her breath caught as the ecstasy took her higher and higher. His fingers bedeviled the salivating lips at the center of her passion, and she moaned loudly.

"Okay . . . okay," she heard herself whisper in half breaths as she reached for him. Once her hand surrounded him, she gently stroked his length, feeling his strength, hearing him groan.

"Devin," he panted, "I have to go to the dresser."

"Huh?"

"I need to go to the dresser. The condoms—" he said between placing kisses across her stomach. Suddenly he withdrew his hands from her body and stood over the bed. He watched her pull herself into a loose ball in the center of the bed. Her eyes were still shut, and again he thought to himself, beautiful.

Devin turned her head when she heard him walk away from the bed. He was magnificently balanced as he walked to the dresser. She loved the way his muscles moved rhythmically, not giving any evidence that he was uncoordinated. To her, he was graceful.

Spark reached into the top dresser drawer and retrieved the condom, turned to the bed and stopped in his steps when he saw her watching him. She had that glow in her eyes again. The one that sent a shiver straight up his spine. It told him what she wanted, desired. He had only seen it once, but already he knew. And he wanted her to have it; he wanted to be the one to give it to her.

Devin liked the front view a lot better. She decided that as soon as he turned around to face her. Ripping the side of the package as he moved closer to the bed, he held her gaze as he donned the prophylactic. He leaned onto the bed, kissing her shoulder, her face, her lips.

Ring . . . ring.

"No, not again," Spark hissed, stopping his movement.

"I'm sorry," Devin said, leaving the bed to answer her phone.

Okay. Spark began to believe that maybe it just wasn't meant to be for him and Devin to get into a physical relationship right away. This was the second time that they had been interrupted.

For the rest of the evening, he decided that they would just leave it alone. When it was supposed to happen, it would. He went into the living room and fished for another movie out of the many. When he found the one he wanted, he waved goodnight and walked back into his bedroom.

Devin, who was in a deep conversation with her daughters and then her father, gave him an understanding wave.

CHAPTER 9

Noise from the living room made Spark wake from his deep slumber. In his confusion, he assumed that Devin had left the television on. The room around him was dark as he tried to gain his equilibrium and move off the bed. He briefly focused on the alarm clock resting on the dresser closest to the bed. It was 12:23 a.m. Of course, being who he was, he couldn't help but stumble over the sneakers he had kicked off his feet earlier.

It wasn't until he was on all fours that he recognized one of the loud voices streaming under his bedroom door. "Oh, damn," he hissed, moving quicker toward the door and forgetting to pull on his jeans or a T-shirt.

"Yo. Yo. Cut it out!" he yelled at the top of his voice as soon as he had the door open.

"Who the hell is this?" Vivian screamed at the top of her lungs. She was standing about three feet from Devin, who was standing in front of the television with a shoe in one hand and unsuccessfully clutching the front of a sheet with the other.

After a couple of glances, he finally took notice of the look on their faces and realized he had come into the living room just in the nick of time.

"Vivian, what the hell are you doing here?"

"That's not the right question. The question is what the hell is she doing here?" She pointed her finger directly into Devin's face.

Devin swatted her hand away. "I told you about that hand of yours once, bitch."

"Hey, stop it," Spark said, wisely choosing to step between the two women before his living room became a disaster area. "I think you need to go, Vivian. Leave the key on the table. And don't bother if you have any more. I'm changing the lock tomorrow."

"I'm not going anywhere." Vivian stood directly in front of them both.

She reminded Devin of a model on a photo shoot with the wind blowing to make her hair fan out around her. The girl was about an inch or two taller, maybe ten pounds lighter. They were about the same complexion, and her weave was sewn in perfectly. Her hair came down to hang wildly below her shoulders.

"Yes, you are," Spark replied. He tried to grab hold of one of her arms to escort her out of the house, but when he grabbed her, Vivian moved, pulling him off balance. He tumbled forward, tripping on the sheet that Devin was half wrapped in.

"Bitch," Devin yelled, as the sheet was tugged from her body, "what the hell are you doing? He told you to leave."

Vivian moved quickly toward Devin. Just the thought of Devin standing in the middle of Spark's apartment enraged her. But Devin was ready for her advance.

Devin braced herself for the attack. As soon as Vivian put a hand on her shoulder, Devin grabbed her arm and swung her around hard and fast, causing Vivian to hit Spark's sliding glass door. As soon as Vivian fell to the ground, Devin jumped on her and began hitting her all over the head and shoulders.

Spark recovered from his clumsiness fast. When he turned around, he saw Devin throw Vivian, but didn't get untangled fast enough to stop Devin from pouncing. He was busy trying to unwrap the sheet from his legs and get Devin, who had straddled Vivian as she kicked to get free.

"Okay, stop. Stop it! Come on, break it up," Spark finally yelled as he stood over the two women and began to separate them. They were both still swinging. Unfortunately, the majority of blows were landing on him. He was getting it from both sides as he yanked Devin up and swung her behind him. Then he grabbed Vivian's arm and stood her up while trying to keep Devin at arm's length.

"How you going to have this bitch in my house?" Vivian yelled.

Spark looked at her, stupefied, but kept his grip firmly in place. What the hell was she talking about? "Vivian, this is not your house. What is wrong with you? You never lived here, and we broke up months ago." He turned to Devin, looked her over once, twice. She was so beautiful, especially mad, her eyes flaming, her nose flaring. "Devin, sit down. I'll be right back."

Devin stood where she was, unashamed, and mad as hell. She watched as he tightened his grip on Vivian's arm and half dragged her out of the house. After they were out the door, Devin went to the bedroom to get her nightclothes.

"Who's that?" Vivian asked as soon as they were out the door. "It sure didn't take long for you to replace me."

"She's a friend of mine and none of your business. Now, listen—"

"She can't be too much a friend if you got her sleeping on the couch. What, y'all have an argument?"

"Vivian, why are you acting like this? You have a man, remember? Why are you even here? Look, just go and don't ever come back. I mean it. I'm changing the locks tomorrow, so if you have other keys you might as well just throw them away. I mean it. If you come back here again, I'm going to call the cops." Spark left her standing near her car. He wanted to walk away with his back to her, but because she was crazy and couldn't be trusted, he decided to do a few side steps first just to keep an eye on her.

Devin was back on the sofa by the time he came inside. He stood over her, waiting for her to say something. She didn't.

"Devin, I apologize for that." He realized that this episode wouldn't make her believe that the phone call from yesterday had been his sister.

"Hey, no need to apologize."

Her voice was even and calm, but Spark could tell that she was still mad. She wouldn't even look at him. Her eyes stayed focused on the black television screen.

"You can sleep in the bedroom. I'll stay out here. If she comes back, I'll handle her. She's just crazy, that's all. We haven't been together in months, really. I don't know what made her come over here." But he did know. He remembered seeing one of Vivian's girlfriends in the restaurant earlier when they went to get their food.

"You don't have to explain anything to me." Devin got up and walked to the bedroom door. Consciously, she tried to keep her steps light so he wouldn't think that she cared about what had just happened. She slammed the bedroom door hard.

Spark lay awake most of the night. Half of him wasn't sure if Vivian would come back or not, and the other half of him was worried that Devin would put the brakes on everything that seemed to be building between them. Granted, nothing was written in stone, but he was pretty confident that they were beginning to have some feelings for each other. Unfortunately, Vivian might have just put an end to all of that. He didn't know what to do. He wanted Devin, and it was more than just sexually now.

Either way, in the end, she was going to hate him. Once they got to the bottom of the list, and she found out who he really was and why he was around her, he was in for it. He wanted to just tell her the whole truth because after the wild goose chase, Devin would be madder than if he just told her that Carlissa was his sister and took her straight to her. This wasn't going to be good.

Spark wondered if he talked to Carlissa—no, he couldn't do that. She would make a big scene, blow everything up, and lie. He realized that he knew less about Carlissa's plan than he did about Devin's. What he did know was that Devin just wanted some answers, the truth. But Carlissa wanted revenge. And he also knew that he couldn't let any harm come to Devin at his sister's hand.

In the morning, when Spark awoke from a restless night of tossing and turning from thinking of Devin, he hopped right up and put on his sneakers and went for a morning run. He hadn't jogged in months, but took his old route through the apartment complex to the two-mile walking trail the state had installed around the park six months earlier. The course used to take him thirty minutes to run twice. This morning it only took him forty-five minutes for both round trips.

Spark allowed his body to take over as he tried to clear the images of the night before from his thoughts. He didn't want to think about Vivian's crazy behavior or Devin being mad at him. He definitely didn't want to think about the two of them fighting in his living room or Devin standing before him or astride Vivian with barely any clothes on. Spark even tried to wipe away thoughts of the future.

He knew that in a few hours, Devin was going to be ready to finish her search for C. Harrison, his sister. His life was about to get very messy, and he needed to figure out the best way to deal with it. But not right now. Right now, all Spark wanted was peace of mind. That was something that he hadn't had since before his gambling problem, which, surprisingly, he hadn't thought about since meeting Devin.

Now, bent over panting in front of the door to his house, Spark realized two things: one, he needed to stop smoking, and two, that the peace of mind he sought hadn't come. And it never would until he was able to straighten out the problems that lay before him. And he was in a whole lot of deepness, as his mother used to say. He wasn't going to be able to have Devin in his life because as soon as she found out the truth, she would be gone. Carlissa would never get off his back because that was just the type of person she was. And he was going to have to watch his p's and q's for a while with Vivian. It was only a matter of time before she retaliated, because drama was the girl's middle name.

He breathed in and out deeply before entering his house. As soon as he shut the door, he stopped short as the smell of pork sausage and eggs filtered into his nose. Moving cautiously into the living room, he saw that Devin was in the kitchen buttering the tops of some biscuits.

"Morning," she said cheerfully.

Now he really was puzzled, but he replied, "Good morning to you, too."

"Hurry up and shower so that we can eat and get on our way." She smiled at him. "The food will be ready in a minute."

Ignoring the churning of his stomach, Spark did as he was told. He wasn't quite sure what was going on, but he knew that this was going to be a long day, maybe the worst day of his life. He wasn't in the best mood from that moment forward because he had no idea how to get out of the hot pot of mess that was brewing.

Devin ate quickly. She wanted to get an early start. It was Sunday morning, and as far as she was concerned the night before was history. All it was about to her was protecting herself. She didn't have anything to do with Spark or whomever he was messing with before her, well, not exactly before her, but whomever he was messing with. She was in Delaware for one reason and one reason only, and that was to find Chris's/Richard's supposed-to-be wife. Besides, the woman last night couldn't have meant too much to him if he could toss her out so easily.

And she needed him. So, Devin made his plate just as she heard him come out of the bathroom and smiled sweetly. She watched him eat and washed his plate as soon as he finished.

Spark glanced at his watch; it was only 7:45 a.m. "Devin, I hope you don't plan to leave this early on a Sunday morning to go knock on stranger's doors."

"Well, yeah, I was kinda hoping to get started early."

"We are not going out this early in the morning. It's definitely not a good idea. People are on their way out. I suggest that we wait until later on in the day, maybe start out around three this afternoon."

"Three?" She looked at him incredulously.

"Yeah, three. People do go to church on Sundays, you know. You should at least wait until they are home and relaxed from church before you go barging into their homes."

"Barging? Now it's barging? All I want to do is ask some questions and get some answers." She turned away from him. "What's your problem?"

His problem was that he wanted her so bad that he wasn't thinking with his head at all. And he needed to be using his head in order to get out of the hole that was being dug all around him. But he couldn't say that to her.

"Nothing is my problem, Devin. Look." He got up from the table and walked over to the sink where she was standing. He stood close to her, letting the smell of her perfume float up into his nose. "I want to help you, but you have to go about this the right way."

"You're right, I know. I'm just so anxious to get this over and done with." She looked up at him. He was standing so close, smelling so good. His soap from the shower was still strong as he moved in closer to her.

She couldn't deny the physical attraction. Not only was he fine as hell, but he was also fun to be around and definitely generous. Who else would have let her practically move in on the heels of a brief encounter? Maybe it wasn't a good decision on her side, but he had truly been helpful to her.

Spark moved closer to her lips. He inched in carefully, giving her ample time to reject him if she chose to. They hadn't exactly gotten off to a good start in either the friendship or the sexual departments. Between the constant bickering and ridiculous interruptions, they hadn't been successful at sex.

His hand went around her waist, and he pulled her flush against him as his lips touched hers softly.

Devin was the one who pulled him in, taking the kiss deeper as she almost went out of control. She grabbed him roughly at the waist and pushed her hands under his shirt.

"Devin, we have to talk," Spark found himself saying. He didn't want to say it, but he needed to. He held her hands.

From the look on his face, Devin could tell that the lovemaking she had in mind with this man would not be happening. She was confused. He wanted her, she could tell that from the way he looked at her, not to mention that stiffness that had been against her thigh just seconds earlier. But for some reason, Spark just wasn't trying to go all the way with her. Devin would have thought he was gay if not for the crazy chick that had burst in the house just the night before. So, what was his problem?

"Devin, I value your friendship. I don't want to—

"To what? Mess up what we have? We don't have anything to mess up. Look, we are adults. If we want to have sex, we can. Are you afraid that you will hurt my feelings by not wanting to be serious?"

"No, of course not. I, Devin . . . I like you a lot, maybe more than I should considering that I only met you a couple of days ago."

She put her arms around his neck, pulling him closer to her. "Then show me," she whispered close to his ear.

Spark grabbed her waist to prevent her from moving. He tried to be strong for both their sakes, but when the warmth of her breath grazed the hollow curves of his ear, Spark lost all his power.

"Are you going to stop me again?" Spark asked, running his hands down her sides to grip her hips.

"Are *you* going to stop *me*?" she retorted, looking up at him in a silent dare. Who was going to back down first?

Suddenly, the same urgency seemed to course through both of them as they began to grab and pull at each other's clothing. Devin's shirt went over her head and flew over the counter that divided the kitchen from the little dining area. Spark's shirt ended up on the stove. Her pants hit the floor, followed by his jeans.

Devin kissed his face and neck as he fumbled with the bra hooks behind her. Once he was done with the bra, Spark immediately bent down to place kisses on her breasts and stomach. He pushed at her panties until they wound up on the floor next to her pants.

Spark showed attention to her hips, her thighs, and her waist until he couldn't take it any longer. He stood back up, reaching under her arms and lifting her until she sat on the countertop. Frantically, he pushed his own boxers down and stepped between her legs.

She welcomed him into her space, wrapping her arms and her legs around him to draw him closer. His hardness pressed against her inner thigh as he kissed her hard, running his hands over her back and bottom.

"Devin—"

"No, don't stop, Spark," she sighed.

"I have to. The condoms are in my bedroom," he announced.

"No, no. I have one in my pants pocket," she said.

Spark looked at her. "In your pants pocket? Why—"

"Don't ask questions. Just get it." Devin continued to kiss him. It had been so long since she had felt the adrenaline that was pumping through her. It was exhilarating, and it was because of Spark.

Spark did as he was told, stooping down to retrieve the package. Quickly, he covered himself and turned back to her. "I'm still wondering."

She continued kissing him as soon as he turned to her. "I was just hoping, that's all. I got it out of your drawer this morning."

"But why?"

"Because I wanted you." It was simple.

Her statement, as simple as it was, turned Spark on more than anything else that had passed between them that weekend. Spark began to return her kisses roughly. His hands skillfully roamed her body, causing her to squeal and squirm.

She was enjoying his attention. Spark was giving her more pleasure than she could handle. Devin realized that her moans were getting louder and louder. She tried to control herself, but she hadn't felt this way in . . . forever.

Spark decided that he wasn't going to make love to Devin on the kitchen countertop, not this time anyway, not the first time. He wanted to make slow leisurely love to her. He wanted her to remember this time if it was going to be the last time.

Picking her up off the counter, he secured her legs around him. She was lighter in his arms than he expected. Devin was kissing his forehead, the top of his head, his ear. She was all over the place. To slow her down, Spark thought he would suckle the brown nipple that was close to his mouth. That only seemed to excite her more as she screamed out and held him tight.

His ego wouldn't let him loosen his hold on her. Instead of paying attention to where he was going, he grabbed the nipple between his teeth and suckled harder. Spark forgot about the jeans on the kitchen floor until they had wrapped themselves around his feet.

Spark quickly fell to his knees to avoid falling hard with Devin in his arms. He landed on the floor next to the dining room table.

"Damn," he exclaimed, a slight pain running up his leg.

"Are you all right?" she asked. "Did you fall or is this where you want me?"

"I want you right here," he said, moving his hips sideways to show her how much as he waited for the pain to subside. "And after I have you here, I can think of a couple of other places that I want you."

Devin smiled seductively as he lowered himself onto her. She closed her eyes as he slowly, very slowly, moved inside of her. The pain was sweet; his sweetness was genuine as he kissed away her tears and spoke to her softly through their lovemaking.

Afterwards, Spark picked her up and laid her on the bed. Luckily, he didn't stumble or fall. He didn't say anything. Just kissed her and walked to the bathroom.

She turned on her side and listened to the steady stream of water hitting the sides of the sink as she smiled to herself and reminisced over the last hour. He'd done it.

He'd absolutely blown her away, absolutely rocked her world, as her older sister Kristal would say. But she would never tell him that. She had to play it cool because, as far as he was concerned, it was what it was. They were both adults having sex. *Damn, those had been her words.*

Oh, Lord, for goodness sakes, Devin thought, pounding her fist into the bed. Now was not the time to start getting emotional over a man she had just met. She was there for a purpose, and it was not to fall in love. It was to find the answers to her many questions about her dead husband.

She watched as Spark came into the room with a washcloth.

"Turn over," he said.

Doing as she was told, Devin let him wash her off without saying a word. She was still trying to come to terms with her situation. Trying to appear relaxed, Devin knew she wasn't fooling him. But he didn't say anything.

Spark walked out of the room. Something was wrong. He could tell. He knew that there was no doubt that she had enjoyed their lovemaking just as much as he had. She'd reacted to him; he'd reacted to her. It was exactly what he'd wanted it to be. After they were finished, he'd wanted to tell her about his feelings for her, but how smart would that have been when their time together was going to be short-lived? Why make matters worse by telling her how he felt when she would hate him even more in the end?

All Spark wanted to do was enjoy the little time they had left. He could only hope that their time together would end on civil terms, but he knew that was unlikely. He walked back into the room and lay on the bed behind her.

She stiffened momentarily before relaxing.

He felt it, but didn't say anything. Instead, he pulled the covers at the foot of the bed over them and placed an arm around her waist.

"Devin—" he started.

"Don't, Spark, don't say anything." Devin cut him off. She didn't want to hear him apologize for their time together, couldn't bear it if he said that it shouldn't have happened.

Instead of saying anything, he snuggled closely behind her and kissed her on her shoulder. How could he let her know how he felt if she didn't want to hear him out?

Spark stirred in his sleep when he felt his hand being moved away from Devin's side. He wanted to hold her to him, but she was already slipping away. Still, he couldn't deny that he enjoyed the view as she walked to the bathroom. When he heard the shower running, he decided to join her.

Devin smiled to herself when she heard the bathroom door open. She hadn't expected him to follow her. The shower curtain slid to the side, and there he was in all his naked, hard glory.

"What you doing in here?" she teased.

"I want to get cleaned up, too, unless you want to get dirty again."

Devin looked at him.

"I'm just putting it out there. It's up to you." He playfully patted her on the behind.

"Well, any other time, I would say sure, but it's already eleven-thirty. Maybe we should get started, because it looks like it's going to rain."

"Okay, have it your way, but you don't know what you're missing," he said as he reached for the bar of soap and began lathering himself.

The problem was that Devin knew exactly what she was missing, a very good lay, but she had to start getting the answers she was looking for. She had to ignore how good Spark looked standing there covered with white suds and smelling all Irish Springy. She had to forget the long strokes he'd used to move slowly inside of her.

No, it was time to do what she had come to do so that she could put that part of her life behind her. Maybe then she could try to pursue some kind of relationship with Spark. Maybe he went to Chicago on a regular basis. She had never asked him why he was there.

Spark's hand on her back brought Devin's mind back to reality.

"Oh, no, you don't," she said, moving out of the way and rinsing off the soap suds he had managed to spread across her back. "I'm out of here, and so are you." She pulled the curtain open and got out.

Spark quickly finished his shower and, dripping wet, followed her back into the bedroom. There wasn't any reason to stay in there any longer than necessary.

CHAPTER 10

Two hours later, Devin sat quietly, patiently, in the passenger seat while Spark took his sweet old time locking up the house and finally getting in on the driver's side. It seemed he had been moving much slower since she left the shower and told him to start getting dressed so they could work their way through her short list.

A slight grin formed on her face as she briefly thought of how she had spent the morning hours lying under him, hovering above him, and . . . maybe he did have good cause to be walking like the living dead. She smiled harder.

"Are you okay?" she questioned as he turned the ignition. He honestly didn't look like he wanted to go anywhere, but she wasn't about to suggest that. She needed to get some answers, and she couldn't let her feelings for—*feelings, she meant friendship*—her friendship with Spark stop that.

"I'm fine," he replied. Putting the car in gear, Spark reluctantly pulled out of his parking spot and headed for the first address she gave him. Even though he knew this wasn't his sister's house, he regretted getting her in the car, letting her direct his driving, and he was going to regret pulling in front of this house because he knew it was all going to backfire on him sooner or later.

"Are you tired?" Devin joked. "Did I hurt you?" She was in a very good mood, considering she was on her way to finding answers that could change her life or at least the life of her children. But it was for her daughters' sakes that she was plunging ahead with finding this woman. She wasn't going to let her daughters become possible victims of their father's past, little as she knew of it.

"Yeah, damn it. Devin, once you get started, it's hard to get you to stop," Spark joked, letting her believe that his lack of enthusiasm was because of drained energy. The statement was true enough. The only time Devin had left the bed was when her daughters called from their cell phone. She'd recognized the ring tone and gotten out bed. Luckily, it was during his down time.

After he made love to Devin the third time, she finally fell soundly asleep. But Spark's pounding heart and guilty soul wouldn't allow him to sleep right away. Instead, he lay next to her and watched her sleep, trying not to let his feelings for her grow stronger. It was a losing battle. There was no denying that he wanted her, maybe more than he should. But even as he knew that it was an unwanted, worthless emotion while in his present predicament, Spark couldn't fight what was quickly building within him. He couldn't fight the feelings that were pulling him closer and closer to her, and he wasn't quite sure that he wanted to.

His head was throbbing from all of the thinking going on. Never in his life had he wanted something to work out so badly for him . . . well, except for the time he was in Philly trying to outrun some fellas who had let him join them in a game of dice, then realized that he had switched the dice and was playing with his own personal loaded ones. But he was young then. He'd had no idea what he wanted in life.

Now he knew. He was much older and a lot wiser. Spark also realized that, no matter what, he was going to get the short end of the stick. Inside, his stomach was tightening as he tried to figure a way out of the madness. At this point, it had nothing to do with whose side he was on. There was no more Carlissa's side.

"Spark," Devin chimed in. "You aren't paying me a bit of attention. I'm sitting here trying to flirt with you, and you're ignoring every word I say. I believe that you're tired of me already. That's not a good sign. I mean, I know it's been a while for me, but I didn't think that I was that bad in the sack."

Spark gave her a side glance, a smile coming to his face. Deciding to play along with her charade, he said, "Honestly, I didn't want to say anything. But I could tell that it had obviously been a while for you. I guess you'll get better with practice." He smiled to himself. There wasn't anything that Devin needed to practice. Her lovemaking had him wanting more. Spark couldn't seem to get enough of her. She was insatiable, unreserved, and uncontrollable, all in one. He loved that.

"Oh, is that so?" Devin hit him across the shoulder playfully. "Well, then I guess since I'll likely be leaving tomorrow, we'll never find out if I learned anything, will we?"

Tomorrow? Spark panicked. That was too soon. Too soon to let her go. Too soon for her to confront his sister and risk the truth being exposed. And definitely too soon for her to hate him. He smiled outwardly, but inside he was crying. This could not be happening to him.

"Devin, though I don't want to blow up your head, I can honestly tell you two things. First, you are very good at what you do, and two, I most definitely plan to see if you know anything else. I don't care if you learned it from me or already knew it." He meant to gently pat her on the leg, but his hand involuntarily stayed in place and he squeezed her knee.

"Stop before you make me blush," she laughed. "I have a compliment for you as well. In bed, you're hardly as clumsy as you are out of it. You have perfect coordination."

He laughed with her. "I think we had better change the subject before I turn the car around. We can always go home and see who has improved the most in the last few hours."

"You would love that, wouldn't you?" She smiled.

"Yes, I would," he replied honestly, *for more reasons than one.* At that moment, Spark wanted nothing more than for Devin to tell him to turn around and take her home and make crazy love to her. At least that way, he would be safe for another day. Have another day with her in his home. But he knew that would never happen. He was resigned to getting this first visit over with while he prayed for a solution to his problems to come his way.

Devin looked out the passenger-side window as he took Exit 8 south off Interstate 95. Although the sky was darkening fast with promise of a terrible storm in the near future, her excitement grew as she realized they must be close to their destination. Hopefully, they could move this along quickly. If luck was on her side, the first name on the list would be the right one, and they could be on their way back to the house before the rain came.

She had no idea what she was going to say to the woman, this C. Harrison. In her mind, it had been so simple, but realistically, there was a strong possibility that her presence would not be received well by her husband's first wife.

She watched the signs quietly. Miller Road. Baynard Boulevard. Harrison Street. Instantly, she did a double take and tried to look down the street, but he was moving too fast. He took the next left, and she began to count numbers. Twenty-fifth Street. Twenty-sixth Street. Twenty-seventh Street. Finally, he parked the car.

"Well," he said, "we're here."

She didn't move. Devin tried to calm her nerves.

"Are you okay?"

"Yeah," she said with a sigh. "It just wasn't until this moment that I wondered if maybe I was making a mistake."

"Do you want to leave?" he eagerly suggested. "You don't have to do this right now, you know." Spark knew it was wrong of him, but if she copped out, his problems would be solved, if only temporarily. That was better than nothing.

"No," Devin stated firmly. She had never backed down from anything in her life, and she wasn't about to start now. This was important if for no other reason than to say that she had tried. Before she lost her nerve, she opened the car door and got out. Spark was right behind her. She didn't say anything. Knowing it was none of his business, she was still thankful that he was there to offer her his support.

Devin approached the door apprehensively. The cranberry, two-story house with white-trimmed windows seemed to loom over her. Was this really a good idea? Would finding the answers she was seeking be beneficial to her or her daughters? Doubt clouded her head just like the clouds covering the sky.

Even with Spark right behind her, she felt her determination waver more. She wanted to turn around and get herself together, but just then the front door swung open. Two teenage girls burst out of the house. Their laughter filled the air until they saw Devin and Spark standing in front of them. Then they quieted down.

"Hi," the tall, caramel beauty said, bouncing the basketball beside her with confidence and agility. "Can I help you?" Her equally tall friend stood next to her with a questioning look on her face.

"Um, hi, yes," Devin began. "My name is Devin Al- I mean, Avery. I'm from Chicago, and I am looking for a Crystal Harrison. Does she live here?"

"No," the girl replied. "I'm her older sister, Dana. Crystal moved out or ran away two weeks ago with that crazy girlfriend of hers." Dana stopped talking long enough to look at Spark again. "Are you friends of hers?"

"Well, I just—"

"We are in town visiting and we're trying to get up with her," Spark interrupted. "Do you know where she moved to?"

"Nope, when Mom found out that she was gay, she had a fit and kicked her out. I know she's with that girl, but I don't know where they live. She hasn't even tried to get in contact with me. So, if you happen to find her, tell her that she could at least give her sister a call. I don't care if she's gay or not. And tell her that she better get her behind back in school before they expel her. Then Mom really will have a fit."

"Okay," Spark said. "Thanks for your help. If we see her, we'll let her know." Spark put an arm around Devin's waist when she didn't readily turn to leave with him. "Come on, baby. We'll try to see her next time."

"But—"

"She's not here. Let's go." Spark cut her off and led her to the car in silence. Once inside, he continued, "They didn't know anything."

"You don't know that. We didn't ask them any questions," she replied.

"Devin, think about it. The girl is a lesbian and the younger sister of the girl we were talking to. Dana can't be any more than seventeen or eighteen years old."

She sat quietly, brooding over his statement. He was right, but she didn't have to verbally agree.

"Are you looking for a woman or a kid?"

"A woman, of course."

"Then I think it's safe to say that you can mark her off the list." After pulling off, Spark looked at the sky again. It was steadily growing darker. "I think that maybe we should grab something to eat and head on back to the house. It's about to pour down any minute."

"We don't have time to stop at one more house?" she asked, half whining. "I really wanted to get through this list as fast as possible. There are only three people on it. How far away is the next house?" She passed the piece of paper that she had written the address on to him.

Spark looked at the paper and cursed under his breath. He didn't want to tell her that it was less than ten minutes away. The sky was darkening, and he knew that rain was minutes away.

"This is the last house, Devin. And you better make it fast. We're going to get caught out here in the storm. And I, for one, don't do thunderstorms."

"You're scared of thunderstorms?" she asked, looking at him incredulously.

"I respect the Lord's work, like I'm sure your mother taught you to. I listened to my mother."

"Yeah, right," Devin laughed.

"I'm not scared of thunderstorms." Spark turned the car toward the Riverside projects located on the east side of town.

"Chelesa is my daughter. What you want with her?"

"Well," Devin said, stepping closer to the door, "I was just hoping that she could answer a few questions for me. I really need to talk to her. Do you know if she'll be home any time soon?"

"You'll probably see that girl before I will. She comes and goes as she pleases, and keeps forgetting the fact that she has two children living here." The woman looked from Spark to Devin. Her curiosity growing, she continued, "But anything you have to say to Chelesa, you can say to me. I guess she'll be here sometime today."

"I could just leave my name and—"

"How about we just try back later?" Spark interjected. He knew exactly what Devin was about to say, and it was definitely the wrong thing to say. This woman would be ringing her phone off the hook until she got answers to her own questions. He grabbed Devin's hand and pulled her slowly toward the car. "Thank you for all of your help," he yelled to the lady over his shoulder. "We'll be in contact."

To his surprise, Devin didn't resist. She followed him willingly, and even more surprising, quietly, to the car. She even giggled softly when Spark tripped over a twig on his way around to the driver's side. She put her head down and hid her face when he got in.

"I guess you saw that, huh?"

"You know I don't miss anything. Spark, I'm surprised that you still have two arms and two legs. You're dangerous."

"At least I'm smart enough to know who to give my information to. You were about to give that lady your whole life story. I don't even know your phone number."

"I don't think she was going to do anything wrong. What could she do with a number, anyway, but call me? I think I have a pretty good sense of character. After all,

I agreed to stay at your house, didn't I, and I didn't know you from a can of paint."

"True that, but you do know me a little better now, don't you?" he asked, taking her memory back to the morning's activities.

"Yes, I do," she agreed with a smile. "And might I add, I trust you a great deal. Spark, you didn't have to do anything for me, but I appreciate the fact that you were willing to help me with this even though I still haven't given you all the details. And because I trust you, after we get back to the house, I'm going to tell you everything, at least everything I know."

In that moment, Spark's guilt grew. She trusted him, and that was what he'd thought he wanted. Right now, he wasn't sure of what he wanted. Instead of holding a conversation, Spark fell victim to his thoughts as he berated himself for what he was doing.

Devin tore into the Italian sub as if it were her last meal. It was possibly the best sub she had ever had. And with chips and a Tahitian Treat soda, her meal was complete. On the way home, Spark had stopped at a G & P sub shop and ordered their dinner. He was across the table chewing on a turkey sub.

She really was appreciative of everything that he had done for her over the past couple of days. He didn't have to give her a ride to Delaware, let alone let her stay in his house, make her feel at home, and provide food. And the way he'd made her feel when he was making love to her that morning—Devin didn't want to think about it as her stomach turned to jelly once again. She didn't want to think of his hands roaming up her thighs and across her stomach, his lips touching her body softly about her neck and breasts, and especially the way he spread her . . .

"Devin . . . Devin?" Spark shook the dining room table. "Devin?"

"Huh, oh, I'm sorry. My mind was somewhere else."

"Obviously. You looked like you were enjoying yourself."

"I was." She smiled.

He looked at her strangely, unaware that she was thinking of him. "Your phone was vibrating on the living room table."

"Oh," she replied, going into the living room to retrieve it. "It was my girls. I gotta give them a call."

Spark finished his meal as he watched her enjoying her phone call. In his opinion, Devin was a very pretty woman, but when she smiled, she was beautiful. Her whole face lit up. He found himself wishing that he could make her smile all the time.

He watched her on the phone, expecting her to hang up any second. She knew that she shouldn't be on the phone in the middle of such a bad storm. Now, if lightning happened to hit the house, she would be deaf or dead. He had already tried to get her attention and tell her to get off the phone, but she happily chirped along with her daughters as if God wasn't at work here.

As he listened to Devin laughing on the phone with her girls, it struck him that he was missing something in his life. He'd never had kids of his own, and his nieces were the only family that he truly enjoyed being around. His parents were deceased, and his sister drove him crazy. The girls loved him despite his faults. They never laughed about his clumsiness. And even when Carlissa berated him in front of them, they never saw him as the failure that she claimed he was. He missed them. He missed laughing and talking with them. He would call them later just to see how they were doing. They'd called him a couple days ago, but he hadn't answered because he didn't want to make the mistake of telling them that he was home.

It was still pouring down outside. The lightning and thunder ripped through the sky loud and hard, and Spark wondered if the apartment would hold up it was creaking and cracking so badly. But the apartment always did that in the mist of a storm. He had turned off all the lights except for the dining room area, where they ate. It wasn't his fault that he had listened to his mother's ranting when they were little and taken it to heart.

Momma had always said to turn off the lights and sit quietly while God did his work. No TV, no phone, no nothing. Some people stood in front of a big bay window and watched, some people continued business as usual with every electrical apparatus they owned working to full capacity, but Spark had listened, maybe a little too well, to his mother.

He hit the switch to the dining room light as soon as he finished his food, threw away his trash, cleaned up Devin's little mess and walked into the living room. Devin lounged on the sofa, still chatting away. He sat opposite her and listened as she asked questions about her brothers and sisters.

Devin finally ended her conversation with her girls. They were telling her how much fun they were having at their grandparents' house, about the new pool her father had purchased, and the barbecue they were planning for the upcoming weekend. Devin told them that she would be home by then. She had already figured that it shouldn't take them long to locate the last person on the list. She was apprehensive, but she had come this far and she wasn't going to give up—not now.

"What's wrong?" Spark asked, noticing the worried look that crossed her face after she hung up. "Something wrong with the family?"

"Oh, no," she smiled at him. "They're great. I miss them so much. I wish you could meet my family. They would really appreciate the way you're helping me. It wasn't as if they were happy about me coming, but they realized that it was something that I had to do."

"I understand."

Devin continued, "You don't." She paused, deciding that she was going to tell him the truth. It was the least she could do for all the help he had given her. "My ex-husband and I were together for a little while before he asked me to marry him. Chris was a great guy. He loved me, and he loved our girls. I know that with all my heart.

We were so happy together. Then one day, he was killed. Just like that."

Spark moved closer to her when he heard her voice begin to break. He put an arm around her for comfort.

"He was shot in the head leaving his job. The cops never found the killer. For a while, they believed it was a robbery, but it wasn't as if Chris was flashy or wore expensive clothes. He was an ordinary guy. He liked nice things, but he didn't flaunt what he had. I just don't understand why someone would go after him. They didn't take anything. His wallet was still with his clothes. So was his watch and wedding band. They didn't take anything but his life."

"Devin, you don't have to talk about this if you don't want to. I don't want you to be upset or sad."

"No, I want to tell you why I'm here. After he was brought to the hospital, a nurse called me and said that she had found a phone bill in his suit jacket. That was how I found out that my husband was dead, an old phone bill. I was able to see him in the hospital room. But when the funeral home went to the morgue to claim the body, they were informed that his brother had already come and claimed his body. One time, a long time ago, a co-worker and I had gone out to lunch, and I was surprised to see Chris at the restaurant talking to some man that I had never seen before. They looked as if they were arguing, but when I walked up Chris acted as if everything was okay and introduced his brother, who was in from out of town. Chris had always said that he wasn't close to his family."

She looked at Spark. "You know how things happen and you don't pay much attention to them until after the fact? Then everything that you should have seen comes crashing back to you at once. I should have questioned that, and a lot of other things that I didn't."

"Well, Devin," Spark said, "you can't know everything. You loved your husband, and your husband loved you. That's all that really matters."

"But it's not. Spark, I have daughters who have questions. What am I supposed to say to them when they ask me about their father?"

"You tell them that he loved them very much. I'm sure they remember that."

"Then one night, I received a call from a man who told me that Chris loved me and the girls very much, and that I needed to remember that and move on with my life, that Chris would have wanted that. He also told me that he would be in contact with me in the future. That was two years ago. I still haven't heard from that man yet." Tears began to roll down her face again.

"Devin, I know you don't want to hear this, but you can't let yourself get upset. I'm not sure that you could have just moved on with your life like the man suggested, but you did have to be strong for your daughters. They needed you."

"Yeah, you're right."

"You have every right to be angry, but holding in anger can hurt you in the long run. Believe me, I know."

"At first I was angry. They stole my husband from me. I didn't get to go to my husband's funeral. I never got to say goodbye to him, my kids didn't get to say goodbye. And I still don't have any closure. For the past two years, I've been functioning, just functioning, for my daughters' sakes. And now that I have a chance to be free of the pain and misery that I've had to deal with, I want it. I want my life back. Is that too much for me to ask?"

"Of course it isn't." He pulled her closer, offering comfort while running his hand up and down her back.

"Then on top of all that, I get this letter from some woman in Delaware claiming to be his wife. I was going crazy. I kept feeling like I was being followed—"

"Followed?" Spark stiffened. His guilt at the story that Devin was telling him and the toll that the past few years had taken on her was tremendous. Although he wasn't directly the cause of her misfortune, he realized that his presence in Chicago had added to her grief.

"Yeah, you know how sometimes you just get a feeling that someone is around you, watching you? It makes you uncomfortable, well, me anyway. I was always looking over my shoulder. But then for some reason, it was even worse the last two days before I left town."

They both fell silent for a long minute.

"I just want to get to the bottom of all this mess so that I can get on with my life. It's time for me to move forward, and I'm tired, just tired."

CHAPTER 11

Devin laid her head on his shoulder and Spark slowly rubbed her arm as they sat facing the sliding glass doors to his balcony. Through the sheer curtains, he could see God still at work. The heavy rain pellets beat against the glass and the thunder continued to shake the room. He was uncomfortable in front of the glass, but he sat there and watched the sky slowly darken.

He gently kissed her forehead and shifted to a more comfortable position for both of them so that she was lying half on him, half on the sofa. Spark rested under her with his eyes closed and wondered what he should do. His options were still the same. Either he was going to confess that he was the one watching her in Chicago, that his sister was the last name on the list, Carlissa Harrison, and Carlissa had been the one who had sent her the letter full of lies, or he was going to remain quiet and enjoy the little time that they had left.

There were only a few days left to his vacation, and he hoped that she would stay with him until at least the end of the week, but that was hopeless. There was only one name left to investigate, and he knew that she would get up first thing in the morning and be ready to go. Luckily, it was Monday and he could try to convince her to wait until after five to go to the last address because people go to work on Mondays. Hopefully, she would buy it. That would give him a little more time. All Spark wanted to do was to let her know how much he did care for her, how much she had grown on him over the last few days. Maybe, just maybe, if he showed her how much he cared, she would remember that when the walls finally came crashing down on him.

"Devin?" he said in the darkness, his fingers swirling small tresses of her hair. "Devin?"

"Yes, Spark," she replied, her voice heavy with sleep.

"Devin, you know that I care for you, right?"

"Yes, Spark. You wouldn't have kept me in your house and helped me like you have if you didn't. You could have just left me in the airport to fend for myself, but you didn't, and I appreciate that."

"I don't want to think that I was trying to take advantage of you or anything. You know, by what happened—"

She laughed. "Take advantage? I practically had to throw myself at you before you would even touch me. No, you definitely weren't trying to take advantage of me. What makes you think so?"

"Nothing. I-I just want to make sure that after you find out whatever you need to find out that it doesn't change things between us." *That was a stupid thing to say,* Spark told himself. "I mean, I just want you to know that I value you as a friend, and I hope that we can continue to be friends even after you leave. I've had a wonderful time with you these last few days, and I almost hate to see it end."

"Almost? If you're trying to say that you will miss me, why don't you just say that? For what it's worth, I'll miss you, too."

"Will you?"

"Of course. Spark, this is the most fun I've had in a long time. If I weren't here for such an important reason, I'd just stay in this house with you and make love all day and night."

This time, he laughed. "You sure don't ask for much, do you? I doubt very seriously if I'd be able to help you in that department as much as I would want to."

"Sure you would, honey. I have faith in you. We can start practicing now if you would like to." Devin squeezed his left buttock for emphasis.

"All right, girl, you're starting to play with fire," he said as he felt himself begin to harden. He looked down at her as she sat up and began to crawl up the length of his body until she was flush with him.

She moved close to his ear and whispered, "Baby, I am fire."

Something in Spark snapped and he couldn't get her clothes off her fast enough. He didn't care that the lightning and the thunder were practically banging down his door. They no longer existed. All he heard was the unzipping of jeans, the ripping of buttons being pulled from her shirt when he snatched it open, and the rustling of their clothes. He wasn't feeling guilty anymore but he wanted to bring her pleasure, as much pleasure as he possibly could in the short time that they had left.

"Damn," he said under his breath when he realized that he had to go into the bedroom. "Damn," he said again, kissing her hard on the lips, then moving away.

"What are you doing?" she called after him.

"Aaw," he yelled, "my toe. Damn it. We need a condom."

Devin smiled to herself. *Poor baby.* "Did you hurt yourself?" she called out.

"No, I'm all right."

He was such a terrible liar. She smiled more.

Walking back into the room, Spark's mind was once again focused on his mission. He ripped the packet, hurriedly covered himself, covered the sofa with the throw he kept on the back and sat down.

"Come here," he said roughly, pulling her toward him. "I want you."

Devin let out a gasp of surprise when he lifted her up and placed her facing him on his lap. She let herself adjust to having him inside her this way, so fast and so hard.

But the next barrage of thunder sounded so loud that it shocked her, making her body leap forward and start the rhythm of their lovemaking. Spark used his hands at her hip to guide her up, and then roughly bring her back down over him again and again. His lips found the hard, darkened buds of her breasts and he suckled them until it drove her insane. On the next clash of thunder, his teeth lightly bore down on her nipples and she yelled out in pain and ecstasy.

Her arms wrapped around his shoulders as she held on for the ride of her life, a ride full of awakenings and beginnings, although she wasn't ready to admit it. Spark was giving her everything he had, and Devin still wanted more.

Soon, he didn't even hear the storm. He heard Devin's passionate cries as they filled his ear and drove him crazy. They moved at a frantic pace, each determined to please the other first. Devin's hips swirled harder; Spark's hands gripped her hips tighter. He leaned back into the soft cushions, knowing that he was very close to the end, but he wasn't going there without her. Moving his hips wildly, up and down, back and forth, he worked as fast as he could to get her to the same place he was.

Devin felt the curling at her center as it grew tighter and tighter. Her breathing mixed with his as he pulled her close and she rode the rest of the wave of ecstasy against him, grinding with him as he groaned out his release.

Neither of them moved a muscle. Their heavy breathing, glistening bodies, and whispered words were all that gave evidence that they were human, not statues. Spark looked at the wall of mirrors with each flash of lightning. Devin's naked body was still sitting on him, his arms around her. They looked as if they were made that way, fitting perfectly together.

Devin felt him hardening again inside her. She smiled.

"Remind me of what you were worried about. Not being able to go all day and night with me?"

A night of wild lovemaking with Spark caused Devin to sleep very late the next morning. She couldn't understand what had gotten into him last night, but he was like a man possessed, or someone trying to possess her. This morning, she was sore, spent, and satisfied, and she couldn't have been happier. But the more she though about it, the sadder she began to feel. This was probably going to be her last day in Delaware. Once they talked to this last lady, what more could she do? Whether she found the answers she sought or not, it would be time for her to go home. She couldn't stay in Delaware, a strange state, hoping that someone would come along and find her.

She looked at the man lying next to her. His strong back vibrated with each deep intake of air as he slept solidly.

Spark was awakened by the repeated yelling of his name. He fought it because even in his sleepy state he knew that waking meant facing the demons that he had struggled with during the night. After making love to Devin several times more than he thought he could, he had lain awake in the darkness trying to fight off his guilt and his worry. He knew that daybreak would bring a deadline to the choice that he had to make, and he was still in a huge mist of confusion.

What should he do? He wanted to sit her down and explain as much to her as he could before taking her to his sister's house. But he didn't want to see the disappointment that was sure to appear on her face, or even worse, the hate that would show in her eyes.

He had tried to make everything up to her during their lovemaking. He wanted to show her that he cared about her more than he could verbally admit. Spark wanted to love Devin, but it was about to be over before it had even started. Before nightfall, she would hate him and be on her way back to Chicago. It was inevitable. The only thing he could do at this point was try to preserve what little friendship between them he could.

"Yes, baby," he finally answered, lazily reaching out to grab her, any part of her, and pull her close to him.

Devin inched closer to the bed. She was nude, and his hand against her thigh instantly excited her. "Here. Your phone is vibrating."

"I'll check it later. Come get in the bed," he said, knowing exactly who was on the other end. He wasn't ready to face the music quite yet.

"They're just going to call back. It's been ringing for ten minutes straight. It might be important." She climbed over him and back into the bed, leaving the phone in his hand and nuzzling close to him under the covers.

"Believe me, it's not."

"Is it your friend?"

"No," he replied, falling back flat on the bed in defeat.

"What's wrong, Spark?"

"Nothing. Don't worry yourself about it." Looking at

the alarm clock, he saw that it was 10:25 a.m. His stomach growled as he sat up in the bed. The phone began to vibrate again. There wasn't any use in putting off the inevitable.

"Are you hungry?" Devin asked from behind him. "I can make you something to eat real quick."

"Thanks, baby. I'd appreciate that." He watched her climb off the bed and head toward the bathroom after grabbing his robe from the closet door. *He was going to miss her.* "Hello," he said into the phone in a quiet voice. He didn't want to risk Devin hearing the conversation before he was ready to talk to her.

"Uncle Spark?" The two voices said in unison.

"Yeah, hey, my baby girls," he said cheerfully, recognizing his nieces' voices on the other line. "What are you two up to?"

"Uncle Spark, listen," one of the girls said. "We called you because mom is on her way over to your house, and she is really mad. We had to warn you. She found out you were back in town."

"Damn," Spark hissed. "Thanks, girls," he said. "I'll call you later."

"Bye, Uncle Spark," they chimed together.

Spark was so thankful that his nieces knew their mother well. He threw the phone down and practically jumped, actually fell, into the gray sweats he pulled out of his dresser drawer. *Damn, damn. Carlissa lived only fifteen minutes away.* Picking himself up off the bedroom floor, he rushed into the living room and looked around for Devin.

"Devin," he yelled.

"I'm down here," she replied from the kitchen, bent down in the refrigerator. "You know, you really need to go food shopping."

"Yeah, yeah. Um, look, I must talk to you. It's real important." He didn't know what he was going to say, but he knew that he had to say something—fast.

"What's wrong? You look like you've seen a ghost." Devin walked to him with concern clearly displayed on her face. She could tell that something was seriously wrong just by the tone of his voice and the way he was fidgeting. "What is it?"

"Look, I don't want you to be mad at me or hate me for what I'm about to say. I would have told you much sooner, but I just didn't want to lose you. I can't explain it, Devin, but you've brought me more happiness in the last few days than I've felt practically my whole life. I just didn't want it to end." He was holding her hands, her arms. He pulled her close to him. "You're going to hate me. I know you are."

"Spark, what are you talking about? What's going on?"

Suddenly the doorbell rang repeatedly and there was banging at the front door.

"Spark?" She looked at him curiously.

"Devin," he started, trying to get as much out as he could, as many words as he could, to make her understand his position. "I didn't expect for this to happen. I didn't expect to start caring for you, to even like you. But I do. She's my sister, and she's been holding some things over my head. I wanted to tell you the truth, I swear. I didn't even want to go, but she made me do it. Just know that I do care for you very much. I do. And everything I did to you or with you was because I cared for you, no other reason. No matter what anyone else says. Please just believe that I care for you, Devin."

"Spark, what the hell's going on? She paused, fear gripping her. The look in his eye was so desperate and wild. "What is it? Tell me!"

The pounding on the door persisted. The ringing of the doorbell continued as well.

"Who's that?" Devin asked.

"Did you hear what I just said, Devin?" He deliberately ignored his sister's pounding. She wasn't going anywhere. Spark knew that if he didn't open the door until eight that evening, Carlissa would still be standing there.

"I heard you, Spark. But you're not telling me anything. Who is at the door?"

Spark sat down, but he held her hands and pulled her into the circle of his arms. "Devin, the last thing I ever wanted to do was to hurt you!"

"Hurt me? What, are you married or something? Is that your wife at the door?" She moved away from him. "I've been staying with a married man all this time? Why didn't you tell me?"

For an instant, a quick instant, Spark almost wanted to let her believe the lie, but he knew that his sister wouldn't let it lie once she heard Devin's name. He was in deep, and there wasn't any way out of it but the truth.

"That's my sister," he said, following her to the bedroom.

Devin grabbed her bag and began filling it with her belongings. "Yeah, right. Your sister, my ass. Your sister wouldn't be trying to bang down your door like she is. Spark, you don't have to lie to me. I went into this whole thing willingly. I practically threw myself at you even when you tried to resist. So, fine, I'll take the blame, but all you had to do was tell me the truth. You could have said, 'Hold up. I'm married.' "

She shoved her legs in her jeans and pulled them up hard. Her T-shirt over her head, Devin threw his robe at him in disgust. She put on her socks and sneakers, then went to the bathroom and began putting her few cosmetics, toothbrush, comb, and other personals, into a smaller bag. The whole time Spark was on her heels, trying to convince her that he wasn't married.

"Devin, please, stop it. Just stop it. I'm not married. That is my sister at the door."

"Whatever. I'll just call a cab or catch a bus or something. Where's the bus stop?"

"I'm not letting you catch a bus. Please just sit down and let me explain." Spark grabbed her arms, and after a moment of protest, led her to the living room sofa. She sat her on the couch, and he knelt before her.

The doorbell began ringing again.

"Devin, please forgive me." Spark looked her right in the eye. His eyes matched the desperation in his voice. "I am so sorry for what I've done, for any way that I've hurt you." She needed to believe him.

The ringing and banging continued.

"What the hell is going on? Just tell me, Spark. Tell me. Who is at the door?"

"Devin, Carlissa Harrison is—"

Devin stood up immediately. He held onto her hands.

"Carlissa Harrison is at the door. Open it!" she yelled, trying to move toward the door. "What is she doing at your door?"

"That's what I want to talk to you about. Please sit back down," he pleaded.

"No. Tell me now," she replied.

"She's my sister," he admitted, tightening his grip on her hands when she tried to pull away. "Please wait. Let me explain, Devin."

"Explain? Explain what? That you've known for almost two days that I was looking for her, and you didn't tell me? That you . . . you played me. You kept me here knowing damn well where she was. Why did we even go to the other houses?" She kept trying to pull away from him, but Spark wouldn't let her go. He grabbed her waist and held on even as she pushed and punched at him for release. "You had no intention of taking me there, did you?"

"I was going to tell you everything. Please, just listen."

"Listen to you for what? More lies? I'm going to open that door, and we're going to get to the bottom of this."

"Wait, before I open the door, I've got to tell you everything."

"There's more? You knew Chris or Richard, didn't you? What were you doing in Chicago anyway? That wasn't a coincidence either, was it?"

Spark got quiet. He didn't want to tell her, but he knew that Carlissa would as soon as she came into the house. She had a way of making everything sound dirty, degrading.

"Devin, I was in Chicago because of you. I'm so sorry. If I had known that you were hurting so bad, I would never have done it. I would never want to hurt you."

"Why not? You don't know me. We only met three days ago. I'm nobody to you, right?"

"Devin, that's not true. You know that's not true."

"So, meeting at the airport, you giving me a ride here, to your house and conveniently letting me stay with you, making love to me, that was all a part of your plan."

"None of that was my plan. Not after the airport. I swear to you, Devin, meeting you was the best thing that ever happened to me. I truly care for you. I didn't mean for it to happen, damn it. That's why I didn't want to make love to you. I knew I was starting to have feelings for you, but my sister had me by the balls. That's why I had to go to Chicago for her. As soon as I met you, I liked you. But I didn't know the person you were when I was foll—" Spark stopped talking immediately. He had said way too much. He knew it by the look in Devin's eye.

"Following me in Chicago? That was you?" Devin swatted at his head until he released her, and he didn't let go easily.

Spark took the beating because he felt he deserved it. No one could hate him more at that moment than he hated himself. "Devin?"

"That was you? I was scared out of my wits. Afraid for myself and for my kids. I thought someone was trying to kill me, Spark. And it was you the whole time."

"My sister made me do it," he pleaded, sounding more pathetic by the minute. "But after I met you, I couldn't do it anymore. I didn't tell her that I was back in town. I didn't tell her that you were here. But now she knows. That was my nieces calling me earlier to tell me that she was on her way over here."

"Well, she obviously knows something, so let her in. I want to get this over with so I can go home."

"Devin, before I let her in, please just hear me out first, please."

"No, let her ass in here now. I don't care what your side of the story is. You have lied to me enough." Devin was ready for the same fight that it sounded like the person on the other side of the door, Spark's sister Carlissa, was ready for. She was tired and fed up, and she wanted to be out of Delaware. For the first time, she was truly sorry that she had ever come to the damn place. But to her dismay, her pity didn't stem from Spark's lies or his inability to tell her the truth, but from the pain that suddenly shot through her heart. She had really felt a connection with Spark, and she had hoped that after everything was over they could build some type of relationship. Her wishing was all for naught.

Spark was still on his knees, still trying to plead his case, but she wasn't willing to hear a word he was saying. He might as well be talking to the wall. He did care for her a lot. And he wanted to say what he had to say before Carlissa blew into the house making all kinds of accusations and making him sound more like a fool. Carlissa was crazy most of the time, especially when it came to her fantasy about her ex-husband. He didn't want Devin to get hurt by her lies.

"I'm going to open the door now," he said. "Devin, please don't let what she might say harm you. My sister is good at distorting the truth." He looked at her, and it hurt him more to see her hurting than it did for him to be hurting himself. Spark reached out to touch her arm, but she moved away. Her arms crossed, lips in a tight line, she was preparing for war.

CHAPTER 12

Carlissa spent her time outside letting her anger build. She continuously rang the doorbell, constantly beat on the door, and repeatedly cursed at her brother. She didn't care if anyone heard her. She wasn't going anywhere until she got into his house and got some answers. What was he doing back? When did he get back? And who the hell was the woman staying in his house?

When she saw her the night before, Vivian told Carlissa about the fight of two days ago, which meant that Spark had come back to town at least two days before and hadn't bothered to let her know that he was there. He hadn't called to tell her any more about Richard's widow or the daughters, twin daughters, she was supposed to have in Chicago.

She rang the doorbell again. To her surprise, her brother opened the door.

"Move out of the way," she said.

"Whoa, what do you want?" Spark said, holding his position in front of the doorway. "What are you doing over here making all this noise?"

"Move out of the damn way, boy," Carlissa screamed, pushing at him so she could get into the house. "I know you got somebody in there."

"Carlissa, what do you want? This is my house. You can't just barge in here anytime you want." Although he had allowed her to do it numerous times in the past, he was fed up today. He was a grown man, and this was his house. It was so hard for him to understand how Carlissa had been able to become a high-level service manager for one of the largest banks in the state. She could act just as ghetto as Vivian, who didn't have anything going for her, when she wanted to. "And you better calm the hell down." His voice was loud and forceful.

Carlissa was a little taken aback. Spark had never dared to speak to her that way, and how dare he do it now? She was the older sibling. She had taken care of him when his gambling habits had caused him more problems than he could handle. She was the one in charge here.

"Who in the hell are you talking to like that, Spark?"

"I'm talking to you. You are not going to come in here with that mess. Not this time. I have company in *my* house, and *you* are going to respect that." He noticed that she quieted down, but Spark wasn't fool enough to trust her actions. Carlissa was sneaky. That was why she and Vivian got along so well.

He moved out of the way. Carlissa gave him a look that would have stopped the air from coming out of his lungs if she were truly as powerful as she thought she was.

"Go in there and have a seat," he said in a commanding voice. Spark was determined to keep control of this situation for as long as he possibly could.

"Whatever," she whispered under her voice.

"I'm serious, Carlissa," Spark replied as he followed her. He was more nervous than at any other time in his life as he quickly moved in front of his sister before she reached the top of the stairs and saw Devin standing there.

"So," Carlissa said, when she reached the living room, "this is your little friend, the one that Vivian was fighting."

"Yes, that would be me," Devin replied.

"I'm surprised at how fast you work," she began, looking back and forth between the two. She really didn't care that Spark was back in town and had picked up some girl as soon as he got back. She was only concerned with why he was back and why he hadn't called her. Vivian's rendition of the night of the fight wasn't of importance to her except for the fact that Spark was back in town. "When did you get back in town? Why didn't you call me?"

"I've been in town for a couple of days, and I didn't call you because I didn't want to be bothered."

"So that you could screw your little friend here all day?"

"So that I could get to know her better, if you must know." He kept his voice calm as he went over to Devin. She didn't acknowledge him.

Devin stood in the same spot he had left her in earlier. Her arms were still crossed as she silently assessed her dead husband's first wife. Carlissa was nothing like she had imagined. There was no way that Chris could have been in love with this woman. No way. Carlissa was loud and obnoxious, rude and very inconsiderate of others. She was the total opposite of him.

"I suppose you saw Vivian somewhere, and she told you that I was home."

"Yes, she told me about the little scuffle she had the other night. But I could care less about that." She walked over to the dining room table and sat down, having already given Devin a thorough once-over and deciding that she was unimportant, just another short affair her brother was having. "All I care about is the fact that you are not in Chicago anymore, and you didn't tell me that you were back in town. Why did I have to damn near bang your door down before you opened it? Were you having sex or something?"

"Carlissa, you are such a bitch."

"I know. Anyway, no updates on little Ms. Devin Albridge?"

Devin was quick with her movement, but Spark was quicker. He grabbed hold of her arm and kept her next to him, right next to him, in the living room.

"Carlissa, I came back into town three days ago," he said, a devilish look in his eye. It was now or never, and he figured that it was just as good a time as ever. He was tired of being her little errand boy. Carlissa had a rude awakening coming, and he wanted to be the one to give it to her. Spark hoped his sister would choke on her own saliva when he told her that Devin was standing right next to him. "I didn't let you know because I didn't want to be bothered by you."

"So, when I called, you were already back?"

"Yes," he answered. He could see the anger build in her eyes. "But I didn't want to be bothered." If he could, Spark was going to use this as an opportunity to prove to Devin that he didn't like doing what he did for his sister, but he had to. He truly liked her, and he hoped that she could see that, even if it did mean the end of their relationship. At least she would know the truth.

"Have a seat," he said to Devin. "Please. Let me get my sister straight."

She didn't know why, but she listened to him and sat in the chair closest to her with her back to the wall. Devin didn't know what he was up to, but she wasn't going to be caught by surprise either.

"Now, Carlissa, I left Chicago for two reasons, the first being that I didn't want to be there in the first place."

"You agreed to go," Carlissa yelled.

"No, you made me go," Spark corrected.

"Damn right. You owe me a lot of money," she said, standing and pointing her finger in his direction. She knew that she couldn't beat Spark, but she could darn sure give him a run for his money. "You'd be dead right now if it wasn't for me paying off your debts."

"And you've been holding that over my head for the last two years. I'm not a gambler anymore, Carlissa. If you really gave a damn about me at all, you'd be glad that I've made changes in my life. You'd be happy for me, but all you know how to do is use people."

"You're an ungrateful bastard, you know that? After Mom died, I practically raised you. I lost a lot because of you. And this is how I get paid back. All you had to do was go up there and find out what she was up to, what she knew about Richard, and where the money was, and you couldn't even do that."

"Because it's wrong," Spark insisted. "Carlissa, that woman never did anything to you. You hate somebody who never even knew you were alive."

"He is my husband, Spark."

Here we go again with her fantasy. Carlissa stood in front of him, and for the first time, Spark saw how weak she really was. She needed to hold onto the distorted memories of a failed marriage in order to justify her own being. He felt sorry for her, but he was determined to make her see the truth.

"Carlissa, Richard divorced you years ago, before he even left Delaware, not long after the girls turned three. You drove him crazy. Don't you remember? He had to get away from you."

"That's not true."

"Then you stopped him from seeing the girls."

"No, he left me and the girls. He never tried to see them again."

Spark shook his head. How in the world could he and his sister have been in the same place and have seen two different versions of a situation?

"Carlissa, I was there, too. Richard never pretended to be in love with you. He tried to be your friend for the girls' sake, but you made it impossible for him to even do that. You drove him away, just like you do every other man in your life, including me."

"First of all, Richard loved me. Secondly, he only left me because of Willis Demby. If he hadn't left, he never would have met that woman in Chicago and started another family. He didn't even feel obligated to tell her the truth, gave her a fake name. That's how much he loved her."

Devin tried to sit by patiently and listen to what this woman was saying. She knew that she would get much more information from her if Carlissa didn't know who she was. Spark knew it, too, and she assumed that was his plan because he kept looking at her after every comment Carlissa made, but that last comment was the last straw.

Devin stood up and looked Carlissa directly in the face. "Lady, you don't know what the hell you're talking about. My husband loved me. He might not have loved you, but Chris loved me." She was moving closer to Carlissa. It was important that the woman knew who she was and heard what she said.

Spark jumped in front of her and kept her at bay. At the same time, he saw the look on Carlissa's face as she realized that Devin was right in her face, not in Chicago, but in Delaware, in her brother's house.

"You no-good son of a bitch," she hissed at Spark. "You brought his wife here with you. Are you crazy? I'll kill you." She turned her eyes on Devin.

"Kill me, then," Devin yelled back. "I don't know what kind of hold you have on your brother, but I'm not afraid of you. Talking about my husband. You don't know anything about our relationship. *You* must be crazy."

The two women advanced toward each other, and again, Spark knew he was going to be the one who ended up with most of the bruises. But he put a hand on each of them and pushed them as far away from each other as he could.

"Why is your ass here?"

"I came here looking for you," Devin replied. "Because I wanted to meet the woman who was writing me, talking about how my husband was her husband. And now that I've seen you, I'm not impressed at all. You sent your brother all the way to Chicago to spy on my family. You're sick. Well, now I'm here. What do you want with me?"

"I want to know where Richard hid the money," Carlissa blurted. "It's mine now. I'm his first wife, his only wife, and whatever he has left is mine."

"Chris didn't have any money except for the money he worked for. You are delusional."

Carlissa tried to go after her again, but Spark was right there to take the blow. Her nails dug into his neck, and Spark pushed Carlissa away in order to recover. "Damn it, Carlissa, you got to go."

"I'm not going anywhere. It seems to me that as smitten as you are with her, you failed to tell her all there is to know about Mr. Richard Harrison. I knew they would catch up with his ass one day. That's why I kept every piece of mail he ever sent the girls, every package that came with a stuffed animal or clothes or toys. I knew that one day I was going to have to track his whereabouts and find my money."

"What money?" Devin asked, throwing her hands high in the air.

"I'm not telling *you,*" Carlissa said, putting her hands on her hips. "At least one thing has come from all of this. I can rest easy knowing that you don't have the money either."

"I don't want any money. Unlike you, I loved my husband for himself. I'm not trying to change history just so I can fatten up my bank account. And I'm not using some flunky brother to do my dirty work for me." Devin regretted saying it, but that was how she felt. She was ready to go. She had done what she wanted to do, talked to the woman who was Chris's first wife, as crazy of a talk as it was.

"Don't tell me that I didn't love Richard!" Carlissa yelled.

"I don't have time for this, lady. You are going to see things the way you see them, and I'm going to see things the way they were. So, basically, we're getting nowhere. How about you stay on this side of the world, and I'll stay on my side. If you want to believe there's money, then you're free to do so. Spark, I'm on my way to the airport. Thank you for your hospitality."

Devin calmly walked toward the bedroom. She stayed on guard because she had to pass Carlissa to do so, but Spark stayed between them, moving Carlissa back into the dining room until Devin was out of her way.

He didn't want her to leave, not yet. Not without her understanding how he really felt.

"I can't believe you," Carlissa said as soon as Devin was out of earshot. "You just turn your back on your family like it's no problem."

"What do you mean, turn my back? Carlissa, you are a real piece of work, you know that? You don't give a damn about anybody but yourself. Not me, not the girls. All you think about is money."

"And all you care about is a piece of ass. Is that what it is, Spark? Did she screw you real good and whip you that fast?"

"Get out!" he yelled, letting his anger at her surface. "If it weren't for the girls, I swear I would disown you in a heartbeat."

"Yeah, right," she replied, walking down the steps toward the front door, "until the next time you need me."

"Don't worry about that."

"I'm still your sister, Spark. You can't do anything to change that."

He remained quiet, but oh, how he wished there was some way he could change it.

"I don't want you to leave like this, Devin." Spark sat in the chair, watching as she carried her bags toward the living room.

She didn't answer. She didn't want to leave like that, either, but what choice did she have? Devin had trusted him, almost fallen for him. It was good that the truth had come out when it did. She would have been devastated if she had allowed herself the time to fall head over heels in love, or even worse, invited him into her daughters' lives.

"Devin—"

"Don't say anything, Spark. Just let it go. This happened for a reason."

"But I can't just let it go. I want you to stay in my life."

She looked at him. If only he had said the same thing to her without the lies between them. Devin looked at her watch. Her taxi should be there any minute.

"Let me take you to the airport. It doesn't make sense for you to pay all that money when I will burn up only about ten dollars in gas."

"They gave me a flat rate, but thank you anyway. I just think this way is for the best."

"Well, at least let me help you carry your things to the door," he suggested.

She stopped in her tracks. "You want to help me, Spark? Why don't you help by telling me the truth?"

"I tried to, but you wouldn't listen."

"Well, you've got ten minutes. Try now. Tell me what you know about Chris."

Spark sat back in the chair and let out a long deep breath. He was going to tell her everything he knew about Richard and pray that she didn't resent him.

"First, I have to apologize for Carlissa. The woman is crazy. That's the only excuse I can offer for her. But she is my sister, Devin, and as much as I hate her, I love her. And I love my nieces."

Devin didn't say anything, just looked at him dead in the face. He was apologizing for Carlissa's actions, but wasn't apologizing for his own. Maybe he had tried to apologize to her before, but she wasn't listening to that. He was desperate and about to get found out. *A desperate man will say anything.* As much as Devin wanted to believe that he truly cared for her, the words that her mother had repeated often during her upbringing stayed in the back of her mind.

"Devin, please listen to me. I wasn't trying to hurt you. I didn't want to hurt you. I care for you. When I went to Chicago, I didn't think I was doing anything but a favor for my sister. I owe Carlissa a lot of money. And she's right. If it wasn't for her, I would be dead. I'm sorry, so sorry, Devin. But I thought that as long as I didn't have contact with you, it was all right."

"It wasn't. Do you know how it feels to constantly think someone is watching you?"

Yes. "No, I don't, and I apologize for that. I honestly wasn't thinking about how it could affect you. I didn't think it would as long as you didn't see me. I was just trying to get Carlissa off my back about what she had done for me and how much I owed her."

"What about Chris?" she asked harshly. She didn't want to hear anything about what he had been going through right now. Feeling sorry for him couldn't be on her agenda. All she wanted was the truth and to get home to her children.

"His real name was Richard Harrison. We were great friends growing up. It was a little crew, six of us in all,

Richard, Al, Jay, Robbie, Butch, and me. He was a good guy, a good friend. We did our share of dirt and got into a little bit of trouble every now and then, but for the most part, we were just out to have fun. We graduated high school and were still all hanging together. A few of the guys went to college, a couple of us got jobs, but we were still the best of friends. Richard went to college, right here at the university. He was a smart guy. Then Willis moved into town."

"Willis who?"

"Willis Demby ruined everybody's life in one sweep. He was a hustler, a swindler. We had never met anyone like him before. He was suave and street smart. He had money and women that could blow a young boy's mind wide open. Before we knew it, we were into some heavy stuff, had more money than we knew what to do with, and some dangerous mob connections. But you don't think about that when you're young and the money is real good. You don't have to work. You have more women than you can handle. For a young impressionable kid, that sounds real good.

"Anyway, Willis set us up big time, had us thinking we were living large, but then one of the guys, Robbie, started using cocaine, then heroin. Before long, he was stealing from the money that we had to give to Willis. At first, we covered up for him. We tried to help him, but the more we covered, the bigger his habit got. Eventually, we couldn't hide it any longer, and Willis found out. He didn't trust Robbie anymore and told us to get rid of him or he would. He was one of our best friends. We couldn't do it. Murder was a little further than any of us expected to have to go, and I think that once Willis said it, we were snapped out of a trance. The things that we heard but chose to ignore couldn't be ignored any longer. But true to his word, Willis killed Robbie. He killed Robbie right in front of us."

Spark paused, trying to push the vision of his friend lying on the cold ground with blood pouring from the side of his head out of his mind.

"We all wanted to get out, but there wasn't any way he was going to let us go alive. We were trapped."

The horn of the cab blew outside, but neither of them moved. Devin wanted to leave, but she had to hear the rest of his story. She had to know as much about Chris's past as she could.

"Let them go," Spark finally said after hearing the horn blow a second time. "I'll take you to the airport, Devin." He didn't wait for an answer, but continued with his story instead.

"We did everything Willis told us to do because of threats that he either made to us or our families. Richard changed after Robbie's shooting. He had studied criminal justice in school and had met a lot of people. He was talking about going to the police. We tried to talk him out of it, but looking back, it was the best thing that ever happened to any of us. He came back and told us they said they would look into it, but didn't really seem to believe his story. But without us knowing, he was actually working with them, wearing wires and gathering information. The next thing we knew, Willis and half the people he worked for were behind bars, and Richard was gone."

"I wanted to know what happened to him, but I wasn't going to ask any questions. Luckily, they didn't need our testimonies at the trial. One of the lawyers told me later that part of the agreement for Richard's testimony was that the rest of us would be left out of it. I owe him a lot, because if we had said anything we would have been killed. He gave us the opportunity to make fresh starts with our lives."

Spark turned toward the sliding glass doors that led to his balcony in a brief moment of thanks. Then he turned back to her.

"I mean, I admit that I've made a number of mistakes since then, like my gambling, but that's because I didn't know what to do with myself after not having to do anything for so long. I was still in the same frame of mind, thinking I had money to burn. Now, I'm different. I've been different for years. I work hard every day, I've learned to trust, and more importantly, I'm trustworthy."

She cut her eyes at him.

"Well, I—you know what I mean. I am trustworthy, Devin, and loyal to the people I love. That's why I was so torn between you and Carlissa. I know she was wrong, but she's my sister. You would do the same thing for your family, right?"

Devin didn't answer. "So what about him and Carlissa?"

"I don't know too much about when or where that started. Which tells me that it wasn't long or serious because these were two people that I was around all the time. All I know is that we were hanging out one night, and she found us. We all had dates or women with us that night, and when she saw Richard on the dance floor wrapped up with this fine woman, she practically beat that girl to death. We had to pull her off. That's when I found out that she and Richard had been doing their thing for a minute, but Richard always said they were just friends. She offered it, and he took it. Carlissa wasn't popular, and it wasn't as if men were beating down her door. When she got with Richard, she wasn't able to accept the concept of 'just friends'. In her mind, he loved her as much as she loved him, or what she called love.

"Either she was already pregnant or she got pregnant right after that, and being a good man, he agreed to marry her. There was never any doubt about the kids being his. And he loved those girls. When they were born, he was right there, and spoiled them from the beginning. Carlissa loved the money. I think she loved it most of all. Anyway, she hated Richard when he turned state's evidence against Willis. I mean, *hated* him."

He laughed. "That sister of mine put Richard through hell the whole time they were married. I bet the day he filed those divorce papers was the happiest day of his life. He didn't want to leave the girls, but he didn't have a choice. Carlissa wasn't going to let him take them, and if he stayed, he'd have been dead within a week."

"So, he came to Illinois. That just doesn't seem far enough away to me."

"I think so, too, but look at it this way. When you can't find something you're looking for, where is it usually? Right under your nose. I'm sure he knew they would expect him to move all the way to Nevada or Arizona."

"Well, they found him, didn't they?" Devin wiped at the tear that rolled down her face.

"I guess they did, but at least he had time to live his life the way he was meant to live it. He fell in love. He had two more beautiful daughters. He was happy the day he died. Not everybody gets to live that good."

His words weren't making her feel any better. Devin appreciated the effort, but it was futile. Chris hadn't loved her enough to tell her the truth about his past. He had put her and their daughters in danger. What if they had tracked him down while he was with the kids? What if the girls had gotten in the crossfire? What if they had kidnapped the girls or harmed them? What if? What if? What if?

She put her head down in her hands and cried. For the first time in a long time, she let her emotions take hold of her and let all of the anger and frustration and fear and animosity flow out of her.

"Devin, baby," Spark said, moving to sit next to her on the sofa. "I am so sorry." He felt her stiffen when he put his arm around her and pulled her toward him. "I am so sorry for my part in this. I loved Richard like a brother. I would never hurt anyone that he loved or that I cared for, never."

If it weren't for the fact that her heart was aching so badly, Devin might have taken the time to hear him out.

But none of that mattered now. She didn't trust him. He had been leading her on and lying to her from day one. From the first moment they met, Spark had been plotting on her. She had given this man her body. He had made sweet, awesomely sweet, love to her and lied to her in the same breath. How could she trust him? How could she believe that he wasn't lying to her now? After allowing herself a moment of weakness, Devin straightened up.

"I'm ready to go to the airport," she said quietly. She didn't want to hear any more of his lies. Picking up the bags, she waited until he got up to follow her out of the house. She never looked back, didn't want to remember.

The ride to the airport was miserable for both people who sat in the car without saying a single word. Devin sat in the passenger seat looking as if the world had just fallen in on her. Spark remained quiet after being cursed at for trying to help her with her bags.

At the airport, Spark parked the car in the garage and got out with her.

"Thanks for the ride," Devin said as she exited the car. She didn't expect him to follow her into the airport, and was shocked when he fell into step beside her. "Spark, you don't have to go inside with me. I'm a grown woman."

"I'll just walk you in. Devin," he started. "Please don't be mad at me forever. I honestly enjoyed having you with me these last few days. I know you don't believe me, and I probably don't deserve to ask you this, but please don't let what I did for my sister stop us from having what could be a wonderful relationship. You can't tell me that you didn't feel the same things that I felt when we were together."

She stopped walking, but didn't say anything. Devin looked at him closely, but then turned away. She wasn't ready for this. There were too many things that she had to do to get her life back on track. He was the last person that should be on her mind.

"You felt it, right? Devin, please don't let it end like this. Talk to me."

"Goodbye, Spark," she said before turning into the airport and walking away from him quickly.

Spark stood in the spot right outside the automatic doors that opened from the parking garage to the airport hallway. He watched her walk away from him, walk right out of his life, and he couldn't accept it.

"Are you all right, dear?" the elderly woman asked as she took her seat next to the young woman who tried hiding the tears coursing down her face. "Is everything okay?"

"No," she answered honestly, "but it will be. I just miss my daughters." Devin wasn't exactly lying. She did miss her girls.

"Do you want to talk about it?"

"No, ma'am. I'm fine, really." Devin thought about her girls and how different their lives would have been if their father hadn't been man enough to stand up for what he believed. She couldn't hate him for that. They would never have been born if Chris hadn't relocated. And he had loved her. Devin knew that down to her bones. And she had been madly in love with him, too. She only wished that they'd had more time together and that he had trusted her enough to tell her his secret. But she understood why he hadn't.

It seemed that her trip hadn't been a waste of time after all. She had gotten the answers to all of her questions and much more. Her husband had been a good man, regardless of what people had said when he was found killed gangland-style. People had been so cruel after the comforting and supporting time passed. And although she didn't want to admit it, Spark had showed her that she did have a lot of living left inside her. She had a heart filled with emotions. He had showed her that laughing and having fun was a good thing. He had showed her that she was still a woman, with needs and wants, and that side of her couldn't be closed off.

CHAPTER 13

The energy seemed to seep out of her body the moment Devin closed the front door to her house. All she could think about was the queen-size bed in the master bedroom. Dropping all of her belongings next to the front door, she walked straight upstairs, intending to hop in the shower and then into bed.

Devin woke the next morning still dressed in the clothes from the day before. She couldn't remember falling in bed or even reaching the bedroom. That's what she got for trying to catch a flight at the last minute without checking the schedule.

She'd had to wait in the airport for three hours before another flight to Chicago became available, and even then, she had paid too much to come home. But she had been determined to get away from Delaware.

All that didn't matter now, though, because she was home where she was supposed to be and she had a new outlook on her life. She had faced her problems dead on, and now it was time for her to start living again.

Devin was so glad that she still had a month before school started to get herself together. It was enough time for her to find closure for what she had learned in Delaware. The sooner she did that, the sooner she could move on with her life.

Devin needed to see her children. She missed them terribly, and in her haste to get home, she hadn't even thought to tell her family that she was coming back. Devin figured a surprise would be in order. Glancing at her watch, she took her time getting dressed, not wanting to run into any of her siblings who would be dropping kids off at their parents' house before going to work. During summer break, the majority of the younger grandchildren either stayed at the house or went there every morning.

She would have thought that her parents would have had enough of raising kids having had eight of their own, but they couldn't get enough of their grandchildren. Having so many kids around kept them young and in shape, they said.

The house was full of noise when she opened the door. It was around twelve-thirty, which meant lunchtime in the busy household. Devin didn't ring, simply used her door key and slipped in. In the background, she could hear her mother calling out orders to the older children so as to get through lunch in an orderly fashion.

She walked into the large kitchen that held a formal dining room table on the left side filled with the smaller children and a smaller round table on the right side that was filled with the older grandkids. Devin smiled to herself. This house had always been full of chaos.

"It looks like you need more help," she commented, smiling at her eldest niece, Pamela, who was trying to help out.

The twins both jumped out of their chairs, shouting at the top of their voices until they reached their mother. Their action prompted all of the other kids to shout and cheer.

"Aunt Devin," Pamela said, blowing out a long stream of air, "I am so glad you're back. These kids are off the chain."

"Hey, Mom," Devin yelled to her mother before reaching her to return her hug. "Pam, these kids are just like you and your brother were when you were younger. It's just more of them now."

"Yeah, I know." Pam was a sophomore in college, with privileges that a lot of girls her age didn't have. Her father was the CEO of a major publishing company; her mother was a social butterfly. Pam had connections that she so far had no idea how to use, and she was smart, pretty, and spoiled. Devin had no doubt that she would go far in her career.

With Devin's help, they got lunch done much quicker. Then the kids returned to playing. The older kids went outside, the boys playing basketball on the makeshift court her father had put together, the girls staying close to the porch and playing jacks or cards or reading books and gossiping.

"Mom, I still don't understand why you don't just open up a daycare center. The house is big enough. You could be making a lot of money."

"Baby, I don't need any money. I have love. That's much more important."

Devin had been having the same conversation with her mother for years. It was bad enough that all the grandkids came here after school, but some weren't in school yet, and her mother insisted on watching them. She wouldn't let any of her children take their kids to daycare centers or preschool. Instead, they stayed with her and she taught them. By the time they started school, they knew their alphabet, numbers to twenty, how to spell and write their names, and their addresses and phone numbers. On top of all that, Brenda wouldn't take a red cent from any of her children.

But to show their appreciation, the siblings were always bringing something to their parents' house. John brought a deep freezer full of food, which he kept filled, Charles had an addition built onto the house for when the kids stayed over, Troy had a new fence put around the yard. Every time their father said he needed something new, he had it within two weeks. The girls, in turn, assisted their mother with the household chores, shopping duties, and taking care of each other's children.

"Come on, baby." Her mother sat down on the living room sofa and patted the space next to her. "Tell me all about your trip. Is everything okay? Did you find what you were looking for?"

"Well, I can honestly say that I found out a lot more than I thought I would. It seems that Chris relocated here because of some things he was involved in when he was younger. He testified against some people in the mob."

"Wow, and he never told you about any of it?"

"Not one thing. Apparently, he wanted to keep his friends out of trouble so he basically put his own neck on the line. In the process, he had to lose touch with his daughters. That must have hurt him a lot."

"We saw how he was with your girls. He doted on them, spoiled them to no end."

"Yeah, I just wish he had talked to me."

"And worry you to death? Why would a man who loved you as much as Chris did put extra burdens on your shoulders?"

"I know, but—"

"No, buts, Devin. That man loved you. That's the bottom line. You should be happy and thankful because most people don't get that kind of love in a lifetime."

Devin was quiet as she contemplated her mother's words. She was thankful because Chris had given her love she hadn't known before him. He was her first true love, and he had blessed her with two beautiful daughters. She just wished he had loved her enough to tell her the truth.

"So, how did you get all the information you needed so soon? Did you have a hard time getting around? Where did you stay? Was it a nice hotel?"

"Mom . . . Mom. One question at a time," Devin commented. "I made friends with a nice gentleman who helped me a lot."

"A man," her mother replied, a shimmer flashing through her eyes. "Where did you meet him? And he helped you just like that?"

"He was a nice man. I met him at the airport, and we started talking. He told me he was from Delaware, and we just hit it off from there."

"So you exchanged numbers, and he helped you find your way around?

"No, he gave me a ride to Delaware and let me stay at his house after I couldn't get a hotel room. Then he drove me where I needed to go."

"You stayed with a strange man?" Brenda shook her head. "I don't know if I like the sound of that, Devin. What if he had hurt you?"

"But he didn't, Mom. I'm right here standing in front of you." This was why Devin hadn't wanted to say anything to her mother about her time in Delaware. She asked too many questions and wanted too many answers.

"Yeah, well, you have to be careful out there. What if something had happened to you? Who would take care of the girls? They've already lost one parent. They can't afford to lose another one. You have to be careful."

"Okay, okay, I get it." Devin knew that if anything ever happened to her the last thing she would have to worry about was who would take care of her daughters. More likely than not, the family would be arguing over who would take them. But sometimes, you just had to know when to shut your mouth and not argue back to your parents.

"Was he a nice gentleman?"

"Yeah," Devin whispered quietly, "he was." Some small part of her had been missing Spark since he stood watching her in the airport garage. She thought about him often, but always forced the images to the back of her mind as soon as she realized what she was doing.

Her mother looked at her closely. She knew that look, had seen it in the eye of every one of her girls a time or two. This time she didn't ask a lot of questions. She made one simple statement.

"He must have been a special man to offer his services like that."

Devin didn't reply; she changed the subject. "Did the girls behave?"

"You know they did. Why you asking a silly question like that? Tell me more about Delaware."

"There isn't anything else to tell. It looks just like here. Housing developments, apartments, of course. Our city is bigger, but there's a small city there, and a lot of roads, just like here. I didn't really get to do a lot of sight-seeing. It rained one day, a terrible storm, so we had to stay in." A smile crossed her face when she remembered how the storm had frightened Spark.

"You stayed at the man's house the whole time you were there? His wife didn't mind?"

"He's not married, and he has his own place."

"Oh, well. Does he have children?"

"No, no kids."

"Umph, he sounds like a catch to me. Single man, no children, working, his own car and house. I'm surprised he hasn't been snatched up by now. What's wrong with him?"

"There's nothing wrong with him. He was very supportive and nice, until he—"

"What happened? Did he try something funny with you?"

"Of course not, Momma. I, um, I don't want to talk about it. It's not important. What's important is that I'm home now with my girls and my family where I need to be. I found the answers I was searching for, and now I can move on with my life."

"That's good. It's been far too long since I've seen you smile and laugh. I think this trip was just what you needed. About this gentleman you met . . . are you two going to remain friends?"

"I doubt that very seriously. He was just there to help me out."

Brenda noticed the sadness that filled her daughter's eyes. It made her heart ache. Devin obviously had some kind of emotional tie to this man, but she wasn't willing to discuss it. Brenda didn't pry. Many mistakes with her children in the past had taught her to stay out of their personal lives as much as possible.

"He sounds like a very good man and maybe a good friend. You shouldn't write him off so easily."

Devin didn't reply. She wished that she had other options, but after everything was said and done, she doubted if she had any other choice.

Over the next few weeks, Devin worked hard to get back into a normal routine, but thoughts of Spark constantly stayed on her mind. She found herself at her parents' house more than ever because her house seemed to remind her of him. By him, she didn't mean her dead husband, but Spark. And every thought of Chris seemed to filter down to Spark's sister, then eventually to Spark. She was driving herself crazy.

One day, she went into Chris's office with a firm determination to clear out the rest of his things and turn the room into a family room. After sitting behind his desk for close to half an hour, Devin hadn't moved a thing. She hadn't opened any drawers or lifted a piece of paper. Instead, she walked out of the room and drove to her parents' house, where the girls were still staying for the rest of the summer.

The following weekend was her birthday, and she knew that her family would be planning a big barbecue for her. It was amazing that with a family as large as theirs, she was the only member who didn't share her birthday month with someone else. Usually their family gatherings were to celebrate the birthdays of at least three or more people. She loved feeling so spoiled and special. It was the only thing that remained of her childhood when she was the spoiled baby child. But at the rate their family grew, she was sure that it wouldn't last much longer. Someone was bound to have a baby in August sooner or later.

Soon, her mind would be occupied with getting the girls ready for the school year, and she relished the thought for once. At least school shopping would take her mind off Spark for a week.

CHAPTER 14

This time the walk through the all-too-familiar airport arrival terminal was done with more focus, more determination. Each stride was smooth and firmly placed with an eagerness to reach its destination. He didn't stumble or trip in the tunnel on his way from the plane to the terminal. There was nothing to be unsure of or self-conscious about; there was no time for that. He had come back here for himself this time, not because he had been ordered. And this time it counted a lot more than it had the last time.

Spark was on another mission, but this was a mission of the heart. Although he very seriously doubted that she would agree with his proposition, he couldn't allow her to just walk out of his life the way she had. No, that wouldn't work. One way or another, she was going to stay in his life. Spark was adamant about that.

As he sat in the waiting area of the rental car office wishing he had a cigarette, Spark thought that this wasn't the craziest thing he had ever done in his life. In fact, this was the most sensible idea he'd had in a long time. He wanted, no, needed, to beg for Devin's forgiveness and regain her trust for his own sanity. Ever since she'd left him at the airport three weeks earlier, Spark hadn't been able to get her off his mind. He couldn't count the number of times he had picked up the phone to call her.

Unfortunately, back then his nerves hadn't been as strong as his determination was now.

It had been in those three weeks without her that he'd realized how much he missed having her near him. In less than a week's time, he had grown used to her being around him as if she had always been there. He was miserable without her. The only relief he'd received during those weeks after Devin left was the phone calls from his nieces. In his voice, they could hear that he was unhappy, and after finally prying the reason out of him, they had both encouraged him to go to Chicago and tell Devin how he felt. It was funny how sometimes the best advice came from children.

His sister wasn't speaking to him anymore. The day after he dropped Devin off at the airport, Carlissa was back out at his house bright and early, banging on the door and ringing the doorbell. She was a damn pain in the ass, and he hadn't been in the mood for her. He was sad, mad, miserable, and damn near depressed. He didn't want any company, especially not her. It was bad enough that Vivian was calling his phone every hour. He had to eventually turn his ringer off altogether.

Something told him not to let Carlissa in, but she was making so much noise outside that he really didn't have a choice. In retrospect, Spark figured that he should have let someone call the cops on her. At least then he would have had a few days to think about his next move. She'd stood at the door with her hands on her hips as if he had done her a great disservice. Spark just shook his head at her and led her into his house.

"What do you want, Carlissa?" he asked. "I'm not in the mood for this, so please make it short." He felt as tired and beaten as if he had just run a marathon.

"Where is your little friend? I came over here to talk to her. I want some more answers."

"Her name is Devin. And she is Richard's widow." He thought a reality check was necessary, even if it was a cheap shot at her.

"I'm Richard's widow."

Obviously, she still wasn't ready to face the truth.

"Whatever. At any rate, she's not here."

"Where is she?" Carlissa walked up the steps, past the living room, and back into the bedroom as if she didn't believe him and as if she paid the bills there.

"She went back to Chicago. Could you please get out of my room? I said that she wasn't here, didn't I? Damn, Carlissa, you don't own the world, you know."

"Oh, she got smart and decided to leave before I whipped her ass?"

"You talk so dumb, you know that? Carlissa, you're damn near forty years old. You ain't whipping nobody's ass. Devin's not even thinking about you. All she came here for was answers. You know, all this could have been avoided if you had just acted like an adult and called her in the first place. I'm sure if you had just talked to her instead of playing your little games you would have gotten your answers a long time ago."

"Boy, what's wrong with you? You sitting around here all crazy looking, talking right dumb." Carlissa looked at him closer as he sat on the couch, hair disheveled, clothes looking slept in. "Don't tell me you fell in love with the little liar. What, you depressed? She left you, too, did she?"

"Is there a point to this visit, Carlissa?"

"Yeah, the point is that you turned your back on me yesterday. Your own family, your own blood."

"Don't start, Carlissa," he replied, lounging back on the sofa. He wasn't giving what she was saying a second thought. Carlissa had been saying those same words since high school every time he didn't do whatever she commanded. She was so dramatic.

"No, I'm serious, Spark. I have never been so upset in my life, my own brother taking the side of a stranger over mine just because she gave you some ass. I didn't think you would betray me for so little."

"I didn't betray you, Carlissa. I just wasn't willing to lie for you any longer. I told you before I left for Chicago that I wasn't going to lie for you anymore. I have been trying to get my life on track, and every single time I do, you ask me to do something dishonest again. You don't love me, Carlissa. All this love and family you talk about is about you. If I don't do what you say, then I don't love you. If I don't say what you want to hear, then I am no longer a part of your family. Honestly, Carlissa, if it were not for my nieces, I wouldn't want to be a part of your family. I really pray they got more from Richard than just their looks because if they turn out to be like you, I feel sorry for them."

Carlissa stood there horrified. Spark had never spoken to her this way. And she never would have imagined that he would. "Spark, I can't believe you said that."

"And I meant it. Carlissa, as long as I have known you, you have been a horrible person. Yeah, you're pretty enough to men when you're just standing there, but as soon as you open your mouth all of that goes away. Why do you think you keep driving off all the good men who have had to deal with you? The only person who will keep you around is Lenny, and that's not because he loves you. It's because you're just as evil as he is."

"I don't have to stand here and listen to this. You're just mad because your little girlfriend found out what a liar you are and hightailed it back to Chicago. You're trying to make me just as miserable and stupid looking as you feel right now. So, why are you lying here in a funk over her when there is a perfectly good woman waiting for you to come to your senses?"

"Who? Vivian? Are you crazy? I don't want that damn girl. She's just as much trouble as you are!"

"Yeah, Vivian. That girl loves you, Spark. Oh, you think little Miss Devin loves you? Now that's a laugh. You want Richard's ex-wife. Ha! She's too high and mighty for you, ain't she?"

"And look at you, all green with envy that the two men you love the most in your life loved her. Carlissa, go home. I don't need you here to cheer me up."

"Oh, don't worry, little brother. I won't be coming back to cheer you up at all. Matter fact, I don't even want to see you anymore."

"Whatever. I don't care about any of that. But I will be seeing my nieces."

Carlissa was silent as she walked toward the front door. She didn't comment on that. It was impossible for her to even try to keep them apart, but she didn't have to let him know that she knew it. If she tried to keep him from the girls, they would have a fit and hate her for it. He would just meet them after school. The school was already under the impression that he was their father as much as he was at their school functions and teacher meetings when she was too busy to attend, which was pretty often.

Spark reported to work the next day, but he didn't joke and talk with the other employees who seemed happy that he was back to work. He had too much on his mind. Once they noticed his somber mood, his co-workers attempted to cheer him up, but all attempts failed. After only a week, he knew that he couldn't go on this way. He didn't want to take the risk of hurting himself or one of his co-workers with his mind constantly wandering to Devin.

In an effort to make things right, he talked to his supervisor and requested a leave of absence, stating that he had to go out of town on emergency business and wasn't sure how long it would take. Spark had already apologized to Devin a dozen times to her face and a million times in his head, but he had to give it one more shot. It didn't matter to him that he was looking disappointment in the face. Before he came back to Delaware, Spark was going to make her believe that he loved her.

Now finally in Chicago, he laughed as he picked up the map of the city that was in the car door pocket. It was an exact replica of the first map he had used to find her. The streets were busy, but Spark patiently maneuvered his way through to his destination. He sat in front of Devin's house for a brief moment, trying to get up the nerve to approach her door. Her car wasn't in the driveway, but there was a brand new gray Ford pickup truck with shiny rims parked there. He wondered who could be driving it. Definitely not her. In the back sat a washer and dryer.

He reached for the sunglasses in the seat next to his as he got out of the car. It wasn't excessively hot, but he was getting progressively hotter under the collar as he prepared to face Devin once again.

"Go ahead," Devin's brother Charles yelled to his brothers as he ran back to Jeff's truck to get the toolbox. He, Troy, Jeff and Chauncey were over at Devin's to take out her old washer and dryer and replace them with the new ones Troy had bought for her birthday. It didn't make any sense how spoiled Devin was. Not that they didn't all spoil each other. To have so many children in a household, it was amazing that they were all still so close-knit, but Devin was the baby. It really didn't matter how old she got. Whatever she wanted or needed or didn't want and need, they practically jumped over each other to get it for her. They had just hung up a huge landscape wall painting by Robert Scott Duncanson, which was a gift from Tia and Kristal.

The man walking apprehensively towards Charles held his attention. He stopped walking, expecting the man to pull out a pen and paper or a tape recorder and ask for an interview. It had happened to him more often than he would have liked of late. Somehow, news had leaked that he and Shelia were expecting twins. It was hard to think of himself as a celebrity now that he had moved back to his hometown. His family treated him just as rotten as they always had. He loved it.

Charles waited for him to say something, but he noticed that the man was so nervous he was sweating through his T-shirt.

"Man, you all right?" Charles asked.

Suddenly, Spark wasn't feeling so good. His hands were shaking, he felt weak and his legs began to go numb. He bent forward, leaning against the truck to steady himself.

"Yo . . . my man?"

"Devin, I came to see Devin," Spark managed to get out. He knew that he should have eaten something before he left home or yesterday or at least the day before, but food was the last thing on his mind, and now he was paying for it. "Do you know Devin?" he asked weakly.

Charles put a hand on his shoulder and bent down to look at his face. He could barely hear what he was saying.

"Yeah, I know Devin. Who are you? Man, you all right? You don't look too good. Let me get Troy." Charles moved away from him to get his brother. Troy was the doctor, not him.

"No. Devin still lives here, right?"

"Yeah. She still lives here." Charles pulled out his cell phone and pushed a button. "Man, come outside." He hung up.

"I really need to see her," Spark stated.

"Not as much as you need to see Troy," Charles replied.

"Troy?"

"He's a doctor. I'm Devin's brother, Charles. Troy is our older brother. And you are?"

"Darnel, but everybody calls me Spark." He tried to put his hand up, but Charles just ignored him. It was too much of a struggle.

"Later, man. Later. Here's Troy now. Troy, this guy here is Spark. He's a friend of Devin's, I guess. He came here to see her, but he looks like he needs to see you more."

"What's wrong?" Troy asked. "Are you in any pain?"

"No, just weak. Real weak."

"Did you take any pills? Any drugs?"

"Nah, man. I don't do drugs," Spark replied, offended.

"Hey, I gotta ask. When's the last time you ate?"

Spark didn't answer.

Troy looked at him. "Yesterday?"

No answer.

"The day before?"

"Maybe," Spark answered quietly.

"Let's get him in the house," Troy said, taking one arm for support. Charles was holding the other. "Jeff, grab that toolbox, please."

"I got it," Jeff replied, falling in line behind them.

"Oh, this is our brother-in-law, Jeff," Charles said.

"What's up, man?" Spark said automatically, not even brothering to turn his head in Jeff's direction.

"Whoa, guys. You think Devin wants him in her house?" Jeff asked.

"It doesn't matter. He's sick," Troy replied.

"I don't know, Troy. You know how Devin is," Charles added. "Besides, we don't know this guy."

"Jeff, just get the door, will ya? We'll sort everything out once we get him inside. He needs to eat something. Jeff, see if Devin has some crackers or soup or cheese in the refrigerator."

"Okay, but when she snaps, it's not on me." Jeff turned toward the kitchen area.

Charles and Troy led Spark to the family room, and he fell onto the sofa. His eyes were closed.

"Troy, don't you think we should find out how he knows Devin?" Charles asked as he watched his brother make the easy transformation to Dr. Avery. "He could be a stalker, for all we know. You know she's been going through it lately."

"Look, guys," he began, "I really appreciate your help. I'm not a stalker. I love Devin."

The brothers looked at each other. This was something deeper than either of them wanted to be a part of.

"I need to see her, talk to her," Spark whined.

Troy had already checked for a fever. Spark appeared to be fine except that he was weak from not eating, and he was a little dehydrated. Jeff came into the room with cheese, crackers and a bottle of water.

"What do you need to talk to her about?" Charles asked protectively.

"I need to tell her that I love her," Spark stated simply.

"Well, why doesn't she already know that, if it's true?" Charles didn't know this man, and he didn't like the fact that they didn't know him, had never seen him before.

"Because—"

"Charles, let the man eat and rest," Troy interjected. "Spark, please excuse him. Devin is the baby sister, and we tend to forget that she is a grown woman now. You should eat these crackers and rest. We will be here for a minute switching Devin's washer and dryer, so why don't you just rest here, and we'll talk as soon as we finish."

"But Devin?"

"She's at our parents' house right now. We're having a family barbecue this afternoon to celebrate her birthday. You arrived just in time. Looks as if you're going to get your chance to talk to her, and a lot of other folks."

Spark was weak, but he wasn't delirious. There was an unmistakable twinkle of mischief in Charles's eyes. The two brothers seemed to be foils, mirror opposites of each other. Troy, the doctor in the family that Devin talked so much about, was personable, as his profession would dictate. Charles wasn't.

"You look familiar," Spark stated as Charles stood over him suspiciously.

"Do I really?"

"Yeah," Spark replied. What was his problem?

"Charles, lighten up, man," Jeff said. "Come on, let's get this done so we can get back to the house. Tia will be calling soon to see what took us so long. Let the man rest. We'll get all our answers soon enough."

"Whatever, man. I'm just not as trusting as the doctor here. And Tia's got you so whipped, it's ridiculous."

"You're the singer, right?" Spark asked. He didn't mean for it to sound insulting, but it obviously came out that way because when Charles turned his attention back to him the look on his face made Spark tense up in preparation for a fight. He might have been weak, and he probably would have lost, but his pride wouldn't let him show either.

"Yeah, I am, why?"

Jeff quickly stepped in Charles's path.

"No reason. I just wondered why you looked familiar, that's all." Spark didn't relax until Charles had turned away with Jeff beside him. He could hear Charles's mumbling, which wasn't quiet, as he stalked off. Jeff was trying to tell him to keep cool and get it together before they reached Troy. By all appearances Troy seemed to be the calm one in the family, and apparently they had a lot of respect for him.

With his eyes closed, Spark slowly ate the crackers and cheese as he listened to the men removing Devin's old appliances and replacing them with the new ones. In his mind, he ran through his speech to Devin. What would he say? How could he apologize any differently than he had the first time? And he wondered what her response would be. Would she be surprised and happy to see him or would she hate him for coming? It would probably help if he had someone on his side, but the brothers were a long shot unless he convinced the singer that he had Devin's best interest at heart. He had to change his tactics.

By the time the guys finished installing the new equipment, Spark was feeling a little better. He sat upright on the sofa and finished drinking the bottled water. Troy approached him first.

"You feeling any better? Seems like you have a little more color in your cheeks."

"Yeah, I do, actually. Thanks, man. I really appreciate your help. I guess I've just had so much on my mind trying to get here that I forgot about a few things."

"Like eating?"

"Yeah, for starters."

"Well, not eating will knock even the strongest man to his knees."

"All I could think about was getting to Devin."

Jeff and Charles walked over.

"Where are you coming from and what's so important that you have to talk to Devin about?" Charles asked immediately.

Everybody in the family knew that Devin had been going through some things since Chris's death, but it seemed that after she got back from her trip to Delaware she had gotten worse. She took care of her children and saw her family as usual, but in her eyes something was missing. They didn't sparkle as they used to, and lately she always had something on her mind. Of course, she didn't talk to them about everything. Most times, the women of the family knew more than the men, and that was exactly how they wanted it.

"I'm from Delaware," Spark started, but hesitated when Charles cursed under his breath.

"I should have known," he said aloud.

"What?"

"Nothing, please continue," Charles said, sending a knowing look to Troy and Jeff.

"I met Devin at the airport when she was going to Delaware. Wait, let me start off by telling you that I have done some things to Devin that I'm not proud of."

"What?" Charles asked incredulously. Was this man crazy, or just stupid? No sensible man would start off a conversation with the brothers about the woman he said he loved like that.

"Wait a minute, Charles," the rational one said. "Let him explain."

"Please do," Charles said, "because that had to be the stupidest thing I've ever heard someone who says he loves your sister say."

Troy turned his attention back to Spark. The other two did the same.

"No, I'm saying that I do love Devin. I was so miserable when she left. I didn't even want to be in my own apartment when she left."

"So, she was staying with you?" Troy asked. "In Delaware?"

Spark looked at Charles before he answered, "Like I said, we, um, met in the airport. By the time we landed, we had become friends. Once we landed, I gave her a ride to Delaware, but we couldn't find a hotel, so I let her stay with me."

The three of them looked at each other without saying a word, each imagining what must have transpired during the stay for him to be here proclaiming his love.

"Just follow us," Troy said as they walked out the back door of Devin's house.

"No, Troy," Charles suggested. "Why don't you ride with him just in case he gets separated in traffic?"

Troy gave him an exasperated expression. He knew that Charles didn't want to be a part of taking Spark to the house. In fact, he wanted to be able to tell Devin that he had nothing to do with any of it.

Troy agreed.

In the car, Spark once again tried to express his feelings for Devin.

"Look, Troy, I really do appreciate this."

"You already said that once, and don't be too quick with your appreciation. All of this depends on whether my sister decides to accept you being here. And I'm going to warn you that she hasn't been in the most accepting mood lately."

"I didn't know it was her birthday."

"Not today. It was Wednesday, but we decided to give her a barbecue today. My family is famous for its barbecues. Oh, and let me warn you that we have a very, very large family."

"Yeah, she told me that there were seven or eight of you."

"Eight, but that's not all. We all have at least three kids, but there are also a lot of cousins, aunts, and uncles, not to mention friends. So, you picked the perfect time to come see Devin. And please don't think that you'll be able to talk to her in private at the house, because you won't. That might be to your benefit because when my sisters get mad it's usually not good to be alone with them."

"I don't expect it to be easy for me to get Devin to come around. And I know how stubborn she can be. She gave me a hard time in Delaware when she was a stranger to the place so I can just imagine what I'm in for here."

"So, what's up with you two? She must have made quite an impression on you for you to come all the way here to win her heart."

"I love her."

Spark's simple statement seemed to hit a spot of understanding in Troy. He had long since hoped that Devin would find another good man to help her raise her children. Chris was a good family man. She needed someone like him.

"So, who are you, really?"

Spark looked at Troy, who was staring at him intensely. He wondered if Devin had taken the time to tell her brothers about the stranger she had met in the airport on her way to Delaware or anything that went on after that.

"My name is Darnel Miles. Look, Troy. I don't know how much your sister told you and your family about me, and I want to be totally honest, but I'm not sure how much she wants you to know."

"Okay. I'll tell you that she hasn't told us anything about her trip to Delaware. She won't let any of us guys in on anything. I'm sure she and the sisters have talked, along with my mother, as they always do, but we were left out of the loop."

"Then I will tell you that I am the brother of Richard's, I mean Chris's, first wife. I met Devin when she came looking for the writer of the letter she received regarding Chris's past. Simply stated, I fell in love with her even when I didn't think I would. I didn't realize it until I watched her leave. So, I got some things together and came here to tell her."

"Simply stated, huh?"

"Yeah."

"Make a left," Troy instructed as he guided Spark into a large development. Houses with large yards lined the long street.

Spark knew he was close when he started to see cars lining the road on both sides. It still took them a while before Troy pointed to a house with small clusters of people in the front yard.

"That's our house," he said.

"I didn't know it would be so crowded."

"Hey, don't say I didn't warn you," Troy countered.

"Maybe I should just go get a room and wait this out. I don't have to go back to Delaware for a few days."

"That's your decision, but if I cared for someone as much as you profess to care for my sister and I came as far as you did, I don't think I could wait a second to tell her how I feel."

"I, um . . ."

Troy smiled. "Just imagine that somewhere in that crowd of people is the woman that you say you love, but she doesn't know it. I can remember what I had to go through to get my wife. If you want her, don't let anything stop you, at least not a large group of people. If you truly feel the way you do, you should be able to shout it in front of a million people."

"Yeah, that sounds good." He looked at Troy. The thought did cross his mind that Troy was setting him up for failure. Maybe Troy was trying to get him in front of these people so that he could be made a fool of, but truth be told, he didn't know a damn one of the folks filling the yard or the house. Nobody knew him, not even Troy and the other men. The only person he was there for was Devin.

Pulling over to the side of the road, he sat quietly trying to hype himself up for what was going to be the toughest battle of his life. Even arguing with his sister would be a piece of cake in comparison. He turned the car off.

"You ready, man?" Troy asked. He wasn't trying to put Spark in a situation that he wasn't ready for. In fact, he really appreciated that Spark was honest but private about his relationship with Devin. He didn't appear to be easily intimidated, especially when Charles put on his older brother hat and started acting like an ass, and Troy hoped that held true in the face of the multitude of people about the house.

"I guess it's now or never. At least, I'll get some kind of feel for her mood. That will let me know just how hard

I'm going to have to work to get back in her good graces."

"See now, that's the spirit. Let's go."

Spark might have had the spirit, but that didn't stop his stomach from weighing heavy with a tight knot. He had every right to be optimistic about his decision to try to surprise her today of all days around all of her family and friends. He forced himself to believe that Troy was a good confidante as he stepped out of the car and walked up the sidewalk with the three men.

The curious glances he received outside from the teenagers and younger adults were nothing compared to the sharper stares he got inside the house, as the age level seemed to increase by ten to fifteen years. During the way into the house, each man stopped several times to talk to this person or that. Each person looked him over as if asking, *Who is he?* No one answered the unspoken question.

In the den, Charles bent over a hugely pregnant woman and kissed her in greeting. Troy explained that was Charles's wife, Shelia, who was Jeff's sister. She was due to deliver their third child any day. He pointed out the two women seated next to her as Denise, their cousin Chauncey's wife, who was Jeff's wife and his sister Tia's best friend, who was also ready to deliver and Shelia's best friend Liz, who was married to Chauncey's youngest brother Greg and also about to deliver. By the time Troy pointed to a few other people in the room, Spark felt the need for a notepad in order to remember names and relationships.

In the main living room of the house, Jeff's wife Tia sat in a corner reading a book to a group of rowdy kids. Troy pointed to a few kids and told him who they were, but he stopped listening after the fifth one. Spark thought it best to concentrate on the adults first, and then work on remembering the children's names and who belonged to whom.

Spark greeted everyone as introductions were made. He watched his feet, solidly placing each foot before trying to make the next step. Troy made sure to point out all of his siblings and their spouses as they passed. They made their way to the kitchen, which was in the back of the large, crowded house.

"Hi, Mom," Troy said, greeting a sophisticated looking, older woman with white hair framing her small face. "We're back. Where is Devin?"

"She's . . ." Brenda paused when she turned and saw the handsome man standing next to her son. "Oh, hi, I'm Brenda, Troy's mother. How are you?" she greeted.

"Hello, ma'am," Spark replied. "You have a lovely home, Mrs. Avery."

"Thank you, dear. Are you a friend of the boys?"

"Uh, not really. I just kinda met them," he answered, looking to Troy for assistance.

"Mom, where did you say Devin was?" Troy interrupted.

"Oh, she's out back with April playing spades. The girls have been beating them all day." Before she let them go, she asked another question with hope in her eyes. "Are you a friend of Devin's?"

Spark stopped in his tracks. "I hope that I still am."

She smiled at him.

CHAPTER 15

Instead of letting him leave with Troy, Brenda asked Spark to take a seat. He was torn between wanting to see Devin and pleasing her mother. But it wasn't a hard decision to make. He pulled out the empty chair at the table and sat between Mrs. Avery and a woman she introduced as Mrs. Daniels, her best friend and Jeff's mother. The biggest bag of potatoes that Spark had ever seen was sitting in the middle of the table. Each woman was peeling potatoes and each had a large bowl in front of her that she threw her peeled potatoes in. Spark desperately wanted to be part of this family, and he needed an ally. Who better than Devin's mother?

He excused himself from the table and went to the kitchen sink where he washed his hands. When he joined them back at the table, he removed his ring, picked up a knife, and began peeling. Both ladies stopped their own peeling to watch him, making sure that there was still potato left once he finished carving. They were impressed by his skill.

Brenda smiled and said, "Usually, the only man in the kitchen on these family days is my son John. He's such a wonderful cook. He could have been a chef, you know, but he chose dentistry instead. What do you do for a living, dear?"

Spark for once didn't lie. He wasn't trying to connive his way into Devin's heart. He explained a little of his past to the two ladies, sure that the others in the room were listening as well. It wasn't that he had ever been ashamed of his past. In fact, if he hadn't gone through some of those things, he probably would be much worse off than he was at that moment. He called his failures lessons that helped him get to where he was now. Before long, they were telling him about their pasts and how they were good friends and had grown up together but then had a terrible misunderstanding because of Jeff and Devin's sister, Tia, and their oldest child, Kevin.

Spark was so engrossed in the story they told that he forgot to wonder where Troy went. He had assumed that his only ally had gone to find Devin, but realized his mistake when he saw Troy standing in the corner flirting with the woman he had introduced earlier as his wife.

"So, dear," Mrs. Avery said, "where are you from?"

"Delaware."

"Delaware? So, you're the young man that helped Devin out when she visited a few weeks ago?"

"Yes, ma'am," Spark replied, expecting the worst.

"Young man, I want to thank you so much for taking care of her." With her last potato peeled, Brenda reached out and grabbed his arm. "You have no idea how much I worried. I am so grateful to you."

"Oh, no, that's not necessary. I believe that even if I hadn't come along, Devin would have taken care of herself quite nicely. She's a tough woman, you know."

"Yes, I know. Sometimes too tough, I'm afraid."

They shared a laugh and stood from the table. As the older ladies began cleaning the shards of potato peeling, Spark lifted one of the bowls filled with potatoes and moved it to the sink. He was about to carry the second one over when the back door opened, and Devin walked into the house.

Devin and her niece Pamela were laughing and joking about beating April at cards. Devin was oblivious to the other people in the kitchen until her niece noticed the handsome man standing with her grandmother. Pam nudged Devin to get her attention when she saw the look the stranger was giving her aunt.

"What?" Devin said, turning in the direction Pam was looking. At once she was flooded with a range of emotions, none of which she wanted to feel. Devin was surprised, elated, excited, flustered, embarrassed, happy, and upset all at once. She just stood there for a second, trying to pull everything in and make sense of it. Spark was standing in her mother's kitchen with her mother, and it looked as if they had been peeling potatoes for some time. The look on her mother's face told her more than she wanted to know. He had obviously been there for a while, and nobody had told her.

Spark put the bowl of potatoes down. Amazingly, despite all of the people in the house, it was suddenly so quiet in the room you could have heard a mouse walk across the floor. He had to say something to her, explain to her why he was there, apologize again for his actions, anything. Spark stepped toward her, aware of the numerous eyes on them.

"Devin—"

"Don't," she pleaded before he could get a word out. "Don't you say anything." She was on the verge of tears, and she was not about to give him the pleasure of seeing them. Whether they were tears of joy because she had missed him so desperately or tears of anger because she didn't want to miss him at all she wasn't sure. But either way, she wasn't sharing them with him. Devin held up her hand to ward him off as he approached her. "Just stop. Don't."

Spark watched several emotions flash in her eyes, including fear. She had no reason to fear him. He loved her. But she wouldn't have it. He could see that in her eyes as well. Though he thought that he might have seen a flash of love, it vanished quickly. Then she ran from the kitchen, down the long hallway and into one of the rooms.

Spark's hopes were dashed in that instant. Then Mrs. Avery came up behind him, put her arm around his back, and smiled.

"Don't worry, dear. My girls are so dramatic. I love these little scenes of theirs. Troy, come, get Darnel a beer and take him out back."

"Darnel?" Troy laughed.

"Whatever, man," Spark replied, following his supposed ally.

Troy continued to laugh, leading the way out the door. "So, Devin's not so happy to see you, huh?"

Spark put his head down. "Well, I'd be lying if I said that I expected her to run into my arms. But you don't seem too surprised that she reacted that way."

"Man, I got five sisters and two sister-in-laws. I'm not surprised by the reactions of any of the women around me." Troy led him to the fence at the back of the house. With all the people in the yard, that was usually the best place for anyone to talk. "Just give her some time. Mom will go in there and talk some sense into her."

Spark didn't understand why Troy was on his side, but he was thankful just the same. "I don't know. I kinda messed things up real bad. If I were her, I wouldn't want to talk to me, either, but I've apologized a dozen times. And I am truly sorry. I just had—"

"Look. When Devin came back from Delaware, she was upset. We all could tell, but she would only let us in on so much. I suppose she told Mom and the girls more than she told us because ten chances to one, Charles would have come after you. He's the one with the mean streak, as you can tell."

Spark laughed. "Yeah, I get that feeling. You'd never know he was a celebrity."

"Our sisters are very special to us, and Devin is the baby girl. We have a hard time realizing that she's grown. But at any rate, you don't have to tell me anything if you don't want to."

"It's not as if I attacked her or anything." Spark said.

Troy's head automatically nodded approvingly. The thought had crossed his mind more than once. He was glad to be able to dismiss it.

"I hurt her feelings. I had to lie to her about some things. And I didn't want to. But I was truly between a rock and a hard place. Stuck right between your sister and mine."

"Yours?" Troy thought about what he had just heard. "So, your sister is the lady who was Chris's first wife?"

"Yeah, but—"

Troy shook his head. "I don't envy you one bit."

"Listen, Troy." Spark began feeling that he needed to explain or at least let some of the frustration out. Regardless of what Troy might say once he heard the story, Spark would feel better for at least coming clean to someone. "A few years ago, I had a big gambling problem. I owed a lot of money to the wrong people. They were going to kill me. I called my sister, and she gave them the money that I owed. Then I owed her, which I think was much worse. After she found out about Devin, she sent me here to spy on her. It was supposed to be the last thing I did to pay off the debt. I didn't want to come, but I didn't want her hanging over my shoulder for the rest of my life."

"Makes sense to me so far, but you would think as she was your sister that you wouldn't have had to pay her back."

"My sister is a piece of work. You have no idea. We're nothing like you guys. Anyway, I came. I figured that I'd spy for a couple of days, tell my sister that I hadn't really learned anything and go on my way. My sister is under the impression that there is a large amount of money somewhere that Chris, well, your Chris, our Richard, stole from the gangster back home he testified against."

"What? Devin told us when she got back that Chris had left Delaware because he got into some trouble, but I didn't know he was in that kind of trouble."

"Man, it's a long story, but Richard did the right thing. He was a really good guy, a really good friend. When Richard turned state's evidence against Willis Demby, he saved our lives because we would still be doing that man's dirty work. We could all be dead. There were five of us that hung together."

"So, you were like brothers?"

"Growing up, we were all each other had. But back to the story. Basically, I kind of arranged for Devin and me to bump into each other on her flight to Delaware. I liked her immediately. Real fast. That had never happened to me before. I wanted to tell her everything right then and there, but I couldn't. Then when we landed, she didn't have a way to get to Delaware. I was going that way, so she rode with me. And then she couldn't find a hotel, so I invited her to stay with me. I enjoyed her company so much over those few days. I loved her wit when we joked around, her kindness when I did something clumsy. I even loved her anger when my ex-girlfriend dropped by and surprised us both.

"But I just couldn't tell her the truth. I was afraid. I kept putting it off until my sister found out that I was back in town and came over snapping. She's a little on the crazy side, and she has bits of fantasy that she has forced herself to believe are reality. She believes that Richard truly loved her. He didn't. He married her because he got her pregnant, but he couldn't take her nasty attitude. Unfortunately, I had no choice but to take it for as long as I could. I love her. She's my sister. But it just became unbearable. And then after everything came out and

Devin left, I realized how much I was missing out of my own life. So, that's why I'm here. I have to get Devin to see how sorry I am and how much I love her. I have never felt love this strong for anyone before in my life."

Troy couldn't help but feel a bit of sympathy for the man. He was practically laying all of his feelings on the line, and had willingly come all the way to Chicago to face whatever Devin was going to throw at him. Troy could imagine that it was not going to be pretty, knowing his sister. "Okay, well, don't tell her that I said this, but I think you're sincere. Not one man I know would have had the courage to face a whole family to get to the woman he loved." He saw Charles approaching and added for good measure, "Even Charles would have to admit that is pretty brave of you."

"What's pretty brave of him?" Charles asked, falling into his brother's trap.

"I was just telling Spark that it was pretty brave or crazy, depending on how you wanted to look at it, that he came all the way to Chicago to profess his love for Devin and to beg her forgiveness, especially in front of a family as large and crazy as ours is. After all," he finished, "you kept your marriage to Shelia a secret for almost a year because you were afraid of one man, her father. Imagine having to face a father, three brothers, and four brothers-in-law."

Charles didn't reply. He knew exactly what Troy was up to, and it hit him hard when he faced up to the fact that he had made some serious mistakes in his own right in order to be with his wife. But instead of giving Troy the satisfaction of agreeing, he simply performed the duties that had caused him to walk over to them in the first place.

"Mom said for you to come and eat. They're making the children's plates now, should be done in a few."

"How is Devin doing?" Spark asked, looking Charles directly in the eyes.

Charles hesitated, slight irritation showing on his face. He looked at Troy and replied before walking away, "She's still in the bedroom with the sisters. They're talking."

Troy smiled after his brother. "Don't worry about it, man. Every time something goes wrong in this family, the sisters and sisters-in-law gather somewhere to help each other. Man, you haven't seen anything like it, and you haven't seen anything yet. Come on, let's go eat."

"I don't want to talk about it, and I don't want to talk to him," Devin told her sisters for the umpteenth time. Why wasn't anybody listening to her?

"Devin, stop being childish," April said. "That man came all the way from Delaware to talk to you. You could at least listen to what he has to say."

"She's right, Devin," Tia added, putting a hand on her baby sister's back. "You need to hear him out. Then if you still don't want to deal with him, so be it, but you have to find some closure with this yourself."

"I have found closure. I don't want to see him."

Kristal stepped forward, her belly full from pregnancy. "Why don't you just stop lying to yourself and us? If you really didn't care for that man in the least bit, you wouldn't be in here crying. You would be out there facing up to him."

Pamela, their oldest niece who, at twenty-two, was enjoying her second year in the confidential folds of the group, chimed in, "Aunt Devin, I don't know much about love and all that, but I saw the look on his face when he saw you, and I saw the look on your face, too."

"It's not going to work anyway. It can't work. He and Chris were best friends. He is Chris's children's uncle. His sister was Chris's first wife. There is no way that woman and I could ever get along, ever."

"Who said anything about getting along with his sister?" Tia asked. "She doesn't have anything to do with you and Spark being in love. And I doubt very seriously if she can stop it. If he really cared what his sister thought, he wouldn't be here, now would he?"

"I think you need to give him a chance. At least sit down and listen to what he has to say," Kristal added. "You know you love him."

"I really don't want to deal with this right now," Devin commented. "I'll talk to him some other time. Just tell him to leave."

"Unfortunately, you have to deal with it now. How are you going to tell a man that just came hundreds of miles to see you that you 'don't want to deal with it right now'? You sound crazy." Kristal stood in front of her with her hands folded. April stood next to her.

Devin couldn't stand it when her sisters were right, especially Kristal, who stood her ground whether she was wrong or right because she felt she was never wrong. April could argue a case from any side until she was blue in the face. And before long, Tia would start with the psychology mumbo-jumbo. They all looked down at her, unwilling to take no for an answer.

"Come on, Aunt Devin. Give the man a chance. You could be letting one of the greatest things to happen in your life slip by. Uncle Chris might be sending this man here for a reason."

Devin looked at her niece sharply. "I don't want to hear any of your romantic notions, Pamela. This is really enough." Pamela was writing her first romance novel. Having a father who owned one of the biggest publishing houses in Chicago did have its advantages. She had been writing articles in one of his romance tabloids for a couple of years. All the poor girl thought about was romance, so much so that she probably wouldn't be able to recognize it when it finally came her way.

Devin stood up and walked between her sisters. She knew they wouldn't let her stay in there too much longer. Besides, they wanted to know what was going to happen. But she already knew what would happen as soon as she saw him again. Her stomach would start to flutter; her heartbeat would quicken. And her desire for him would grow stronger. It was everything that she was fighting against.

In the kitchen, she saw her mother and the others beginning to make plates for the dozens of children that overran the house. There was a line at the bathroom while the kids went in two at a time to wash their hands, starting from the youngest to the oldest. This procedure had been in place for so long that it usually amazed visitors how coordinated and organized the whole affair looked. After washing their hands, the children walked into the kitchen two at a time to get their plates. They were then ushered onto the huge deck to eat. The immediate back yard was filled with picnic tables for the rest of the family, while a makeshift basketball court was built towards the rear so the children wouldn't have to be in the front yard or in others' yards. But of course, there were always a number of neighborhood kids over visiting the grandchildren when they were home. Brenda Avery practically ran the neighborhood teen center, recreation center, and day care—without pay, of course. But plenty of people chipped in to help because they knew that without Ms. Brenda's place their kids would be running wild in the streets.

The sisters came out and immediately began helping to get the kids settled. Once that was complete it was time for the wives to make their husband's plates. The line moved along steadily while Devin, Pamela, and a few of the female cousins stood in line to make plates for the single male cousins. Pamela thought they should make their own plates, but her grandmother didn't like men in her kitchen, except John Jr.

Devin's mother stood next to her. "Make that plate be for your young man," she said, having noticed that Spark sat outside at the picnic table with a table full of men already digging into their plates. Devin had made one plate already, but gave it to her cousin Lawrence instead of walking it to Spark. She should have known that her mother wouldn't let anyone else take him a plate. For a woman so small, she always had control of everything.

Spark waited patiently as Troy had told him. His stomach growled at the sight of the plates in front of him piled high with burgers, hot dogs, barbecue ribs, corn on the cob, and all types of pastas.

"Just be patient, man," Troy counseled as he took a bite of his barbecue chicken. "Devin will be out here soon enough."

"As stubborn as your sister is, I'll probably be on my last breath dying from starvation."

Charles laughed. "You might be better off that way. Here she comes now, and she doesn't look all that happy to me. Uh oh, she's carrying two plates. You're really in trouble now."

Spark wasn't quite sure what that meant. He watched her come his way, practically holding his breath in anticipation. She stopped right by him, looked him in the face, and stated, "Come on," before moving on. Spark got up to follow her, but his foot got caught when he tried to swing his leg over the bench. He caught himself, but barely, and received a look of empathy from Troy and Charles. Shaking it off, he moved over to the empty table she stood next to.

"I hope they work things out," Charles said to his brother. "That poor guy's got it bad."

Troy looked at his younger brother and shook his head. "No more than you did. And at least he's man enough to face her head-on. Besides, I didn't think you liked him."

"First off, I was man enough, so just lay off of me on that. I married the woman I loved, didn't I?" After Troy's nod, he continued, "And secondly, I'm not head over heels for the guy like you obviously are. I don't know him. But he's okay, I guess."

"He loves her. I could tell by the way he talked about her. That's good enough for me."

"My mom told me to bring you a plate. She made one for me and is making me sit out here with you," Devin stated as soon as Spark was seated. She didn't want any misunderstanding on the subject of her forced hospitality.

"Well, I don't want to make you do anything that you don't want to do."

"You're not making me, she is." Her eyes floated to the deck where she knew her mother stood watching to make sure she followed directions.

"Well, happy birthday," he said quietly.

"Thank you," she replied, looking down at her plate.

"Devin." She looked so good, beautiful, he lost track of his thought. "Devin, I came here to talk to you. I have to make you understand how sorry I am about what happened. And I want you to know how much I care about you. I—"

"Stop, Spark. Just stop," she pleaded. Devin didn't want to hear anything about him being sorry. She wasn't ready for his apology. She wanted to stay mad at him because that was the only way she could think to stop the hurt of missing him. She wanted to be able to let him leave when he decided it was time to go back.

"Devin, you have to listen to me." He pushed both plates of food aside so nothing was between them and grabbed hold of her hands. "I am sorry. There is nothing in this world that would have ever made me hurt you the way I did, especially after I found out that I was in love with you. I swear I wanted to tell you from the very beginning, as soon as I talked to you at the airport terminal when I spilled my lemonade. I didn't want to be doing my sister's dirty work. I know how crazy she is. And I knew that half of it was based on some fairy tale that she had stored in that sick head of hers."

"But you still went along with it."

"Devin, I honestly thought that I could come here and watch you for a few days, then report nothing to her. I didn't expect that you would hop on a plane and try to find her. I know that it's hard for you to believe right now, but I do care for you, and I do hope that you'll forgive me because I need you in my life. I didn't realize it until you weren't in it anymore. Baby, the last two weeks have been miserable without you."

"Spark, it's way too soon for you to have any feelings for me at all. How can you say that you love me? How can you say that you can't live without me? You'll survive, and you'll do just fine." She put her head down to avoid eye contact.

"You don't love me, Devin?" He grabbed her hands tighter when she tried to pull away from him. "Look at me. Tell me that you don't have any feelings for me, Devin, any feelings at all, and I'll leave here right this moment."

She remained quiet.

"Tell me, Devin."

Devin tried to look away again. She couldn't say it because she did have feelings for him. Instead, she said nothing. She just stared at him.

Spark bent down and kissed her hand. He'd known that she had feelings for him, that it wasn't a one-sided coin.

"Regardless of my feelings for you, what you did was wrong. You hurt me, Spark. You betrayed me and my trust."

"I'll be the first one to say it was messed up. I was wrong. But Devin, you have to let me make it up to you somehow. I don't know how, but I promise you that I will."

"Spark, just eat your food." She looked around the yard only to find that half her family was focused on their conversation. The last thing Devin wanted to be was the center of all this attention. "We're going to have to talk about all of this later. It seems that we have a large audience, and I am not trying to be the entertainment tonight." Try as she might, Devin couldn't stay mad at this man. She smiled as he clumsily moved his plate back in front of him and began stuffing his face after a brief prayer. "I see you're still as clumsy as ever."

"Sorry about that, but ain't nothing changed since the first time we met except my feelings for you and my relationship with my sister."

"Your relationship with your sister?"

"Yeah, we don't talk anymore. I still talk to my nieces, but, most of the time, they have to sneak and call me on their cell phone on their way to or from school. She knows that I'll snap if she tries to keep them completely from me, and they will, too. For some reason, they love their uncle."

She didn't fall for his weak attempt to broach the subject of love for him.

"I'm sure she'll get over it sooner or later. She'll need you again, soon."

"Nah, I think this is pretty much it for us, but it's been heading down this road for a long time. The situation with you was just the straw that broke the camel's back."

"Maybe you should have stayed in Delaware and tried to fix things with your sister instead of coming here."

"No, I don't think so. I think I made the right decision in going after what is most important to me." Spark looked her in the eyes. He was serious, and it was important that she realize that. He wasn't leaving until it was time for him to go home to pack up his apartment and move back here. All he needed from her was the say-so, and he would be on the next plane out of Chicago to go get his things. But he knew it wouldn't be that easy. He was going to have to do a lot of work to get back in her good graces and gain her trust. And Spark was ready to do it. He didn't have anything but time and the ten thousand dollars that he had saved since his gambling had stopped. It still amazed him how much money he had lost on the pipe dream of hitting it big. He could have been a millionaire by now if he had just saved his own money instead of giving it to slot machines, horse races, and gambling dens.

CHAPTER 16

After everyone ate, the older guys decided that they wanted to play the teenagers in a game of basketball. It was Jeff's idea. So, he recruited Troy, Charles, Chauncey, and Spark onto his team.

The game started out easy and friendly, with the whole family gathered around cheering on their team of choice. Devin had let go of the attitude she was carrying, and put effort into enjoying her birthday. She and her sisters eagerly cheered on both teams. Occasionally, she found herself cheering louder for Spark, who she was surprised to find could play just as well as her brothers.

It was a close game, although the teenagers stayed in the lead the entire time. The older guys seemed to begin to slow down halfway through the game. Instead of running up and down the full length of the court, three stayed at one end on offense and the other two stayed at the other end for defense. They didn't care about the jokes or the fun that was being made of them. At that point, the teenagers really began to show off.

The crowd went wild when Roberta's son dunked the ball backward and when John's son caught an ally-oop. Not to be outdone, the older guys began to put on a performance of their own. It wasn't as impressive as the dunks, but a backward lay-up by Troy brought cheers, and Spark's 360-degree turning toss-up would have been beautiful if he hadn't landed first on somebody's foot, rather than on the ground.

He landed hard and just lay still. Spark wasn't sure if his ankle was broken or not, but it wouldn't have been the first time. He sat up, grabbing his ankle and trying to put on a brave face because he could see Devin rushing onto the basketball court. Somehow, she reached him before Troy, who was only a few feet away.

"Spark," she asked, kneeling next to him, "you all right? I knew it was going to happen sooner or later."

"I'm all right, Devin." He winced, trying to move his foot around. Then he looked at her knowingly. "That's what I get for trying to act like I was twenty again."

"At least you recognize where you were wrong. Next time, just act your age."

"I don't think there will be a next time," he said confidently.

"Oh, dear, are you sure that you're okay?" Brenda asked Spark as he limped his way to the nearest picnic table with the help of Troy and Jeff.

"I'm okay," he assured her, wincing as Troy peeled off his sneaker to examine his ankle.

"Mom, can you tell somebody to run into the house and get me the ace bandages in the bathroom under the sink?" he called after her as she walked away. "We're also going to need a pair of the crutches."

"Crutches?" Spark moaned. He knew it was bad. This wasn't the first time he had hurt himself, broken a leg or ankle, hand or arm. He'd definitely had his share of hospital visits.

"It's not that bad. I can tell just by looking at it that it's not broken," Troy told him. Hearing Spark curse between his teeth when he slowly rotated the foot to the left, Troy added, "But you should get to the hospital so we can get an x-ray of it just to be sure. I've been wrong before."

"It feels like it's broke," Spark complained, "but I can still move it."

"Well, the foot is made up of many bones. It's possible that you broke a small bone, which wouldn't interfere with the movement that much. I'll wrap you up and run you to the hospital."

"Thanks, man. I really appreciate this. Aw, aw, stop. Stop. That hurts a lot more when you turn it that way. Just stop, please. I know you're a doctor and all, but just stop."

"Listen to you," Charles laughed. "A big strong man like you brought damn near to tears by a little sprained ankle."

Spark cut him a look that would have killed him if that were possible.

"Leave him alone, Charles," Devin interrupted. "I've seen you brought to tears by much less. Should I recount the list?"

"Whatever. I was just having some fun. If that were me, you'd all be joining in."

"Let's just take it easy on the new guy," Troy suggested.

"I don't see why. He's here, ain't he?" Charles continued to argue his case until his wife wobbled over, full with their third child.

"Charles, I think I need to get home and lie down. I'm not feeling that well," Shelia said, making Charles forget about everybody else and move fast to gather up his kids.

Sheila wasn't due for two more months, but she'd had a rough time with the last pregnancy, and he wasn't going to take any chances. He scooped up his four-year-old and his two-year-old and walked toward her. "We're ready when you are, baby. I'll see y'all tomorrow. Tell Mom that we had to cut out early."

Everyone said their good-byes as the family left through the back gate. Spark had to admit that he was a little glad to see Charles go. He was a nice enough guy, but Spark could tell that he was not going to be the most helpful in his quest to get Devin. Spark realized that he hadn't even had time to be in awe of his superstar status because of the big brother role he had taken on so vehemently.

"Well," Brenda said as she came back outside with all the supplies in hand, "what's the verdict, Doc?"

Everyone laughed before Devin explained, "Mom, doctors don't make verdicts, judges do. Doctors make diagnoses."

"You know what I meant. How's the boy doing? Is it broken?"

"We're going to take him to the hospital to make sure it's not broken," Troy informed his mother.

"Well, it's almost eight o'clock. Everybody will be gone by the time you get back," Brenda explained. "So, why don't you, Stephanie and Devin go on and take him to the hospital. The kids are going to stay the night here, Troy, and your girls, too, Devin. Take care of yourself, Darnel, dear."

"Yes, ma'am."

"Have you always been so clumsy, baby? Your mother must have had a time with you when you were younger."

"Yes, ma'am. She did."

"Stop with the ma'am. Just call me Ms. Brenda like everybody else, or better yet, you can call me—"

"Let's go, Troy," Devin said loudly, drowning out her mother's last words. She looked at her mother incredulously. The woman had no shame whatsoever. "Where are your clothes, at the hotel?" Devin asked him.

"No, I didn't get a hotel room. I went straight to your house, and that's when I ran into your brothers. My clothes are in the trunk of the rental car."

"He doesn't need a hotel," her mother intruded yet again. "My goodness. How hospitable is that? No, he'll stay at Devin's house. He helped her out by letting her stay out his house when she needed it. I swear, people will think I didn't raise you right." She threw her hands in the air for emphasis, and then walked away.

"You sure are throwing it on a little thick, Mom."

"Darnel is staying at your place, and that's it. The girls will stay here until he goes back to Delaware."

Troy smiled to himself as he helped Spark to the car. "Don't put any pressure on it. Use the crutches."

Spark stopped after two attempts. "You might as well take these things before I kill myself." He looked at Troy. "I've never been able to use them. Sorry." Instead, he supported himself on Troy's shoulder and hopped all the way to Troy's car, which was parked in the front of the house.

"Troy, you should have known that he wouldn't be able to use the crutches. He's just plain uncoordinated," Devin said, following Spark and praying that he didn't trip over a rock or something.

"I bet you didn't say that when you two were in bed," Troy joked back, until he received an elbow in the ribs from his own wife.

The trip to the hospital didn't last long, thanks to Troy's credentials. He was able to take Spark through the clinic in record time. However, the x-rays did show a small fracture. With his inability to use crutches, Troy had no choice but to wrap his foot up, but instead of putting it in a cast, he placed a boot on Spark's foot to immobilize it. That didn't stop Spark from complaining, or almost falling on his face the first time he tried to walk with it, but with a little practice he got it together. He simply walked like a duck with one leg twisted to the side.

Troy dropped him and Devin at her house. By the expression on her face, they could all tell that she wasn't too happy about it.

"Here, let me help you get into the house. Stephanie, take his keys and grab that suitcase out of the truck, please. Devin, go open the front door, will you? God, you'd think you never had company before."

She cut him a look.

So, he antagonized more. "Spark, if she doesn't treat you like the hospitable host that we all know she can be, let me know. I'll tell Mom, and she'll be in a world of trouble. That includes breakfast for you in bed tomorrow morning. After you take this pain medicine, I don't want you on your feet at all. Don't come out tomorrow for anything, and don't get up. Do you hear me, Devin? That's doctor's orders."

Devin had the front door open and shut before they were halfway up the front walk. Spark looked at Troy.

"I don't envy you, man. You got one long night ahead. My advice is to take the pills as soon as you get in and just go to sleep."

"But he won't do that," Stephanie interjected, "because he needs to get everything out in the open and explain himself. He misses her, Troy. Can't you see that the man has feelings for your little sister?"

"Well, if he knew what I know, he'd save that for a couple of days because anything he says to her tonight is going to go in one ear and right out the other. The girl is not trying to hear all that, and she's probably still a little mad that he came. All of my sisters get ignorant when they are mad. He'll be better off following my directions. In a few days, she'll stop slamming things, and then maybe you'll be able to talk to her. She'll still give you the dirty looks, but at least she'll probably listen to what you have to say."

"Troy, you ought to be ashamed of yourself talking about your sisters that way. You know what? I'm going to tell them all what you said about them." Stephanie laughed when Troy quieted down.

"Stephanie, I'm not afraid of my sisters, regardless of what you might think, and if you tell them, then you're a tattletale. And I'm going to have to punish you when you get home."

Spark saw the look that passed between them and knew that was his cue to go. "I guess I'm just going to have to take my chances, Troy, because I'm not leaving here without winning her back. Call me stupid."

"Don't worry, I am. But I wish you the best of luck just the same." Troy helped him into the house.

They heard Devin in the living room. She was spreading sheets over her sofa for a makeshift bed.

"Devin," Spark said, "I really appreciate this."

"No problem, Spark. Just returning a favor," Devin said, turning towards the group, a smile on her face.

"Its time for us to go, hon," Troy said, grabbing his wife's arm and leading her to the door. "Y'all have a good night. Spark, I'll check on you in the morning. Take the pills like I said and get a good night's sleep."

"Thanks for having my back," Spark said to him as he retreated. Then he focused his attention on Devin, who had returned to her work. "Devin, can we please sit down and talk for a minute?"

"I just want to get you set up here so you can rest. There's a bathroom down the hall to the left, second door. I'll get this finished and get out of your hair."

"I don't want you out of my hair, Devin. I want us to settle this."

"Let's not do this tonight. I'm tired. You're hurt. It can wait. Please."

Her eyes were pleading with him, making his determination to talk to her weaken. In concession, he picked up his bag and headed to the bathroom. When he came back out, Spark was disappointed to find that Devin was no longer in the living room. All of the lights on the lower level were out except the one on the end table beside the sofa.

Devin sat in the chair behind Chris's desk and watched the sun come up. She hadn't been able to sleep and had decided to come down to the den. It was time for her to let go of the past and put an end to the confusion the past month had bought. This was the only room in the house that still held Chris's belongings. She had given his clothes to the Salvation Army the month after he passed away. Against their wishes, her brothers had helped her divide Chris's tools amongst them and clean out her garage. They did insist that she keep a few important tools in the garage for emergencies.

This room she had been unable to clean out. Chris had spent a lot of time sitting behind the desk working or reading to the girls on his couch. He had watched his games on the large-screen television and had hooked up the video game system so that he could watch as the girls played. She missed him, but it was time to move on.

Tears fell from her eyes as she began to pack up the books from the wall of shelves. She flipped through the pages of each book just to make sure they were empty, and filled the boxes that had sat in the corner for months. After filling a few boxes, she taped the lids and stacked them near the door.

Spark was awakened by the sound of a loud thump. He sat up slowly, quietly, and listened. He heard her whisper something under her breath, but then there was complete silence. Against his better judgment, Spark decided to make sure she was all right. He hobbled to the doorway and stopped in his tracks at the sight of Devin sitting on the couch crying. Violent sobs caused her shoulders to shake as she covered her face with her hands.

He wanted to console her, but what if she didn't want him near her?

"Devin?" he asked, trying not to startle her. He kept his voice even and as comforting as he could. "Devin, is everything okay?"

She turned away from him, wiping her eyes. "I'm fine, Spark."

"You don't look fine," he said, moving closer and trying not to put too much pressure on his hurt foot. He sat next to her, slowly putting his arm around her shoulders. "Let me help you, Devin."

"I have to do this, Spark," she said, looking at him for the first time. She was trying to be strong and failing miserably at it.

"I know, baby. But you don't have to do it by yourself. That's why I'm here. I want to help you."

Spark held her close, letting her move past her worries and her fears. He didn't move until he felt her pull away.

"It's so hard. Chris was a really good man, and it hurts that he's gone, but it hurts even more to know that he didn't trust me with his secrets. I was with that man for over six years, and its like I didn't know anything about him at all."

"Devin, come on now. I don't see it that way at all. I think that Chris loved you too much to put you in jeopardy by telling you the truth. He gave you exactly what you deserved: a life with a man who loved you with his whole heart. He gave you two beautiful daughters, and he loved you all very much. Why would he burden you with worry? He carried that on his shoulders, and his alone, because he loved you."

"He should have told me. You don't think that we might have been in jeopardy? Whoever killed him had to know about us. What if they had come here and killed us all? What if they wanted to hurt him so badly that they decided to use his family to do it?"

"Okay, now you're starting to reach a little too far. Devin, you're talking about things that didn't happen. No one ever came for Chris's family. That is all in the past, so why even think about it now? It's been two years since his death. If you or the kids were their targets, I'm sure they would have done something by now."

"What if they're still looking for whatever money your sister was talking about?"

"What money? I know that you're not listening to anything that my sister had to say. Chris was a smart man, Devin. He would never have put you or his children in any kind of danger." Spark lifted her head until she was looking him directly in the eyes. "I know that it was a lot for him to carry by himself, but that's what he chose to do because of his love for you, just as you will choose to be strong for your daughters. You have to get yourself together and work through your pain. You know that Chris loved you, and that's all that really matters at this point."

"But—"

"No buts. I am here for you, and I will help you in any way that I can. You know that, so let's get this stuff cleaned up. Your girls will be surprised to see the den straightened and clear of these books. Maybe we could bring some of their toys down here and make it a recreational room for them."

"I don't know. Let's just get this stuff boxed so I can send the books to the youth center. If I call them, they'll send someone over to pick them up either today or tomorrow."

"Okay, let's do this," Spark said, cautiously following Devin to the bookshelf. She explained to him which books she wanted to get rid of and which she wanted to keep for the girls. "Richard always did keep a lot of books. When we were kids, we used to tease him because his mother, rest her soul, made him read every day for an hour before he could come outside. He tried to say that he didn't like reading, but a couple of times we had to cancel or postpone our makeshift football games because he didn't show on time."

"He loved to read. Used to read to the girls every night, nursery rhymes and Dr. Seuss. Then he would tell them stories about *Aladdin* and *Moby Dick*, kiddie versions. And they loved it. He had them so engrossed in the stories that they actually believed in flying carpets and that a big whale might be in the pond by my brother Charles's house. I used to tell him to stop letting them live in fairy tales."

"I think that's right where all children should be. With all the harsh realities of the world, I think its important to keep our children as innocent as possible for as long as possible."

"Yeah, but because of the harsh realities, we can't afford for them to be ignorant of what's really going on. In the long run, that could hurt them. Like now. My girls have to deal with the reality of their father being dead. Nowhere in his storybooks did it say that was going to happen."

Spark put the book he was holding in the box and slowly walked over to her. "Devin, sit down," he said, leading her to the chair. He sat on the desk. "I don't think you need to worry about the girls. They seem to be well adjusted. If they have questions, they will come to you for answers, but you need to be prepared to give them the answers they need to hear. Are you sure that you're ready to do that?"

"Honestly, no, I'm not. I know what they need to hear, the truth. Their father loved them very much. But I don't feel the truth."

"Yes, you do. You just said it less than ten minutes ago. Chris was a very attentive father. I think the problem is that you can't let go of the fairy tale. And when you say that his death wasn't a part of it, you mean that in the story you two were making together he wasn't supposed to die."

She wiped at the tears that fell heavily down her face as Spark's revelation hit home. He was completely right. Chris was supposed to be around for everything. He wasn't supposed to leave her alone to be strong for her kids. He didn't have the right to leave her when she needed him so much. But he had.

"I hate him for putting me in this position. It's been so hard living without him," Devin explained as the tears persisted.

"You don't hate him. You just need to come to terms with what's happened. Do you think that if he had a choice he would have chosen to leave you like this? You have so much confidence in your love for him, why do you doubt his love for you?"

Devin was quiet. She wiped her tears. Spark was right. She should be ashamed of herself for thinking the way she had been thinking about Chris. He had showed her every day they were together how much he loved her, and here she sat doubting him. Quietly, she resumed work. She began to tackle the piles of paper that cluttered his desktop, sorting the papers into three piles: trash, important, and unsure. She would shred the trash, read and file the important papers and discuss the unsure papers with Spark. Maybe he could give her a suggestion on what to do with them.

An hour later, they decided to pause for breakfast. They were both starving.

"I think you should put that foot up while I cook breakfast. Go on into the living room and rest."

"No, I'll sit out here with you." He got a pillow off the couch and followed her to the kitchen. "I'd be bored sitting in there by myself. Besides, I don't want to fall asleep. We got a lot done, and I want to help you finish today."

"Are you sure the foot isn't bothering you? Is it time to take your medicine?"

"I'm fine. That pain medicine knocks me right out. I'll take some later." He put the pillow and his foot in the kitchen chair next to him. "So, when are you bringing the girls home?" Spark was wondering how much time he had to convince her of his feelings.

"Knowing them, they'll be staying at my folks' house until the day before school starts. They love it over there. All the kids do."

"Well, it's easy to see why. I wish I'd had that many kids to play with growing up, and all family. That's even better."

"Yeah, I guess. I'd be lying if I said that I still got along with all of my cousins. For the most part, everyone in the family is still cordial, but I have my picks of the ones I like to be around. I guess it's like that in every family."

"Definitely. I can't even stand to be around my own sister, so you can just imagine how the rest of the family feels about her."

They shared a laugh as they thought about Carlissa. Devin pulled eggs and bacon out of the refrigerator.

"How do you like your eggs?"

"Over medium, but you can just scramble them."

"I know how to cook them over medium."

"Okay, but I don't like the white running at all, just the yoke."

"I said I know how to cook eggs over medium. Why don't you try to call her? I'm sure the girls would love to hear from you."

"I'll talk to the girls later. They call me every day, but Carlissa's problem is bigger than me. I can't help her. It's mental."

"Does she know that you're here?"

"I'm sure she does. She says that she doesn't care or want to speak to me again, but I know she quizzes the girls after every phone call. That's her way."

"And I'm sure she's not too happy about it."

"I'm sure you're right. My sister hates me right now, and there is nothing I can do about it. One day, she'll have to deal with the consequences of her actions, but until she really gets a swift kick in her ass, she's going to keep acting like she's untouchable. I just don't want my nieces to have to suffer because of it."

"I wish the girls could meet one day. Maybe when they're older. I just don't know how to explain to my girls that they have older sisters, who also happen to be twins, without telling them too much of their father's business."

"Kids have a tendency to handle situations much better than adults. You'll be surprised at how well the girls will adapt to each other. Christina and Christal already know about your girls. Carlissa doesn't care who she rants and raves about, which makes it hard for them to maintain those fairy tales that we were talking about earlier."

"And what do they think?"

"My nieces are smart girls. Without Carlissa's knowledge, I have made sure that they know a lot of positive things about their father. I let them know why I thought he left, and that he loved them. They figured out on their own that their mother drove him away, and they did have a very limited relationship with him through his letters and his gifts. Money was sent to them, but this money that Carlissa keeps ranting over didn't really come to light until she found out that he had passed away. Then the money was all she talked about."

"The money that she believes I got."

He shook his head as she bought him a plate with three perfectly cooked eggs, several slices of bacon, and toast. She next down with her own plate. They each said grace, and the conversation was forgotten for the time being.

"Well, it's one-thirty, and that's the last box of books." Spark turned toward the neat pile of boxes in the corner of the room. He counted them, seventeen. Why in the world would a man keep so many books? And that didn't include the books Devin said she wanted to keep for the girls or the encyclopedias. They had four sets. There wasn't that much research in the world.

Spark was moving one set of encyclopedias to a higher level when an envelope fell from its folds. "Devin?" he said, retrieving the envelope from the floor. "Devin, you might want to look at this."

Devin was looked up. She was going through the bag that she had filled with papers from the desk the night she rushed out of the house on her way to Delaware. She wasn't finding anything that she hadn't seen before. Her marriage license, Chris's death certificate, and some insurance information, which she put back in the bag to see what Spark had.

"It's a letter, from Chris," she said, unsure of what she saw in his eyes when she looked at him. Was it insecurity? Disappointment? Fear? Love? In that moment, Devin was torn between two men, one dead and one alive. She loved them both.

But in her hands she held what was possibly the answer to her doubt and fears, the answer to her questions. Answers she needed in order to move on with her life. She briefly looked at Spark again, and then tore open the envelope.

Spark left the room quietly. Even though he wanted to stay, he knew that he had to give her space. Devin had to read the letter and come to terms with whatever was inside. Spark loved her, he wanted her, but there was no way he could compete with a ghost for her affections. She needed to find closure, and perhaps the letter was it.

"I'll be in the living room," he said, though he knew she wasn't listening. Spark nervously retreated. No, she couldn't be with Chris physically, and no, Chris shouldn't pose a threat to what he wanted to have with Devin, but none of that mattered. In her hands was a very powerful piece of paper. That letter could make or break any future that he had with her. Spark was exhausted as he fell back onto the couch in the living room and let his head fall back. He shut his eyes and exhaled.

CHAPTER 17

Dear Devin,

If you are reading this letter, I must be dead. There are so many things that I need to explain to you, and I pray that you will find it in your heart to forgive me for not telling you sooner. I tried so many times, but I just couldn't. I love you too much to put you in the middle of something that isn't your fault.

Devin, I never thought I would meet anyone like you. You brightened my life and made it so much more than I ever thought possible. And I miss you, even now, having to write this letter. I miss you. I love you, and I love our daughters. But now is the time for me to tell you the truth. When you read this, I'll be gone, and I don't want you to find out the truth from anyone but me.

I have been in the Witness Protection Program since two years before I met you. I am in the program because I turned state's evidence against someone that I saw kill a friend in front of me. Please understand my position and accept my apology. I knew that just by becoming involved with you I was putting you in an awful position, but I wanted you so badly. You made me feel so good, and you've given me so much. I wanted to tell you so many times that I have two other daughters from a previous marriage. They are twins, too. I guess it was just in my genes.

I know that this is asking a lot of you, and it's something that I should have done a long time ago, but I couldn't take the chance of connecting the past with the present. Over the years, I've sent my other girls gifts through a friend and talked to them on his phone, but what I really want is for my girls to know each other. My other daughters' names are Christina and Christal, and they live in Delaware. Their mother and I aren't on very good terms, and she may give you a hard time. Her name is Carlissa Harrison. Don't be surprised if she isn't very cooperative; we have a very bad history. If you need help, her brother, Darnel Miles, will help you. He is a good man and one of my oldest friends.

When you finish reading this letter, I want you to contact a friend of mine. His name is Allen Bowen. He is a very old friend and knows a lot about my past. His name is in the bottom drawer of my desk in the black address book under Al B. I have given him instructions on what to do if you should ever contact him.

Devin, I know this is a lot to spring on you, and I ask your forgiveness for not being able to tell you face to face. I just hate to disappoint you.

Please call Al. He can explain so much more to you.

Devin, I will always love you. You have filled me with more love than I could have ever hoped for.

Yours forever,

Chris

Devin wiped her eyes and read the letter again. A sigh of relief escaped her lips as she put her head down in her hands. He had wanted to tell her the truth. He did love her. How could she have ever doubted it?

"Spark," she called after getting herself together. He came into the room as if he expected the worst.

"Is everything okay?" he said, worry etching his brow.

Devin forced a smile to her face. Everything was going to be just fine. She was finally seeing the light at the end of the dark tunnel that had been her life for the past two years. And she was going to reach for it. "Everything is fine. I think I need your help."

"You name it," he said, walking towards her. "Does it have something to do with the letter?"

"Yeah, Chris explained some things to me in his letter. I need to contact a friend of his. Allen. His number is on the bottom of the letter. Did you know him?"

"Allen Bowen?" he said curiously.

"Yeah, Allen Bowen. You do know him."

"Al is one of the guys we used to hang with. After everything went down with the trial, he left town. I never heard from him. So, he and Richard stayed in contact?"

"Apparently so. He said that I should give him a call and left his number.. He also said for me to get in touch with you if I needed your help getting the girls introduced to their sisters. He wanted them all to know each other."

"Well, of course, any real man would want his children to know each other. And he knew that Carlissa would give you trouble."

"Yeah," Devin said. "He said that you were a good guy who would help me."

"And he is right. Regardless of how it may have seemed, Devin, I have wanted to help you in some way from the start."

"Well, you can help me now. Do you know if Allen might live close by?"

"I wouldn't know. After the trial, I never saw him again."

"Well, I'm going to call him and see when we can make an appointment." She picked up the phone and dialed. "You don't have to go back to Delaware right away, do you?"

"Of course not. I'm here for as long as you need me," Spark replied, hoping that his support showed her how much he cared for her. "Devin, does this mean—"

She held up her finger to silence him when the phone began to ring.

It rang several times before the answering machine picked up.

"Hi. I am trying to reach Allen Bowen. My name is Devin Albridge, and I believe that you knew my husband. Would you please return my call at your earliest convenience? Thank you." She left her number and hung up the phone.

"So now we wait," Spark said.

"Yeah. I'm sorry, Spark, what were you saying earlier?"

"Don't worry about it. What time are they supposed to be here for these boxes?"

"They said sometime this afternoon," she said, glancing at her watch. Two-thirty.

"Why don't we move them closer to the door?"

"Good idea. Then I want you to lie down for a while. Take a nap. You definitely need to put your foot up."

"Yes, Mother," he replied jokingly. "I'm not used to being told what to do. Well, not by anyone but my sister, anyway."

"Don't worry," she laughed, going to get another box. "You'll get used to it."

Spark wasn't sure if Devin was aware of what she had said, and he didn't stop to make her aware of it, either. He didn't want her to possibly correct herself. Instead, he went with the flow of the day, joking with her until they had moved all of the boxes to the foyer. Then he rested on the couch and put his foot up on the pillows while she made lunch. There wasn't too much on television, but he managed to find a movie that caught his interest. His foot had started hurting while they were moving the boxes, but he'd tried not to let it show. He could only move so fast, and had found himself passing boxes to her rather than walking them all the way to the foyer. He hadn't liked that.

Spark swallowed two painkillers and leaned back, prepared to watch the movie until she returned. By the time Devin walked into the living room with a tray of sandwiches, chips, and sodas, he was snoring softly.

She didn't want to wake him so she took the food back into the kitchen, wrapped his, and ate quietly. It had been a busy day, and they had gotten a lot done. With an injured ankle, he probably shouldn't have helped her so much, but Devin was grateful that he had. It was good to have someone there while she moved from the past and started looking toward her future.

It was a future that she now hoped included him. It was crazy to think this way, but Devin realized that if she hadn't gone through her doubts and fears and found out about Chris's past, she would have never met Spark. In a way—a very improbable way—it was as if Chris had bought them together.

Devin walked past him as he slept and walked up the steps to her bedroom. She thought about the turn her life had taken. Was she really okay with everything that she had heard about her husband? Even finally finding the letter didn't totally put her at ease. What if the men came after her because they thought she had whatever money Carlissa had been talking about? What if her girls were in danger? What if . . . what if . . . what if? There were still so many unanswered questions. What if Spark was here on another mission from his sister? Was she ready to completely trust him after everything they had been through? Should she trust anyone, including the man she was waiting to call her back?

So many thoughts assaulted Devin as she tried to rest and put her life into some kind of perspective. Her girls would be coming back home. She had to make sure that their lives were not directly affected by any of their father's actions. Except for the fact that she would have to tell them that they had older siblings, she hoped their lives would stay normal.

At the sound of the doorbell ringing, Devin was awakened. After three rings, she rushed downstairs, trying to get to the door before Spark was disturbed. To her surprise, Spark was standing at the front door talking to the men from the youth center. She noticed that her apron was wrapped around his waist and the smell of onions and peppers filled the air.

Instead of going to the door, she sat on the couch and watched as he instructed the men about the boxes. They gave him a receipt and thanked him for his donation and were gone quickly.

"They moved those boxes a lot faster than we did, huh?" she said, as he hobbled towards her.

"Yeah, I guess they're used to lifting things. I was trying to let you sleep."

"Thank you," she said, looking up into his eyes. "I appreciate it." Then she turned to the kitchen. "And what's going on in there?"

"Oh, that would be your dinner, madam." He bowed slightly, extending his arm in the direction of the kitchen.

"It smells good. What is it?"

"Just something I threw together. Smothered steak, baked potato, mixed vegetables, and a small salad. I think you deserve it, and I've worked up a hell of an appetite. Shall we?"

"Yes, we shall. I'm starving, too, but give me one second. I need to call over to my parents' and check on the girls. I'll be in there in a second."

"Are we still riding over there today?"

"Well, that's why I'm calling. It's already five o'clock. I'm sure they're eating now, but I do want to ride over before it gets too late. I just want to make sure they don't have any plans."

Spark nodded and walked to the kitchen. He'd had a good sleep and was wide- awake again. He doubted if he would be sleeping anytime soon. A ride out in the night air might just do the trick for him.

When she came into the kitchen, Spark motioned for her to have a seat. He had put their salads on the table and was making her plate.

"Don't do anything. You deserve to be pampered."

"If this your way of paying me back for letting you stay, you're making me feel bad for never cooking while I was in Delaware."

"One has nothing to do with the other. I am not paying you back for anything. I am pampering you because it's what I want to do. Don't you like being pampered?"

"Of course, I am a woman. I enjoy being taken care of every once in a while."

"Good. I plan on doing just that."

"Spark, I think we should talk."

"No, I don't think so. Just enjoy this evening. We can talk later." He sat down, took her hands, and said a quick prayer. "Let's dig in."

Devin wasn't sure if she was making the right decision by letting the conversation end. Sometimes it was important to get things out in the open before they went too far, and this seemed to be one of those times. With everything going on, they hadn't been able to talk about the effect finding Chris's letter might have on them or if there was still a 'them' to talk about. As friends who wanted to be more than friends, they needed to figure out the best way to build their relationship. Obviously, he didn't want to talk at the moment.

Spark was suddenly worried. He had thought about the future long and hard while Devin slept. Pushing her to make a decision about him right now could be the worst mistake of his life. With everything that was going on, it wasn't fair of him to demand or expect her to think about their relationship. He just might push her in the wrong direction. She was going through too much, and she needed to be focused on getting past whatever Al had to tell them about Richard. Spark intended to be right there to support her, but in all honesty, he knew he also had his own best interest in mind.

What did Al know that he didn't know? And why had Al left so fast after everything went down? Why were he and Richard the only ones who had remained in contact? Butch had left town as soon as Willis was arrested. He'd packed up his girlfriend and their son and moved without giving anyone a moment's notice. After he left, Spark had talked to Butch's cousin Jay and asked what had happened to him. Jay had said that he moved away, and didn't tell anybody where he was going. Jay had also said that he was thinking about doing the same thing. Before long, he did.

"Spark? Spark? What you thinking about?" Devin asked, watching him curiously.

"Just thinking how life changes. You know, when my friends and I were growing up nobody could have told me that I would ever be sitting in Illinois eating dinner. We thought that we would all be growing old together in

Delaware, helping each other raise our children. Now, two of us are dead and the other four have no contact with each other. I'm the only one who stayed in Delaware. I don't know where the other guys went. Life is so simple when you're children."

"That's so true, but God doesn't put you through more than you can handle. Just like your gambling. He had to take you as far as He did with that for you to stop altogether. I know that sometimes it's hard. Believe me, the past couple of years have been very hard for me, too, but I got through them. And it wasn't by myself. I've had a lot of help."

"Luckily you have a good family willing to help each other in any way possible."

"And your sister was there for you when you really needed her. Despite whatever else she's put you through, your sister does have love for you." By the way he looked away from her, lowering his head, Devin could tell that he didn't believe her so she continued. "Don't you have love for her?"

"She's my sister."

"And despite everything she's done, you still love her, right?"

"Of course."

"Well, same goes. She might hold her anger a little longer than most, but she loves you. Maybe you should call her so you two can talk some things over. She probably wants to put an end to all of this as much as you do, but just doesn't know how. It's never too late to save a relationship, especially if the two of you truly want to."

"I hope you're right," he said, looking her straight in the eye. Their gaze held for a split second before Devin turned her attention back to her plate.

The phone's ring broke the sudden silence.

"Get the phone. I'll clean up the table," Spark said, watching her move quickly to the wall phone in the kitchen.

"Hello," she said.

"Hello. May I speak to Devin?" The male voice was deep and friendly. Joy was obvious in his voice.

"Speaking. This is Devin."

"Hi, Devin. This is Al. How are you doing today?"

"Hi, Al. I'm doing very well. Thank you."

"Devin, I can't tell you how surprised and glad I was to get your message today. I've been waiting for a call from you for quite some time. First of all, let me offer my condolences for your loss again. I know it's late, but then again, its never too late, correct?"

"Correct. Again?" Devin was quiet for a second, and then she remembered his voice. "You were the man who called my cell phone that night?"

"Yes."

"And you took Chris's body from the morgue?"

"Yes. I realize that I have a lot of explaining to do, and I'm prepared to talk to you. But before we start, is everything okay? I mean with you and the girls."

Devin found she liked this man immediately. "Yes, we are fine. Unfortunately, I just found the letter this morning. I had a hard time going through Chris's things so I put it off and never really finished." She heard a baby crying in the background and wondered about his family. It was a shame that the two families hadn't been able to get to know each other better.

There was a long silence before Al spoke. "I know that you're used to calling him Chris, so please forgive me if I call him Rich while we're talking. Devin, I want to tell you how much joy you brought into my friend's life, and I want to thank you for that. I've wanted to meet you for so long, but understandably could not. I don't know how much of the story has been told to you. Rich/Chris did tell me that he was writing you a letter in the event that anything happened to him. So, please let me start from the beginning."

Devin sat down at the kitchen table, focusing on the man's hypnotic voice, wanting to hear everything he had to tell her. She ignored the look from Spark as he filled the sink with dishwater.

"Originally, we lived in Delaware. There were about six of us guys who grew up together, tight as a fist. We practically couldn't move without each other." He laughed as he reminisced. "I miss those guys. We got older, and basically, right after high school, met the wrong guy. He was a small part of a big-time drug ring, and he was trying to make a name for himself. So, he got a group of popular and naïve guys to work for him. And even though it was wrong, it was great at first. We had money, women, cars, and apartments. Those are big items for young guys, but then one of our friends began stealing the drugs and then the money."

"Robbie."

"Yeah, Robbie." He paused for a moment. "So, you have heard some of the story."

"Yes, but I'll explain that later. Please continue," she urged.

"Then you know that Willis Demby killed Robbie. He wanted us to do it, but we couldn't. Richard couldn't get over it. It was really a wake-up call to all of us. We wanted out, but couldn't get out. And we needed help. Richard had a teacher at the university who used to work for the government. He talked to the guy, and they immediately contacted someone who could help. He called me late one night and asked me to come over. When I got there, we went for a walk away from his apartment, and he told me that he was going to turn state's evidence and he needed someone he could trust on his side. He was the closest thing I ever had to a brother, so I wasn't going to say no. We agreed that he would tell the other guys that he couldn't get any help. During that time he wore wires and got whatever information the feds wanted. I helped a little just by covering for him, lying if necessary. But he did what he had to do, and he got the evidence that convicted Willis Demby. That was much more than I could have done.

"He didn't know where they were going to relocate him, but he told me that he would send me a coded message when he got there. And sure enough, about a month after the trial, I got a delivery. It was a book, *Frank Lloyd Wright: A Biography.* It wasn't marked, didn't have a return address on the package, and the postage stamp was marked Ohio, but I knew it was from him. I was an architectural major in college. I already had the book on my shelf. I was just happy that he was okay. So, I followed the rest of our plan. We saved a lot of money during the time we worked for Willis Demby, but Richard figured that he couldn't touch it without the feds being in his business. So, I had all of our money and left Delaware and moved in with my uncle in St. Louis. I transferred from the University of Delaware and graduated from Webster University. We've kept in touch over the years.

"Devin, I am so grateful to Richard, I mean Chris, for taking the risk that he did and being as brave as he was. It's because of him that I am able to have my beautiful wife and my newborn son. His name is Richard Christopher Bowen, by the way. There are a few more things that I need to talk to you about, Devin. I am just getting in the house, and I wanted to call you back right away, but I'll be taking a few days off this week. I need to see you in person. So, I'll be driving there on Tuesday. I hope you will be able to see me."

"Oh, definitely, Al. I'm off until school starts. I'll be able to get away, or you are more than welcome to come here. Just give me a call when you get into town. Thank you so much for everything that you have shared with me. I did know much of the story leading up to the trial, but thank you for explaining a little more."

"He loved you, Devin. I don't know how I can say it any plainer than that. I know you don't need reassurance, but I could tell that he did when he first started talking about you. Then when you got married, and when the girls were born, another set of twins, he was simply . . . he loved you."

"I know he did, thank you. I actually have another old friend of yours staying here at my house. He has been a big help to me as well."

Concern filled his voice when he answered, "Are you sure he is a friend, Devin?"

"Yes," she replied, looking at Spark's wide back as he washed dishes. "His name is Darnel Miles."

"Spark? You've got Spark at your house? That nutball. How is he doing?"

"He's doing good."

"You know about Carlissa?"

"Yes, and as far as I can tell, she's the nutball. She actually wrote me telling me that she was Chris's wife, so I went to Delaware to confront her, but she was one up on me. She had already sent Spark here to spy on me. Apparently, he owed her a lot of money for his gambling debts."

Al was laughing when he spoke. "Yeah, that's Spark. I told him that gambling was going to catch up with him sooner or later. It seems that we all picked up some bad habits once we started living high on the hog. For most of us, it was women, but Robbie started with the drugs, Spark started gambling, and Richard started drinking heavily after Robbie was killed. But I'm glad he had the common sense to put things right. I haven't heard from Jay and Butch in a while. Last I heard, Butch had moved out to Arizona, and Jay to Florida. But who really knows?"

Devin knew the question was rhetorical and didn't answer. Instead, she motioned for Spark to get on the phone. "Al, I will see you on Tuesday. Hold on, here's Spark."

"My man," Spark said loudly as soon as he got the phone in his hands.

She could hear Al on the other end just as loud. Shaking her head, she turned away and started drying dishes. Before long, she was finished, and Spark and Al were still rehashing old memories. She told him she was going in the living room. She knew they needed some privacy.

CHAPTER 18

"Mom, I think that you worry too much. Believe me, I am thinking clearly for the first time in months. I feel like a huge weight is being lifted off my shoulders, and I am finally going to have all the answers that I need. It's been so long since I've felt this way. With these answers, I'll be able to come to terms with Chris's death because I'll have a better understanding of why he chose to do the things that he did."

Devin stood in her mother's kitchen helping her put away dinner dishes. After the phone conversation with Al, Devin and Spark had decided to take a ride so she could check on the girls. Spark was in the den with her father and Troy, who had just stopped by to check on their parents before turning in for the night.

"I hope so, baby. Chris will always be with you because of the girls, but it's time that you let go of the past and move on with your life. It has hurt us all so much to watch you try to be strong and go through all this pain by yourself. You know your daddy and I love you to death. We just want to see you happy and know that you're going to be taken care of."

"Whether I find another husband or not, I will be fine. Every woman doesn't have to be married in order to make it."

"All I know is that your father and I aren't getting any younger. He's going to be sixty-five next year, you know. And I know that he worries. He wants to make sure that you are in good hands before he goes to Glory."

"He's always talking about going to Glory. If it will ease your troubles any, please know that I am fine. I am telling you that I am going to continue to be fine." She looked out her parents' back door and watched her children playing in the backyard with a half dozen of their cousins. Her girls were happy, and she was happy. That was all that mattered.

"So what are you going to do about your young man?"

"He's not my young man, Mom. Please stop calling him that," Devin said even as her attention was drawn to the two men sitting at the picnic table also watching the kids.

"Just because you don't think so doesn't mean I'm not stating the truth, dear."

"Mom—"

Brenda put her hand up for silence. "All I'm saying, baby, is that God already has a plan laid out for you that even you can't change. And I believe with all my heart that Chris was a good man and that he loved you very much. I believe that you two had a good marriage and a great relationship. But I also believe that maybe, just maybe, God might have been using Chris to put you right in the position that you're in now. Just maybe, God brought Chris into your life to bring Darnel into your life."

"How can you say something like that?"

"With my mouth, girl. You don't know how the Lord works. I've been telling you all your life that the Lord works in mysterious ways. If you don't believe it by now, you need to read your Bible."

"I believe in my Bible, Mom."

"And you just better. If this family isn't a perfect example of the Lord's work, what family is? How do you think your father and I made it all these years if not by God's grace?"

Devin sat in her seat and listened as her mother went through as many of God's blessings on their family as she could. "Mom, I know. I know the Lord has been good to us. I just don't want to minimize Chris in my life."

"Baby, I'm not asking you to minimize anything. Chris gave you two beautiful children. He was your husband. You loved him. That could never be minimized. But you have to understand that God gave you Chris for a time and a purpose. Now, I don't know what Chris's purpose in your life was, but I'm telling you not to limit the possibilities of that purpose. Chris gave you so much, but maybe one of his purposes was for you to meet Darnel and receive much more. Don't close yourself off to what is good for you."

Brenda pulled her out of her chair and gave her a tight hug. "I love you, Devin. I just don't want you to miss out on a good man for holding on too long to a good man." She looked straight into Devin's eyes. "It's time to let him go, baby."

"I know, Mom, but it's so hard." Tears slowly began to fall down her cheek, flowing harder when her mother attempted to wipe them away. "I don't know what to tell the kids."

"You don't have to tell them anything. You can include Chris in your relationship with Darnel. It's not about making him an enemy to your relationship. You're not disrespecting him. And Chris would want you to be happy. He was your friend. He was Darnel's friend. Why would the two of you want to make his memory your enemy? The both of you need to embrace it because he left four daughters behind who still need to be raised around love, and who need to learn a love for each other."

Devin sat back in the chair. She wondered how her life had gotten so confusing.

Was she really making it much harder on herself than it had to be? Could it really be as simple as her mother had suggested?

Spark was so relieved when Troy joined him and Devin's father in the den he stood up and shook his hand and gave him a hug. For the past half hour, he had been trying to divert Mr. John's interest off him and onto the baseball game they were supposedly watching. He hated baseball, but he was willing to do almost anything rather than answer questions he didn't know the answer to.

"Troy, my man," he said with enough zeal to make Troy look at him questioningly.

"Ah, hey Spark, what's up?" Troy said, walking over to give his father a hug. He noticed that his father had a small grin on his face, and figured out what was going on. "What are you guys up to?"

"Nothing much, son. Just sitting here with Devin's young man trying to get to know him better."

Troy smiled. "Is that all?"

"Yes, that's all. What else would I be doing with him?"

"Oh, I don't know. Giving him the third degree, maybe." He looked at his father and then back to Spark. Neither confirmed or denied his suspicions, but the look on Spark's face said it all. "I know you aren't asking him a bunch of questions. Devin isn't going to like that." He sat down next to his father.

"I'm that girl's father, she's not mine. I can ask anything that I want. She's got you boys all afraid of her or something. I'm not afraid of nary one of my children. I bought y'all in this world, and I can take you out."

"Okay, Pop. I hear ya," Troy agreed. His father was getting old. For a long time, he'd refused to face the fact that John Sr. wouldn't be around much longer. It was something hard for all of them to come to terms with. How was he supposed to forget how young and active his father had been just a short time ago? Slowly but surely he had seen him slowing down. He still did work around the house and kept busy, but the athletic man was gone. He watched more than he played now. The kids kept him active, but he was still slowing down. "Pop, don't you think Spark is a good man?"

"Of course I do. That's why I'm sitting here asking him if he is going to marry my daughter. The boy acts like he's scared to answer."

"Maybe it's too soon to be asking him those kinds of questions. Spark and Devin haven't known each other that long."

"Well, he's staying at her house, isn't he?"

"Yes," Troy said, hunching his shoulders.

"And she stayed at his house when she went to Delaware, didn't she?"

"Yeah, Pop, but—"

"Son," John said, looking directly at Spark, "I realize that I'm getting old, but please don't mistake me for senile. I'm not too old to know what happens between a man and a woman, and I'm not too blind to see that it has already happened between you and my daughter."

"Sir, I—" Spark was between shock and uncertainty. He didn't know what to say to Devin's father after such a blunt statement and was glad when he didn't get the chance.

"You don't have to say anything. Just don't try to pull the wool over these eyes. It's obvious that there is something very strong and perhaps very special going on between you and Devin. But for some reason, you're both fighting it. Now, I knew right off the bat that you care for my daughter or you wouldn't have come all the way up here to apologize. You could have done that on the phone. You're here because you want something, and I'm hoping that it's her."

"Mr. Avery, I do love your daughter, but I realize that there are some issues that need to be worked out before I can even approach her that way. I don't think that she will think I'm sincere with everything going on right now."

"Not sincere, huh? Well, I think you sincerely care about my daughter. But look, young man, I'm getting old real fast, and I don't have time to be waiting on you."

"Dad," Troy said, trying to interrupt his father and calm him down. The look he received quieted him.

"Young man, my daughter loves you. I can see that. Why can't you? What are you waiting for?"

"I don't want to rush her," Spark responded, uncertain of how he should answer. "Once everything is clear about Richard, I'm sorry, Chris, we'll be able to talk more freely about the future."

"You young people are always waiting and waiting and more waiting. Don't you realize how short life is? You have to grab what you want before you lose it. I guess you won't realize that until you're my age. Then you'll be sitting around with a lot of shoulda, coulda, wouldas. Believe me, that's not a good place to be."

"I understand, sir, but if I rush her, she might turn away from me."

"And you're probably right with that daughter of mine. All of my daughters are stubborn, even more stubborn than the boys. That's why I don't get involved with them. I let the missus handle that stuff. I just don't get in it."

Troy and Spark passed a glance between them. If John Avery hadn't just been trying to get into Spark's business, they didn't know what he was doing. But instead of pointing that out, they decided it would be easier on both of them if they turned their attention back to the baseball game.

The next two days, Devin didn't sleep well. Not only was she wondering about her meeting with Al, but she was also struggling with having Spark sleeping on her living room sofa. She had been tempted more than once on both nights to invite him into her bed because she knew that he could ease her nerves and calm her fears, but she hesitated and stayed strong. Devin didn't want Spark to feel as if she was using him or that her feelings weren't genuine. Her feelings, which were a problem in themselves, were making this whole situation more complicated. She knew that she had to talk to him sooner or later. He had tried every night before they went to bed, but she'd told him each time that she had to get everything situated with Al and find out everything he knew about Chris before she could even consider moving into another relationship.

Spark told her that what she didn't understand was that they were already in a relationship and that she just refused to acknowledge it. And true to his word, he had stayed there and was waiting patiently for her to be ready. It wasn't fair to him, she knew, but having him there helped her. She wasn't afraid to find out whatever was in store for her because she knew that Spark would be there to help her through it. He was putting his own life on hold for her.

Devin should have told him to go back to Delaware, but she needed him. She was keeping him from his family, and she knew it was wrong, but she wanted him with her. He hadn't tried to make amends with his sister as she had advised. But he talked to his nieces at least three times a day. She could tell that he missed them. Each time, he could hear his sister in the background yelling, not at the girls, but at the man she was seeing. Then he would get off the phone, complaining that his nieces didn't need to be in that situation.

To make herself feel better, she promised that she would let him go back even if she didn't want to. He needed to check on the girls and see that they were all right for himself.

The morning that they were to meet Al, Spark and Devin were both unusually quiet. Each mentally contemplated how their lives might or might not change after meeting with Al. He was the only person left who could help straighten out the mystery that was Richard Harrison/Christopher Albridge. But would he give them the answers they were hoping for?

As far as Spark was concerned, he wanted whatever answers Devin needed to make her whole again and ready to accept him into her life. And he didn't think it was being selfish to think this way. Her father had said it two days ago: Life was too short. Spark didn't want to wake up years later and hate himself for not going after the woman he loved. He was giving her the time she needed to straighten out her past and her heart, but as soon as that chapter in her book of life ended, he was determined to have his name in the first line of the next one. And to Spark, the meeting with Al was the last paragraph of that chapter of her life.

Devin was ready to move forward with her life. She wanted to move forward, but in order to do that, her past had to be firmly behind her, not a burden that she carried with her into a new relationship. She needed to have her answers and come to terms with them before she could even consider being with Spark.

Devin watched him now sitting on the sofa, supposedly watching television. She knew he wasn't because his eyes kept following her from one end of the living room to the other.

"Could you sit down? Your pacing is nerve-wracking."

"No, I can't sit down," she said. "Why isn't he here yet?"

"He'll be here when he gets here, Devin. He called and said that he had just checked in, and he was on his way. He probably wants to freshen up first. Come here." Spark extended his hand to her and waited for her to accept his offer. "Sit down here and talk to me."

She took his hand and allowed him to pull her down next to him. "Spark, I'm really not in the mood to talk right now. I want Al to get here and tell us whatever it is that he knows."

"And he will, but a watched pot never boils."

"What?"

"The longer you stand there waiting for him, the longer it will take him to get here. So, chill. He'll be here." Slowly, he ran his hand up and down her arm to help calm her nerves. His nerves stood on end. This was the closest she had been to him since he first came to visit.

She was leaning against him, and, gradually, she felt herself relaxing.

"Devin?"

"Yes, Spark," she answered, slightly turning to face him.

"I only want what's best for you," he said.

"I know. Spark, I owe you an apology. I have no right to push you to the side like I have and expect you to wait on me."

"After what I put you through, I deserve it. Besides, I'd wait for you forever, don't you know that? Listen, Devin, no matter what happens or doesn't happen between us, I want you to know that I do care for you and I consider you a friend. That's another reason why I'm still here. I want to make sure that you're okay before I go back to Delaware. And I can wait until Al leaves to talk to you about us. I know how important this is to you."

Devin knew that what her heart was telling her was true. She knew that Spark was a good man, and despite their brief history, she could trust him. He did care for her, and it was all right to want a man that she was desperately attracted to and hopelessly in love with. There was nothing wrong with that, and not even Chris would want her to be without it.

She wanted to kiss him. She was going to kiss him.

Then the doorbell rang.

Devin was nervous and excited when she went to the front door. Spark was right behind her, just as nervous. She opened the door, and Al stood in front of her. He wasn't at all what she imagined. He looked serious. He was dressed in a dark jogging suit with a baseball cap covering most of his face and was carrying a black gym bag. When he stepped into the house, Devin realized that Al was taller than both she and Spark. Standing well over six feet, he would be hard to hide in a crowd. His frame was lanky, but he looked strong. The thin mustache on his brown, handsome face made it hard to figure his exact age. Devin couldn't believe it was the same jovial man she had spoken with on the phone until he smiled. A gold-toothed smile. That smile seemed to change the whole atmosphere of the room in a flash, brightening it.

"Devin?" he said curiously, waiting to be invited fully into the house.

"Yes," she replied, just as he scooped her into his arms for a brotherly hug.

"It is so nice to finally meet you. You are just a beautiful as Richard said, and just as short."

"Thanks, but I suppose that everyone is short to you." She moved aside so he could speak to Spark.

"Spark, my man. What's up?"

"You, Al. Just you. How are things?" Spark said as the two men shook hands and quickly embraced. "It's been a long time, man. How you been?"

Devin followed the two men into the living room, listening to them as they got reacquainted.

"Al, would you like something to drink? Bottled water, beer, cranberry juice, soda— "

"I'll take cranberry juice. Thank you. You have a very nice house, Devin."

"Thanks." Devin went into the kitchen to get their drinks.

"So, man," Al said to Spark, "how long have you been in Chicago?"

"Oh, not quite a week yet. After the way I hurt her in Delaware, I felt it only right that I come back here and apologize, but then I hurt my foot, and then when I was helping her clean, we found the letter from Richard telling her to call you. I didn't want to leave her by herself, so I decided to stay around."

"Oh, what about her family? They don't mind you staying here?"

"Not really. Her children are at her parents' for the rest of the week. She has a pretty large family, but they're cool. Only one brother really gave me a hard time when I first got here. But I don't blame him."

Al didn't get the feeling that his old friend was telling him the whole story. Something just didn't seem right.

"And Carlissa, how's she doing?"

"She's just as crazy as ever. I called the girls today, and she was in the background yelling at that knucklehead she's got living there. This one is supposed to be a bail bondsman. And I guess he's making money, but probably not as fast as she spends it."

"Your sister always was money-hungry. So, how did you hurt your foot?"

"Playing basketball with some of Devin's nephews. I should have known better."

"Still clumsy as hell?"

"Man, nothing has changed."

Both men grew quiet when Devin walked back into the room. She gave Al his drink, then Spark his, and set her bottle on the living table.

Spark's cell phone rang. He looked at it, and then frowned when he recognized the number. He didn't answer, instead silencing it and putting it on the table.

Devin looked at him suspiciously.

"Vivian," Spark said to Devin.

Al watched as her face also turned sour, but she took the seat next to Spark. He observed Spark's hand squeeze her knee comfortingly and wondered what was really going on between the two of them. When had it all started?

"Okay, well, there's no use in prolonging the inevitable," Al said after a sip of his cranberry juice. "So, here's the whole story. When Richard realized what he was going to do, he came to me like I told you before. We sat down and laid out a plan because we both wanted out. He was turning state's evidence and going into Witness Protection."

"Witness Protection? So that was the reason for the name change." Devin smiled. "I just thought that he didn't want to give me his real name after . . . I'm sorry." She wiped at the tears forming. "I just assumed that—"

"No, Chris Albridge became his legal name. He didn't just run after testifying. The government gave him a whole new identity. Devin, he didn't lie to you. He just couldn't tell you the whole truth."

Spark passed her the napkin that was under his drink. He put his arm around her briefly for support.

Al noticed, again wondering what had transpired between them.

He continued. "So, when the trial was over, I waited for my sign, then I left town, too. He already knew that I was going to my family in St. Louis, and he had already memorized the address. I waited for him to contact me there. Then we met up here. What nobody knew was that Richard had money, a lot of money, saved up. He told me that Willis Demby had him moving a lot of weight that none of us knew about. At any rate, he didn't mix the money for those side jobs with any of the money we made. Instead, he put the money from the side jobs into a safe that he kept locked up at the storage he rented in his mother's name."

Spark's phone rang again, and he ignored it.

"Are you sure you don't want to answer that?" Devin said, irritation clear in her voice.

"No, I don't. Devin, I don't know why she's calling, and I'm not answering it."

"Maybe you should," Devin replied, looking him right in the face, almost daring him to when the phone rang again.

Both seemed to have forgotten that Al was sitting in the room until he cleared his throat. Spark turned the ringer off, and put the phone in his pants pocket.

"I'm sorry, Al," Devin said, snapping her eyes Spark's way. "Please continue."

"Go 'head, man," Spark encouraged.

"Okay. Um, the last day of the trial, I had all of my belongings in my car. I stopped at the storage locker and picked up Richard's safe and left Delaware for good. Richard never touched that money. He told me that he didn't want the government or the mob to be able to trace any of it back to him. So, I've been holding it. I invested a small portion with his consent and put some in an IRA account. Then after you had another set of twins, we talked about starting a college fund for the girls."

"So, there was money? That's the money that Carlissa was talking about?" Devin asked.

"I don't know how Carlissa would have known about it. Maybe he told her something, but to my knowledge, I was the only one he ever told. At any rate, I brought the papers for you to have a look at. All of the accounts are in my name, and I listed my four *nieces* as beneficiaries." Al pulled the papers out of the black gym bag he carried and placed them on the coffee table. "I can switch them over to you at any time. I have you listed on the IRA as a joint owner. The money has just been sitting there collecting interest. I started out with a small amount, but as I began to make more money, I slowly put more into the account. I had to do it that way so as not to draw too much suspicion to myself. Richard, I mean Christopher, and I talked a lot about what he wanted to do with the money. One thing I know for sure is that he was trying to make sure that you and the girls were taken care of if anything should ever happen to him."

Devin wiped away more tears.

"With the money that has been put away, you really don't have to worry about anything. You have enough money for you and the girls to live pretty comfortably for a long time. Their college funds have more than enough money in them to take care of anything they could possibly need. The IRA account is overflowing with funds that have not been touched at all."

"But how?"

"Devin, I'm an architect with a degree in accounting. I have a very successful architectural firm that is primarily housed in St. Louis with a lot of high profile clients. I also have offices in New York and California. I know you can't tell by looking at me, but I'm a very wealthy man. I'm smart, and I'm loyal. Christopher was one of my few accounting clients, and now you are."

"I just don't understand all of this," she said, glancing at a solemn Spark for help. She was comforted by the squeeze of his hand as his arm went back around her shoulder.

He was contemplating their future. Would she still want hin? And what could he really offer now that she had more money than she needed? "So, exactly how well off is she now, Al?"

Al looked at what he now suspected was a couple, although he wasn't quite sure how it happened, and nodded to Devin for approval to continue.

"Oh, yeah, please. You can say anything in front of Spark," Devin confirmed.

"To be exact, with all of the college funds, the IRA, and the cash that I am still holding in the safe, you have a total of four million, three hundred sixty-three thousand, four hundred seventy-two dollars and ninety-one cents. I also have a ledger with a list of all the transactions and balances, if you'd like to see it." He lifted it out of the bag. "The girls' college funds are each worth one hundred twenty-five thousand, the IRA has three million, and the rest I have in the safe—cash."

"But all this time, and he never said anything. He could have—"

"Devin, there were a lot of times that Christopher wanted to take that money and help you two out of some of your problems. I know things weren't always easy for you, but believe me, and Spark will agree, he did the best thing by separating himself from it. He was taking a chance just by keeping in touch with me. Even though we barely talked more than twice a year, we had ways of communicating."

"Devin, Chris suspected that Willis Demby's men had found him almost three months before he was killed.

He contacted me through another friend. But he wouldn't do anything that might cause them to harm you or that would make you worry. So he did what he had to do and quietly let it happen. He knew they expected him to be flown back to Delaware for burial, and he didn't want you there. I claimed his body and with the help of his federal agent took him back to Delaware for the funeral as per his wishes. He made me promise not to contact you, but I had to call and try to give you some comfort that night after finding out that another funeral home came for the body after I left. Christopher never wanted to stray too far from his roots. And he is buried with his mother and father."

Spark tried to comfort Devin the best he could, but she was crying hysterically. "Devin, baby," he said, without concern for Al's pricking ears. "Baby, you have to keep it together. These are the answers to all of your questions. Now you know that Richard did love you more than anything in this world. He loved his children, and he made sure that you were all provided for."

Al spoke again. "Devin, I can tell you four things for sure. One, Richard loved you more than you will ever know. Two, he didn't want you at the funeral for your own good. Three, he was a good man, in life and in death. And four, he wouldn't want you to go through this alone. Richard would want you to continue living and for you to enjoy your life, because those are his children that you are raising. You have to be happy and strong and go through this for your children's sake."

"Richard, you're right," Devin said. "I am strong. I've made it through these past years with my sanity intact. It's been hard, but I have a large family who support me unconditionally. My girls haven't noticed anything different because I've kept my problems away from them, like a mother should. They are wonderful girls. And I'm happy." She glanced at Spark. "I am happy. I've got good friends who I trust. You know, my mother told me the other day that God makes things happen for a reason, and I believe her. For some reason, I know that I'm going to be all right. I miss Richard, but I will always have the memories of him to share with my girls and his girls. I might have to wait a while, but when I meet them, I'll let them know how much their father loved them."

"As I told you before. I'm here for you and Richard's daughters in any way I can be of service. That is the least I can do to repay him for his trust and the way he helped me over the years. It's getting late, and I'm sure you have a lot to talk about so I'm going to get going. Devin, you think about what you want to do with the accounts. I'm only a phone call away. I'm staying at the hotel tonight, but leaving first thing in the morning. I don't know if you need this or not, but I took some of your money out of the safe." He dug into the bag and pulled out a banded wad of twenties. "It's only five thousand because I didn't want to travel with a large amount, but if you need any more before I get a chance to bring the safe, don't hesitate to call me."

"Oh, Al, thank you so much for coming today. Are you sure you don't want to stay for dinner?"

"No, I'm good. The wife is up here with me. We convinced her mother to keep the baby so we could have a bit of alone time. So, I will take her to dinner, and wine and dine her clothes off her." He smiled, and again Devin felt she had found a good friend in him.

"Well, man," Spark said, "you have a safe trip home. Hey, maybe we could all get together in the morning for a quick breakfast before you go. We would love to meet your wife."

"Now that is a great idea. How about you come to the hotel tomorrow morning around eight?"

"We'll be there." They walked him to the door.

Al turned around to say one more thing. "I wasn't going to say anything, but it's kind of obvious that something is going on between the two of you. I don't know what it is, but I think it's a good thing. And if I might add," he looked at Devin, "I think Richard would approve also. Spark's clumsy and he has a checkered past, as we all do, but he's a good man with a good heart." He shook Spark's hand, gave Devin a hug, and left.

"Do you feel better now that you have your answers?" Spark asked on their way into the living room. They had just finished washing the dinner dishes and were stuffed from the large meal she'd prepared. Devin was feeling so good by the time Al left that she poured her energy into her cooking. She'd made yams, macaroni and cheese, deviled eggs, stuffed chicken breasts, and greens. Then she'd baked a pineapple upside-down cake.

She let him lead her to the sofa, her fingers twined with his, and lazily leaned against him.

"I'm fine. Full and fine. I feel like a huge burden has been lifted off my shoulders. I felt terrible when everything first started coming to light. I actually believed that I was not a good enough wife to Chris because, if I had been, he would have told me all about his past. I thought that he didn't love me enough to share his whole self. But now I know more about Christopher than I could have believed. Now I know how good a man he really was and how lucky I was to have him in my life. And thanks to him, I don't have to worry about the kids financially. I know that they will be taken care of, no matter what might happen to me. So, yeah, I feel better now."

"Well, you had to have known that your kids would always be taken care of with the type of family you have. I would think that would be the least of your worries."

"I know that my family would take care of my girls without a second notice, but I'm a mother and we worry about things whether it's warranted or not."

Spark nodded his head in agreement. "Finally, you know that Chris loved you."

"I always knew that. It was just that I was going through so much, and there were too many things coming at me at one time. I didn't know which way I was going or where to turn."

"I'm sorry that I had any part in that, Devin. I love you. I would never do anything to hurt you. I had a hard time hurting you when I didn't know you. That's not the type of guy I am."

"I know that."

"But do you know how much I care for you?"

"Spark, I know that you care for me. I care for you, too. I missed you when I left Delaware. And I know I didn't show it, but I was glad to see you when I walked into my mother's kitchen that day. I was just confused because I didn't want to have feelings for you. I wanted to hate you, but I didn't. I don't want you to leave now, but—"

"Then I won't," he said, turning her to face him. He searched her eyes. "Devin, if you want me to stay, I'll stay. I have some money saved up. I'll look for an apartment, if you want me to. I know this might be a little complicated for the girls to understand. But all you have to do is tell me to stay."

"That wouldn't be fair for me to do. You still have obligations in Delaware. And you need to talk to your sister and straighten out that whole mess with her. Spark, I have no doubt that you care for me, and I'm not going anywhere. I'll be here."

Spark was about to concede to her, but then he thought of what her father had said to him. Time was too short to waste, and tomorrow wasn't promised to anybody. He had to go after what he wanted, and he had to do it right now. Spark turned her to him; he put his hands on either side of her face, and demanded her complete attention.

"Devin, look at me, listen to me. I love you. You are worth more to me than words can explain. No sunset can replace the beauty of your eyes. No amount of heat can warm me more than your smile. And no joy compares to the thought of being with you forever. My goal is to show you your value to me, and I pray that you will trust and believe in the message I send you. I feel the completeness that being with you brings, and I know you feel it, too. We belong together. That's why I'm not willing to leave Chicago until I know you will be waiting for my return."

He wiped the tear from her cheek with his thumb.

"Don't cry, baby. There's no need to cry."

"Yes, there is," Devin said, hugging him tightly. "I almost lost you because I didn't want to let go of the past. I was pushing you away, keeping you at arm's length because I felt even more betrayed and hurt when I came back from Delaware. And I doubted that you cared for me at all."

"And now you know the truth about that, too. Devin, I've made a lot of mistakes in my life, more than I care to count, but having feelings for you, despite what my sister said, was not one of them. I can't live my life for Carlissa. That's why I came out here. And you can't live the rest of your life for Richard. We have to live for ourselves because if we're not happy, we can't make anyone else happy."

"Spark, I know you're right. And I'm sorry."

"No, I'm sorry. If I had been honest in the beginning, we probably wouldn't have gone through any of this."

"That's not true. We still needed to go through everything to get to this point. Speaking of going through things, how many more times did Vivian call you?"

"A lot," he answered, pulling out his phone and looking at the missed calls. "Oh, wait a minute, the girls called a lot, too."

"You should call them back. Make sure everything is all right."

Spark held her, placing gentle kisses across her forehead, and then backed off, saying, "You should go to bed. I'll call them and let them know that I'm going to book my flight for tomorrow."

"When will you be coming back?"

"As soon as I can. I'll have to pack up the house and call my supervisor to let him know I'm leaving. I would like to give them two weeks notice because they've been real good to me over the years. I'll tie up a few other loose ends and be back as soon as possible. While I'm gone, could you look into a few apartments for me?"

"Okay. Anything in particular?"

"Something as close to what I already have as possible. I don't need much. I'll be driving back and be able to look into some jobs right away."

"And I'll get my dad and brothers to look for something, too. I'm sure Chauncey and Jeff could use some help with the clubs."

"No, thank you. I'm not too big on the club scene. I've had more than enough of that. But I would appreciate any other help they can give me."

"I'm going to take a shower and head to bed," Devin said as she rose from the sofa. She tightened her lock on Spark's fingers as she moved.

"You going to come up?" she asked, smiling at the surprised look on his face.

"Let me call the girls, and I'll be right up there," he said, placing a light kiss on her cheek.

"Be careful not to trip. Matter fact, stay here. I'll come back down. I don't want you to hurt yourself."

They both laughed.

"Yeah," he agreed. "That would probably be the best idea." He watched her go up the steps, then sat back and dialed the number to his nieces' cell phone.

CHAPTER 19

After the phone conversation he'd had with his nieces, Spark didn't wait until the next day to fly home. He told Devin what had happened, and they got on the computer and booked him a seat on the next flight going to Philadelphia. Carlissa was his sister, and no matter what problems they had between them, it was all about family in the end. And even though he realized there was no way that he and Carlissa would ever have the kind of sibling affection that Devin and her sisters and brothers did, he had to take a step toward building some kind of relationship with her.

He only rang the doorbell once before entering the house. It was Vivian who he saw first, stretched out on the downstairs sofa. He didn't know why, but having her watch his nieces disturbed him more than he could say. He immediately asked for his nieces, ignoring the look on her face. He didn't know what her problem was, and wasn't about to start a conversation with her.

She threw her leg over the edge of the sofa invitingly. He ignored her.

"Where are they?" he repeated. How in the world could he have ever thought he had feelings for Vivian? She was so far removed from the type of woman he wanted in his life. She was absolutely nothing like Devin.

But then he saw his nieces standing near the staircase down the hallway, looking scared and sleepy. As soon as they saw that it was their uncle, they both ran into his arms and began crying. He was alarmed.

"Hey, hey, pretty ladies. No tears, no tears," he encouraged, holding them tightly. "I'm here for you."

"Their mother is in jail," Vivian said matter-of-factly, "what do you expect them to do? They've been crying all night."

Spark just looked at her as he held onto his nieces tightly.

"Hey, I tried to call you several times, but I guess that bitch wouldn't let you pick up the phone. So, I told them to call you." She walked away from the three of them and went to the kitchen.

"Girls," Spark started, bending down to be face to face with them, "I want you two to go upstairs and get dressed. Then pack a few clothes. You're coming to stay with me."

After they did his bidding, he followed Vivian into the kitchen. She was standing there pouring a cup of coffee like it was a regular day and all was well in the neighborhood.

"Excuse me," he said furiously. "What exactly is the situation?"

"Like I said, your sister is in jail. She called me yesterday and told me to get my ass over here right away. Right after I got here, all of these damn cop cars surrounded the house. She was like, stay here with the kids. So, here I am."

Spark just looked at her. She was dumb as hell. He couldn't believe he had ever seen anything of worth in her. But a fat ass and tight jeans used to count for something with him. He was madder at himself than anyone.

"Vivian, the kids told me that the cops came here and arrested her last night, but they couldn't give me all the details. So, *exactly* why did they arrest her?"

"She killed Lenny and that girl he was cheating on her with," she replied nonchalantly, walking back to the living room.

He followed her.

"What? And you couldn't get on the phone when I called the girls back, knowing that I needed to know what the whole story was? How dumb can you be?" Spark was instantly furious again. This stupid-ass girl had the nerve to sit in front of him watching television when his nieces' world was falling apart. Without thinking, he grabbed her by the arm, pulled her to her feet, and started for the front door.

Vivian looked up at him in shock. "What are you doing?"

"I'm getting rid of your dumb ass. I will take care of my nieces from now on, thank you. You really do have a problem, you know that?" Before she could respond, Spark was shutting the door in her face. "Goodbye, Vivian."

"But—"

Spark waited for both girls to come back downstairs. He looked at his nieces, then stood to hug each one. "Don't worry, darlings. We are going to be just fine. I'm going to find out what is going on with your mother, and we will take it from there. I am so sorry that I wasn't here for you. But everything is going to be okay."

"It was scary, Uncle Spark. There were police everywhere, and they wrestled Mommy to the ground and handcuffed her. She was screaming and fighting them."

"I know it was scary, but you don't have to worry about that any more. I will get to the bottom of everything, okay? Now, when does school start for you?"

"Next month."

Spark shook his head slowly. He was hoping to be back in Chicago fairly soon, and wondered how that could happen now. Mentally, he made a to-do list, the top item being to call Devin as soon as possible. Then he needed to talk to his sister. He was moving to Chicago either way; it was just a matter of whether to pack up one house or two.

"Spark, I understand. You have to make sure that your sister is okay. She needs you now more than ever. How are the girls holding up?"

"As well as can be expected, I guess. I mean, I don't know what to say to them. That damn Carlissa. She's really messed up this time. I called the station and spoke to the detective in charge. They've got her on two counts of manslaughter. And they have evidence and eyewitnesses. She didn't even try to hide what she did. Apparently, Lenny was seeing his baby's mother again.

Carlissa must have suspected something and followed him. They met at a bar. Carlissa walked in, saw them kissing, pulled out her gun, and shot them both, the woman in the face and Lenny in the neck. Right in front of everybody. She's snapped. The detective said that she's at the jail under mental observation because they don't want her to harm herself. And the prosecutor is trying to push for premeditated murder. This is so crazy. I can't believe this is happening."

"When are you going to be able to see her?"

"I made an appointment for next week, Monday. The girls start school next month. I don't know what to do. It's like I'm between a rock and a hard place. I thought I would be coming back to Chicago in a couple weeks. I was planning to pack night and day."

"Well, you can't really do anything until you talk to your sister. I mean, you're going to have to make space for the girls either way, so start packing up your unimportant things and put them in storage until you're ready to come back. I'm going to wire you some money."

"No, no, no. I have money in the bank."

"It's not for you. It's for Chris's, I mean Richard's, daughters. This is their money, too. So, I'll Western Union it. You start packing and hire movers to pack Carlissa's place if it comes to that. You don't have to do it all yourself. Besides, I hate the thought of you carrying lamps and mirrors from the house to the curb." She laughed.

"Hah, hah, very funny. What I should do is have a garage sale for both houses. I'm going to talk to the girls. I'll give you a call back after they're asleep."

"That's a good idea. Yeah, call me back later."

"And Devin, I love you."

"I love you, too, Spark."

Spark sat quietly in the small room. The shock of what was going on in his life had to be evident to the ten or so other people, each at their own table, sitting in the tightly guarded room. Although he had been in a prison before, he never thought he would be visiting the Baylor Women's Correctional Center, and definitely not to visit Carlissa. It had been seven days since her arrest.

Even though he realized there was no way that he and Carlissa would ever have the kind of sibling affection that Devin and her sisters and brothers did, he had to take a step at building some kind of relationship with her. Spark knew that her reaching out to him was a slim possibility, so it was up to him.

Carlissa followed the other prisoners into the gloomy looking room. She had never been so unsure and frightened of anything in her life. Since she had been arrested, she hadn't said more than a few words to anyone. She was afraid to make friends, didn't know who to trust, and hated having to look her brother in the face after the way she had been behaving since, well, forever. But she needed him.

All of the mistakes and mess-ups he had made in the past, all of the times he'd called needing her help, she had eagerly thrown in his face, saying how he was nothing but a big problem. And look at her now. She had been the one going around thinking she was the invincible and that she could get away with everything. She was the problem.

For the last week, Carlissa had had more than enough time to review her life. She had made so many mistakes, pushed so many good people out of her life because she couldn't fathom that she wasn't the most important person in the world. She was stupid. Her own children didn't come before her own desires. She had spent the last days and nights in her cell contemplating the things she had done wrong, starting with Richard. In retrospect, the only thing she had ever done right was give birth to her girls, and she had complained the whole time she was pregnant with them.

Her guilt and tears put her to sleep every night.

She walked into the room with her head hung low. Her brother stood at a table across the room, and she couldn't bear to look him in the face. Tears threatened her eyes, and her throat grew tight as she tried to calm herself. She would have given anything to be able to run, but she had to face him just as she had to face the consequences of her actions. The consequences of thinking she was untouchable.

Spark's heart dropped when she walked into the room. He had never seen her look so drab and inconsolable. He had never seen her without makeup and expensive clothing. Never seen her shoulders slumped low or the top of her head. Carlissa always walked with her head so high that the bottom of her chin was visible. He instantly pushed the thought that she had killed two people aside, and only saw his sister hurting. Despite their problems, he loved her. As if they had a mind of their own, his arms rose, but even more surprisingly, she fervently moved into them.

He held her, and she held onto him. In that moment, neither had to speak or apologize. Everything they wanted to say to each other but couldn't was conveyed in the hug. Spark didn't want to let her go because her tears told him that she needed the embrace. He held onto his sister until the guard mentioned that they needed to separate and sit down.

Spark started the conversation. "Carlissa, what happened?"

"I don't know. I just snapped. Spark, I swear, I didn't mean to kill them. I was only trying to confront them, but then that bastard started cussing at me, telling me that he didn't want to be with me anymore and that I wasn't worth anything. And she jumped in my face, pushing me upside my head. Next thing I knew, I reached into my bag and pulled out the gun. I don't even remember shooting it. It was like I blacked out or something."

"Carlissa, you know you're going to be doing a lot of time behind this, don't you?"

"Darnel," she said sadly, looking her brother directly in the eye for the first time during the visit, "please take the girls and raise them. Take them to Chicago with you. I want you and Devin to raise them. I want them to be with their sisters."

Spark's mouth dropped open.

"I know you're going to move up there. The girls told me that was where you were, and I know you love her.

I've been so stupid. My priorities have been so twisted. I haven't given my girls the proper upbringing. If it weren't for you, I'm sure their priorities would be messed up, too. You and Devin can give the girls a good life."

"Carlissa—"

"I'll sign anything you need me to. I'm facing a long time, if not life, in here. I can't do anything for the girls but this. Please let me make at least one good decision as far as my daughters are concerned."

"Of course I'm going to take the girls. I didn't think that you would want them around Devin, though. I honestly thought I would have a big fight on my hands."

"Let's just say that I've had a lot of time to think. And I realize that my thinking over the years has had nothing to do with the realities of the world. And I have been wrong about a lot of things."

"Well, it's good to know that you're thinking clearly. I'll go to the courthouse tomorrow to get emergency custody papers drawn. The girls and I have been to the house. We packed up their rooms. I put most of their stuff with my things that will be going to Chicago. Devin is looking for a place for us, me and the girls."

"I thought you would be moving in with her."

"No, we decided that we didn't want to spring everything on either set of twins all at once. They need to ease into some things. But today Devin is supposed to be telling her girls that they have sisters."

"I want you to sell the house. Call Shelia, that's my agent, you remember her, right?"

"Yeah, she tried to hit on me at your closing."

"Yeah, and you hit her, too, didn't you?" She looked at him. He hadn't thought she knew.

"Uh, yeah, I did."

"Anyway, she will help you put the house on the market. I realize now is a bad time, and it might take a while to sell, but at least it's almost paid off. You should be able to get a very good profit from it either way. She'll be able to bring the papers in for me to sign, or at least she'll be able to get in contact with my lawyer."

"Carlissa, is there anything you need?"

"Spark, at this point the most important thing is for you to take care of my girls. Please make sure the girls don't forget about me. I know I won't be able to see them that often with you being in Chicago, but I would like to write them and vice versa. I do love them, Spark."

"I have no doubt of that, Carlissa. You signing over custody proves that as far as I'm concerned. Is there anyone you need me to call? What about your job? Any friends that I don't know about?"

"The only people who ever really cared about me are with you, and as long as I know they're all right, I'm all right. Can you do me a favor? Tell Devin that I am sorry. I apologize for everything that I've done to her and you. I know it's hard to believe, but it's true. I've been an awful person and a terrible sister. I'm sorry, Spark."

Spark looked at her, again surprised, not so much by what she said, but by the sincerity evident in her eyes.

"I'll tell her," he replied. Deep down, Spark wished that he had seen this side of his sister a long time ago. He wished that they could have had the time to get to know each other and that it hadn't taken something like this for them to act civil to each other.

Just then, the guard announced that visiting time was over.

Carlissa looked at him sorrowfully. "Could you bring the girls by to see me before you leave?

"Of course I will. I'll bring them next week. And call us tonight if you get a chance. They need to talk to you."

He stood and opened his arms to her again. And again, Carlissa went into them. She wasn't the dominating older sister anymore; she was just his sister, and she needed him for the first time in his life. Spark was determined to be there for her.

"I love you, Carlissa," he said, squeezing tightly.

"I love you, too, Darnel," she whispered, tears clouding her vision as she pulled away from him.

He watched her leave. She didn't turn around as she walked out of the room. But for some reason, Spark was able to smile because he knew that they had made progress on their relationship. And to be honest, he was impressed with her. She was thinking so much more clearly, feeling remorseful for her past actions, and opening up about her feelings. All of those things were positive acts in his mind. And, you had to find the good in every situation, right?

Spark wanted to go home and give her lawyer a call. Although there was no doubt that she would be doing a significant amount of time, he hoped there was some way they could get her sentence reduced.

EPILOGUE

They stood over the flat granite headstone that marked the grave of Richard Joseph Harrison. Under that name was another name in parentheses, Christopher David Albridge. The six of them stood as a family, each mourning the loss of their loved one in a different way. For the past three years, they had been coming back, but this time was different.

Each year, they came to Delaware for a brief family vacation during the summer. The family had strong connections here. It was where the girls' father was born; it was where one set of twins was born and where their mother had been imprisoned at the Baylor's Women Correctional Center for the past three years. She had fifteen years left to serve without a chance for parole.

When Spark returned to Delaware three years prior, it was to get his nieces, pack up his apartment, resign from his job, change his mailing address, and get in his car for the drive back to Chicago. He was determined not to let the opportunity to be with Devin pass him by.

One day he had spoken to her father on the phone and told of his plans to come back to Chicago, find a job, and marry his daughter. And that was what he did.

After visiting his sister and talking to her lawyer and realtor, he put her house on the market and packed up his apartment. He and his nieces had a huge garage sale and set up an account for his sister that would send money to her prison account every two weeks.

He and Devin talked every night on the phone as he worked hard and fast getting everything in order. With Devin's blessing and help, he and his nieces moved back to Chicago and lived in an apartment owned by her brother John Jr. John Sr. called a few of his old friends, and Spark found himself in a manager's position at an oil refinery just outside of Chicago.

He and Devin focused all their energy on the girls, making sure they were comfortable with each other and the situation until the four of them were inseparable. And when Spark asked Devin to marry him, he presented rings to all five ladies. When they got married a year and a half later, each lady had a ring for him. Devin's wedding band went on his finger, and the girls' smaller bands were placed on a chain that he wore around his neck daily.

Spark was blessed, and he knew it. This was the emotion flooding his soul as he stood over the grave of a friend. They were able to bring Richard into the folds of their family for their children's sake, and he was able to honor the friend who had risked his life to save the lives of others. If it weren't for Richard being brave enough to put a stop to the madness so many years ago, he knew that he wouldn't have found the peace and serenity in his life that he had with Devin.

For the two sets of twins, the visit was to mourn a father they barely knew, barely remembered except for the stories they were constantly told by their parents. The girls, ages sixteen and eleven, were as close as sisters could be and the older girls, Christina and Christal, were very protective of their siblings, Tionne and Dionne. They had no idea what their father had done; all they knew was that he was a good and honest man. Devin reminded them of that whenever they needed a little encouragement with their schoolwork or when they started to follow too much behind their cousins. She would say, "The world doesn't need more followers, it needs more leaders."

They watched as their mother moved forward to place a large bouquet of flowers on the grave, and moved back when Spark motioned to them so Devin could have some private time.

"Hey, Chris," she started. "As you can see, the girls are growing up fast. Pretty soon, I'll have a houseful of women. Oh, how I wish you were around to enjoy them. Every year, I come to you and say the same thing. I wish you could have trusted me enough to talk to me, but this year is different. I have come to terms with your decisions. And I have to tell you something."

"Spark and I finally married last year. He's a good man, Chris. But you already knew that, didn't you? And he's a wonderful father to the girls. Al was his best man. He's become a very good friend to all of us, and the girls simply adore their godfather. He has another baby on the way. I say this all the time, but I'm going to stop questioning the Lord's will. He knows what's best, and everything that was done was for a reason.

"We'll be taking the girls to see Carlissa after we leave here. She's doing quite well. I was surprised last year when she told Spark that she wanted me to visit as well as the girls. I've talked to her on the phone a few times, but haven't seen her since . . . anyway, I can tell by our phone conversations that she's changed a lot. Carlissa is nothing like she was the first time I crossed paths with her. Spark said that she was also taking business classes."

Devin smiled when the wind blew. She liked to think that was Chris's reaction.

"Yeah, that's what I said, but Spark said she's doing quite well. I think it's good for her. At least it keeps her mind busy. I have to go. We'll be back next year around the same time. God bless you, Chris."

Devin stood and felt the wind blow around her again. She turned toward her family just in time to see Spark trip over a headstone. The girls immediately began laughing as they all reached down to help him up.

"Chris, that wasn't funny," she said, laughing as she looked up toward the heavens.

The winds blew.

ABOUT THE AUTHOR

Michele Sudler lives in the small East Coast town of Smyrna, Delaware. Busy raising her three children, she finds time for her second passion, writing in the evenings and on weekends. After attending Delaware State College, majoring in Business Administration, she continues to work in the corporate banking industry. Enrolling back in school, she is currently working hard on time management skills in order to balance family, work, and school.

Waiting in the Shadows is her sixth novel and third Avery family romance. Her other Avery novels are *Intentional Mistakes* and *One of these Days. Stolen Memories,* introducing the Philips family, who promise to be an interesting lot, was released in February 2008. *Three Doors Down,* the first novel dealing with the memorable Jarnette brothers was released in September 2008. *Best Foot Forward* was released in June 2009. Also, be on the lookout for the second Philips family novel, *Stolen Jewels,* in April 2010.

Besides spending time with her children and writing, Michele enjoys playing and watching basketball, traveling, and reading. She would love to hear what you think about her novels. Please send any comments to her email address: *micheleasudler@yahoo.com.*

2009 Reprint Mass Market Titles

January

I'm Gonna Make You Love Me
Gwyneth Bolton
ISBN-13: 978-1-58571-294-6
$6.99

Shades of Desire
Monica White
ISBN-13: 978-1-58571-292-2
$6.99

February

A Love of Her Own
Cheris Hodges
ISBN-13: 978-1-58571-293-9
$6.99

Color of Trouble
Dyanne Davis
ISBN-13: 978-1-58571-294-6
$6.99

March

Twist of Fate
Beverly Clark
ISBN-13: 978-1-58571-295-3
$6.99

Chances
Pamela Leigh Starr
ISBN-13: 978-1-58571-296-0
$6.99

April

Sinful Intentions
Crystal Rhodes
ISBN-13: 978-1-585712-297-7
$6.99

Rock Star
Roslyn Hardy Holcomb
ISBN-13: 978-1-58571-298-4
$6.99

May

Paths of Fire
T.T. Henderson
ISBN-13: 978-1-58571-343-1
$6.99

Caught Up in the Rapture
Lisa Riley
ISBN-13: 978-1-58571-344-8
$6.99

June

Reckless Surrender
Rochelle Alers
ISBN-13: 978-1-58571-345-5
$6.99

No Ordinary Love
Angela Weaver
ISBN-13: 978-1-58571-346-2
$6.99

2009 Reprint Mass Market Titles (continued)

July

Intentional Mistakes
Michele Sudler
ISBN-13: 978-1-58571-347-9
$6.99

It's In His Kiss
Reon Carter
ISBN-13: 978-1-58571-348-6
$6.99

August

Unfinished Love Affair
Barbara Keaton
ISBN-13: 978-1-58571-349-3
$6.99

A Perfect Place to Pray
I.L Goodwin
ISBN-13: 978-1-58571-299-1
$6.99

September

Love in High Gear
Charlotte Roy
ISBN-13: 978-1-58571-355-4
$6.99

Ebony Eyes
Kei Swanson
ISBN-13: 978-1-58571-356-1
$6.99

October

Midnight Clear, Part I
Leslie Esdale/Carmen Green
ISBN-13: 978-1-58571-357-8
$6.99

Midnight Clear, Part II
Gwynne Forster/Monica Jackson
ISBN-13: 978-1-58571-358-5
$6.99

November

Midnight Peril
Vicki Andrews
ISBN-13: 978-1-58571-359-2
$6.99

One Day At A Time
Bella McFarland
ISBN-13: 978-1-58571-360-8
$6.99

December

Just An Affair
Eugenia O'Neal
ISBN-13: 978-1-58571-361-5
$6.99

Shades of Brown
Denise Becker
ISBN-13: 978-1-58571-362-2
$6.99

2009 New Mass Market Titles

January

Singing A Song…
Crystal Rhodes
ISBN-13: 978-1-58571-283-0
$6.99

Look Both Ways
Joan Early
ISBN-13: 978-1-58571-284-7
$6.99

February

Six O'Clock
Katrina Spencer
ISBN-13: 978-1-58571-285-4
$6.99

Red Sky
Renee Alexis
ISBN-13: 978-1-58571-286-1
$6.99

March

Anything But Love
Celya Bowers
ISBN-13: 978-1-58571-287-8
$6.99

Tempting Faith
Crystal Hubbard
ISBN-13: 978-1-58571-288-5
$6.99

April

If I Were Your Woman
La Connie Taylor-Jones
ISBN-13: 978-1-58571-289-2
$6.99

Best Of Luck Elsewhere
Trisha Haddad
ISBN-13: 978-1-58571-290-8
$6.99

May

All I'll Ever Need
Mildred Riley
ISBN-13: 978-1-58571-335-6
$6.99

A Place Like Home
Alicia Wiggins
ISBN-13: 978-1-58571-336-3
$6.99

June

Best Foot Forward
Michele Sudler
ISBN-13: 978-1-58571-337-0
$6.99

It's In the Rhythm
Sammie Ward
ISBN-13: 978-1-58571-338-7
$6.99

2009 New Mass Market Titles (continued)

July

Checks and Balances
Elaine Sims
ISBN-13: 978-1-58571-339-4
$6.99

Save Me
Africa Fine
ISBN-13: 978-1-58571-340-0
$6.99

August

When Lightening Strikes
Michele Cameron
ISBN-13: 978-1-58571-369-1
$6.99

Blindsided
Tammy Williams
ISBN-13: 978-1-58571-342-4
$6.99

September

2 Good
Celya Bowers
ISBN-13: 978-1-58571-350-9
$6.99

Waiting for Mr. Darcy
Chamein Canton
ISBN-13: 978-1-58571-351-6
$6.99

October

Fireflies
Joan Early
ISBN-13: 978-1-58571-352-3
$6.99

Frost On My Window
Angela Weaver
ISBN-13: 978-1-58571-353-0
$6.99

November

Waiting in the Shadows
Michele Sudler
ISBN-13: 978-1-58571-364-6
$6.99

Fixin' Tyrone
Keith Walker
ISBN-13: 978-1-58571-365-3
$6.99

December

Dream Keeper
Gail McFarland
ISBN-13: 978-1-58571-366-0
$6.99

Another Memory
Pamela Ridley
ISBN-13: 978-1-58571-367-7
$6.99

Other Genesis Press, Inc. Titles

A Dangerous Deception	J.M. Jeffries	$8.95
A Dangerous Love	J.M. Jeffries	$8.95
A Dangerous Obsession	J.M. Jeffries	$8.95
A Drummer's Beat to Mend	Kei Swanson	$9.95
A Happy Life	Charlotte Harris	$9.95
A Heart's Awakening	Veronica Parker	$9.95
A Lark on the Wing	Phyliss Hamilton	$9.95
A Love of Her Own	Cheris F. Hodges	$9.95
A Love to Cherish	Beverly Clark	$8.95
A Risk of Rain	Dar Tomlinson	$8.95
A Taste of Temptation	Reneé Alexis	$9.95
A Twist of Fate	Beverly Clark	$8.95
A Voice Behind Thunder	Carrie Elizabeth Greene	$6.99
A Will to Love	Angie Daniels	$9.95
Acquisitions	Kimberley White	$8.95
Across	Carol Payne	$12.95
After the Vows	Leslie Esdaile	$10.95
(Summer Anthology)	T.T. Henderson	
	Jacqueline Thomas	
Again My Love	Kayla Perrin	$10.95
Against the Wind	Gwynne Forster	$8.95
All I Ask	Barbara Keaton	$8.95
Always You	Crystal Hubbard	$6.99
Ambrosia	T.T. Henderson	$8.95
An Unfinished Love Affair	Barbara Keaton	$8.95
And Then Came You	Dorothy Elizabeth Love	$8.95
Angel's Paradise	Janice Angelique	$9.95
At Last	Lisa G. Riley	$8.95
Best of Friends	Natalie Dunbar	$8.95
Beyond the Rapture	Beverly Clark	$9.95
Blame It On Paradise	Crystal Hubbard	$6.99
Blaze	Barbara Keaton	$9.95
Bliss, Inc.	Chamein Canton	$6.99
Blood Lust	J. M. Jeffries	$9.95
Blood Seduction	J.M. Jeffries	$9.95

Other Genesis Press, Inc. Titles (continued)

Bodyguard	Andrea Jackson	$9.95
Boss of Me	Diana Nyad	$8.95
Bound by Love	Beverly Clark	$8.95
Breeze	Robin Hampton Allen	$10.95
Broken	Dar Tomlinson	$24.95
By Design	Barbara Keaton	$8.95
Cajun Heat	Charlene Berry	$8.95
Careless Whispers	Rochelle Alers	$8.95
Cats & Other Tales	Marilyn Wagner	$8.95
Caught in a Trap	Andre Michelle	$8.95
Caught Up In the Rapture	Lisa G. Riley	$9.95
Cautious Heart	Cheris F Hodges	$8.95
Chances	Pamela Leigh Starr	$8.95
Cherish the Flame	Beverly Clark	$8.95
Choices	Tammy Williams	$6.99
Class Reunion	Irma Jenkins/ John Brown	$12.95
Code Name: Diva	J.M. Jeffries	$9.95
Conquering Dr. Wexler's Heart	Kimberley White	$9.95
Corporate Seduction	A.C. Arthur	$9.95
Crossing Paths, Tempting Memories	Dorothy Elizabeth Love	$9.95
Crush	Crystal Hubbard	$9.95
Cypress Whisperings	Phyllis Hamilton	$8.95
Dark Embrace	Crystal Wilson Harris	$8.95
Dark Storm Rising	Chinelu Moore	$10.95
Daughter of the Wind	Joan Xian	$8.95
Dawn's Harbor	Kymberly Hunt	$6.99
Deadly Sacrifice	Jack Kean	$22.95
Designer Passion	Dar Tomlinson Diana Richeaux	$8.95
Do Over	Celya Bowers	$9.95
Dream Runner	Gail McFarland	$6.99
Dreamtective	Liz Swados	$5.95

Other Genesis Press, Inc. Titles (continued)

Ebony Angel	Deatri King-Bey	$9.95
Ebony Butterfly II	Delilah Dawson	$14.95
Echoes of Yesterday	Beverly Clark	$9.95
Eden's Garden	Elizabeth Rose	$8.95
Eve's Prescription	Edwina Martin Arnold	$8.95
Everlastin' Love	Gay G. Gunn	$8.95
Everlasting Moments	Dorothy Elizabeth Love	$8.95
Everything and More	Sinclair Lebeau	$8.95
Everything but Love	Natalie Dunbar	$8.95
Falling	Natalie Dunbar	$9.95
Fate	Pamela Leigh Starr	$8.95
Finding Isabella	A.J. Garrotto	$8.95
Forbidden Quest	Dar Tomlinson	$10.95
Forever Love	Wanda Y. Thomas	$8.95
From the Ashes	Kathleen Suzanne Jeanne Sumerix	$8.95
Gentle Yearning	Rochelle Alers	$10.95
Glory of Love	Sinclair LeBeau	$10.95
Go Gentle into that Good Night	Malcom Boyd	$12.95
Goldengroove	Mary Beth Craft	$16.95
Groove, Bang, and Jive	Steve Cannon	$8.99
Hand in Glove	Andrea Jackson	$9.95
Hard to Love	Kimberley White	$9.95
Hart & Soul	Angie Daniels	$8.95
Heart of the Phoenix	A.C. Arthur	$9.95
Heartbeat	Stephanie Bedwell-Grime	$8.95
Hearts Remember	M. Loui Quezada	$8.95
Hidden Memories	Robin Allen	$10.95
Higher Ground	Leah Latimer	$19.95
Hitler, the War, and the Pope	Ronald Rychiak	$26.95
How to Write a Romance	Kathryn Falk	$18.95
I Married a Reclining Chair	Lisa M. Fuhs	$8.95
I'll Be Your Shelter	Giselle Carmichael	$8.95
I'll Paint a Sun	A.J. Garrotto	$9.95

Other Genesis Press, Inc. Titles (continued)

Icie	Pamela Leigh Starr	$8.95
Illusions	Pamela Leigh Starr	$8.95
Indigo After Dark Vol. I	Nia Dixon/Angelique	$10.95
Indigo After Dark Vol. II	Dolores Bundy/ Cole Riley	$10.95
Indigo After Dark Vol. III	Montana Blue/ Coco Morena	$10.95
Indigo After Dark Vol. IV	Cassandra Colt/	$14.95
Indigo After Dark Vol. V	Delilah Dawson	$14.95
Indiscretions	Donna Hill	$8.95
Intentional Mistakes	Michele Sudler	$9.95
Interlude	Donna Hill	$8.95
Intimate Intentions	Angie Daniels	$8.95
It's Not Over Yet	J.J. Michael	$9.95
Jolie's Surrender	Edwina Martin-Arnold	$8.95
Kiss or Keep	Debra Phillips	$8.95
Lace	Giselle Carmichael	$9.95
Lady Preacher	K.T. Richey	$6.99
Last Train to Memphis	Elsa Cook	$12.95
Lasting Valor	Ken Olsen	$24.95
Let Us Prey	Hunter Lundy	$25.95
Lies Too Long	Pamela Ridley	$13.95
Life Is Never As It Seems	J.J. Michael	$12.95
Lighter Shade of Brown	Vicki Andrews	$8.95
Looking for Lily	Africa Fine	$6.99
Love Always	Mildred E. Riley	$10.95
Love Doesn't Come Easy	Charlyne Dickerson	$8.95
Love Unveiled	Gloria Greene	$10.95
Love's Deception	Charlene Berry	$10.95
Love's Destiny	M. Loui Quezada	$8.95
Love's Secrets	Yolanda McVey	$6.99
Mae's Promise	Melody Walcott	$8.95
Magnolia Sunset	Giselle Carmichael	$8.95
Many Shades of Gray	Dyanne Davis	$6.99
Matters of Life and Death	Lesego Malepe, Ph.D.	$15.95

Other Genesis Press, Inc. Titles (continued)

Meant to Be	Jeanne Sumerix	$8.95
Midnight Clear (Anthology)	Leslie Esdaile Gwynne Forster Carmen Green Monica Jackson	$10.95
Midnight Magic	Gwynne Forster	$8.95
Midnight Peril	Vicki Andrews	$10.95
Misconceptions	Pamela Leigh Starr	$9.95
Moments of Clarity	Michele Cameron	$6.99
Montgomery's Children	Richard Perry	$14.95
Mr Fix-It	Crystal Hubbard	$6.99
My Buffalo Soldier	Barbara B. K. Reeves	$8.95
Naked Soul	Gwynne Forster	$8.95
Never Say Never	Michele Cameron	$6.99
Next to Last Chance	Louisa Dixon	$24.95
No Apologies	Seressia Glass	$8.95
No Commitment Required	Seressia Glass	$8.95
No Regrets	Mildred E. Riley	$8.95
Not His Type	Chamein Canton	$6.99
Nowhere to Run	Gay G. Gunn	$10.95
O Bed! O Breakfast!	Rob Kuehnle	$14.95
Object of His Desire	A. C. Arthur	$8.95
Office Policy	A. C. Arthur	$9.95
Once in a Blue Moon	Dorianne Cole	$9.95
One Day at a Time	Bella McFarland	$8.95
One in A Million	Barbara Keaton	$6.99
One of These Days	Michele Sudler	$9.95
Outside Chance	Louisa Dixon	$24.95
Passion	T.T. Henderson	$10.95
Passion's Blood	Cherif Fortin	$22.95
Passion's Furies	AlTonya Washington	$6.99
Passion's Journey	Wanda Y. Thomas	$8.95
Past Promises	Jahmel West	$8.95
Path of Fire	T.T. Henderson	$8.95
Path of Thorns	Annetta P. Lee	$9.95

Other Genesis Press, Inc. Titles (continued)

Peace Be Still	Colette Haywood	$12.95
Picture Perfect	Reon Carter	$8.95
Playing for Keeps	Stephanie Salinas	$8.95
Pride & Joi	Gay G. Gunn	$8.95
Promises Made	Bernice Layton	$6.99
Promises to Keep	Alicia Wiggins	$8.95
Quiet Storm	Donna Hill	$10.95
Reckless Surrender	Rochelle Alers	$6.95
Red Polka Dot in a World of Plaid	Varian Johnson	$12.95
Reluctant Captive	Joyce Jackson	$8.95
Rendezvous with Fate	Jeanne Sumerix	$8.95
Revelations	Cheris F. Hodges	$8.95
Rivers of the Soul	Leslie Esdaile	$8.95
Rocky Mountain Romance	Kathleen Suzanne	$8.95
Rooms of the Heart	Donna Hill	$8.95
Rough on Rats and Tough on Cats	Chris Parker	$12.95
Secret Library Vol. 1	Nina Sheridan	$18.95
Secret Library Vol. 2	Cassandra Colt	$8.95
Secret Thunder	Annetta P. Lee	$9.95
Shades of Brown	Denise Becker	$8.95
Shades of Desire	Monica White	$8.95
Shadows in the Moonlight	Jeanne Sumerix	$8.95
Sin	Crystal Rhodes	$8.95
Small Whispers	Annetta P. Lee	$6.99
So Amazing	Sinclair LeBeau	$8.95
Somebody's Someone	Sinclair LeBeau	$8.95
Someone to Love	Alicia Wiggins	$8.95
Song in the Park	Martin Brant	$15.95
Soul Eyes	Wayne L. Wilson	$12.95
Soul to Soul	Donna Hill	$8.95
[illegible] Comfort	J.M. Jeffries	$8.95
[illegible] Standards	S.R. Maddox	$6.99
[illegible]	Sharon Robinson	$8.95

Other Genesis Press, Inc. Titles (continued)

Still Waters Run Deep	Leslie Esdaile	$8.95
Stolen Kisses	Dominiqua Douglas	$9.95
Stolen Memories	Michele Sudler	$6.99
Stories to Excite You	Anna Forrest/Divine	$14.95
Storm	Pamela Leigh Starr	$6.99
Subtle Secrets	Wanda Y. Thomas	$8.95
Suddenly You	Crystal Hubbard	$9.95
Sweet Repercussions	Kimberley White	$9.95
Sweet Sensations	Gwyneth Bolton	$9.95
Sweet Tomorrows	Kimberly White	$8.95
Taken by You	Dorothy Elizabeth Love	$9.95
Tattooed Tears	T. T. Henderson	$8.95
The Color Line	Lizzette Grayson Carter	$9.95
The Color of Trouble	Dyanne Davis	$8.95
The Disappearance of Allison Jones	Kayla Perrin	$5.95
The Fires Within	Beverly Clark	$9.95
The Foursome	Celya Bowers	$6.99
The Honey Dipper's Legacy	Pannell-Allen	$14.95
The Joker's Love Tune	Sidney Rickman	$15.95
The Little Pretender	Barbara Cartland	$10.95
The Love We Had	Natalie Dunbar	$8.95
The Man Who Could Fly	Bob & Milana Beamon	$18.95
The Missing Link	Charlyne Dickerson	$8.95
The Mission	Pamela Leigh Starr	$6.99
The More Things Change	Chamein Canton	$6.99
The Perfect Frame	Beverly Clark	$9.95
The Price of Love	Sinclair LeBeau	$8.95
The Smoking Life	Ilene Barth	$29.95
The Words of the Pitcher	Kei Swanson	$8.95
Things Forbidden	Maryam Diaab	$6.99
This Life Isn't Perfect Holla	Sandra Foy	$6.99
Three Doors Down	Michele Sudler	
Three Wishes	Seressia Glass	
Ties That Bind	Kathleen S	

Other Genesis Press, Inc. Titles (continued)

Tiger Woods	Libby Hughes	$5.95
Time is of the Essence	Angie Daniels	$9.95
Timeless Devotion	Bella McFarland	$9.95
Tomorrow's Promise	Leslie Esdaile	$8.95
Truly Inseparable	Wanda Y. Thomas	$8.95
Two Sides to Every Story	Dyanne Davis	$9.95
Unbreak My Heart	Dar Tomlinson	$8.95
Uncommon Prayer	Kenneth Swanson	$9.95
Unconditional Love	Alicia Wiggins	$8.95
Unconditional	A.C. Arthur	$9.95
Undying Love	Renee Alexis	$6.99
Until Death Do Us Part	Susan Paul	$8.95
Vows of Passion	Bella McFarland	$9.95
Wedding Gown	Dyanne Davis	$8.95
What's Under Benjamin's Bed	Sandra Schaffer	$8.95
When A Man Loves A Woman	La Connie Taylor-Jones	$6.99
When Dreams Float	Dorothy Elizabeth Love	$8.95
When I'm With You	LaConnie Taylor-Jones	$6.99
Where I Want To Be	Maryam Diaab	$6.99
Whispers in the Night	Dorothy Elizabeth Love	$8.95
Whispers in the Sand	LaFlorya Gauthier	$10.95
Who's That Lady?	Andrea Jackson	$9.95
Wild Ravens	Altonya Washington	$9.95
Yesterday Is Gone	Beverly Clark	$10.95
Yesterday's Dreams, Tomorrow's Promises	Reon Laudat	$8.95
Your Precious Love	Sinclair LeBeau	$8.95

Order Form

Mail to: Genesis Press, Inc.
P.O. Box 101
Columbus, MS 39703

Name ______________________________
Address ______________________________
City/State ____________________ Zip ____________
Telephone ____________________

Ship to (if different from above)
Name ______________________________
Address ______________________________
City/State ____________________ Zip ____________
Telephone ____________________

Credit Card Information
Credit Card # ____________________ ☐ Visa ☐ Mastercard
Expiration Date (mm/yy) ____________ ☐ AmEx ☐ Discover

Qty.	Author	Title	Price	Total

Use this order form, or call 1-888-INDIGO-1

Total for books ____________
Shipping and handling:
$5 first two books,
$1 each additional book ____________
Total S & H ____________
Total amount enclosed ____________

Mississippi residents add 7% sales tax